本书是西北民族大学2012年中央高校青年项目（项目号zyz2012005)的成果

文学术语

关桂云 著

Jim Rogers 校

中国社会科学出版社

图书在版编目（CIP）数据

文学术语/关桂云著. —北京：中国社会科学出版社，2017.3
ISBN 978 - 7 - 5161 - 9819 - 3

Ⅰ.①文…　Ⅱ.①关…　Ⅲ.①文学—名词术语—英、汉
Ⅳ.①I - 61

中国版本图书馆 CIP 数据核字（2017）第 021496 号

出 版 人	赵剑英	
责任编辑	陈肖静	
责任校对	刘　娟	
责任印制	戴　宽	

出　　版	中国社会科学出版社	
社　　址	北京鼓楼西大街甲 158 号	
邮　　编	100720	
网　　址	http://www.csspw.cn	
发 行 部	010 - 84083685	
门 市 部	010 - 84029450	
经　　销	新华书店及其他书店	

印刷装订	北京君升印刷有限公司
版　　次	2017 年 3 月第 1 版
印　　次	2017 年 3 月第 1 次印刷

开　　本	710×1000　1/16
印　　张	14.75
插　　页	2
字　　数	230 千字
定　　价	66.00 元

目 录

A

D

F

G

H

I

Q

R

S

T

A

Adventure Fiction（冒险小说）

Adventure fiction is a genre of fiction whose main theme is often formed by an adventure with exciting risks, physical dangers and fast-paced actions. The key protagonist is so nimble and courageous that he or she is able to fight against strong enemies and survive in very dangerous situations. According to critic Don D'Ammassa[①], "adventure fiction is an event or series of events that happens outside the course of the protagonist's ordinary life, usually accompanied by danger, often by physical action. Adventure stories almost always move quickly, and the pace of the plot is at least as important as characterization, setting and other elements of a creative work."[②] Adventure fiction often overlaps with science fiction, romance and spy thrillers. *Robinson Crusoe* (1719) written by Daniel Defoe[③]is viewed as a notable adventure fiction.

---

① Don D'Ammassa is a critic and author, famous for *Blood Beast* (1988) and *Servants of Chaos* (2002).

② Don D'Ammassa, "Encyclopedia of Adventure Fiction" *Facts on File Library of World Literature*, Infobase Publishing, 2009, pp. vii – viii.

③ Daniel Defoe (1660—1731) was an English writer, best known as the author of *Robinson Crusoe*. He was one of the earliest practitioners of the novel.

冒险小说是小说的一种，其主题往往是带有刺激的危险、身体的威胁和激烈的打斗的冒险活动。主人公机智勇敢，能够打败强敌，脱险存活。根据批评家堂·德阿玛莎："冒险小说是发生在主人公日常生活之外的一件事或者一系列事件，经常伴有危险和打斗。冒险故事往往情节发展迅速，情节节奏至少与作品中的人物塑造、场景以及其他的因素同等重要。"冒险小说与科幻小说、传奇小说以及谍战片有共通之处。丹尼尔·笛福写的《鲁滨逊漂流记》（1719）就被认为是著名的冒险小说。

Aestheticism or the Aesthetic Movement（唯美主义）

In the 19th century, there appeared many literary and art movements, among which Aestheticism was one of the most prominent that rose in the late 19th century and withered away soon. It concentrated on the doctrine of "art for art's sake", which was first coined by Victor Cousin[①]in 1818. Aesthetes criticized Mammonism and Utilitarianism, thinking them as the ugliness of the industrial age. They held that art should serve no political, religious, moral, didactic or other purpose. Oscar Wilde[②]was the milestone of aestheticism, and his being put into prison because of his homosexuality in 1900 was generally thought as the end of the trend.

在 19 世纪，出现了很多文学艺术运动，其中唯美主义是兴起于 19 世纪末很快又衰败的最著名的运动。它以维克多·库辛在 1818 年首次提出来的"为艺术而艺术"为核心。唯美主义者批判拜金主义和功利主义，认为这是工业时代的丑陋面。他们认为艺术不应该有任何政治、宗教、道德、说教或者其他的目的。奥斯卡·王尔德是唯美主义的里程碑，他在 1900 年因为同性恋而被捕入狱，这通常被认为是唯

---

① Victor Cousin (1792—1867) was a French philosopher as well as the founder of "eclecticism".

② Oscar Wilde (1854—1900) was an Irish writer, notable for *The Picture of Dorian Gray* (1890) and *The Importance of Being Earnest* (1895).

美主义的结束。

Allegory （寓言）

Allegory is a narrative and literary device with a long history and vigorous vitality. It is widely used throughout the world in almost all literary forms. To some extent, it is an extended metaphor with hidden illustration and profound philosophy through symbolic figures, actions, imagery, or events.

John Bunyan[①]'s *The Pilgrim's Progress* (1678) is the most notable allegory in English. In addition, John Dryden[②]'s *Absalom and Achitophel* (1681) and John Milton[③]'s *Paradise Lost* (1667) are also representatives of the genre.

寓言是有着悠久历史和旺盛生命力的叙事文体和文学体裁。它在整个世界几乎所有文学形式中广泛应用。从某种意义上讲，它就是通过象征性人物、动作、意象或者事件而进行暗示和讲述深刻道理的比喻。

约翰·班扬的《天路历程》（1678）就是最为著名的英文寓言。除此之外，约翰·德莱顿的《押沙龙与阿奇托菲尔》（1681）和约翰·弥尔顿的《失乐园》（1667）也是寓言的代表作品。

Alliteration （头韵）

Alliteration (also called "initial rhyme" or "head rhyme") is an important term in stylistics which can be traced back to Old English. It is the

---

① John Bunyan (1628—1688) was an English Christian writer, best known for *The Pilgrim's Progress*.

② John Dryden (1631—1700) was an English poet and critic, best known as the king of Restoration literature. So the Restoration period is also called the "Age of Dryden".

③ John Milton (1608—1674) was an English poet, pamphleteer and man of letters. His *Paradise Lost*, written in blank verse, is considered as the greatest epic poem in English.

repetition of the first consonant sounds in some neighboring words. Shakespeare is a master using alliteration. In his works, there are many examples, such as: crafty confusion, fantasy of fame, delight and dole and so on. So alliteration "depends not on letters but on sounds". For example, know-nothing is alliterative, while climate change is not.

头韵（也被称为"首字母韵"或者"开头韵"）是文体学中的一个重要术语，可以追溯到古英语时期。它是指相邻单词的第一个辅音重复使用。莎士比亚是使用头韵的大师。在其作品中例子俯拾即是，例如："装糊涂、虚名、喜与悲"等等。所以头韵"取决的不是字母而是发音"例如，know-nothing 是头韵，而 climate change 就不是。

Allusion（典故）

Allusion, as a figure of speech, is an indirect or covert reference to an event, person, place, mythology or literary work. Because allusions are not identified clearly, readers should be knowledgeable enough to make the connection themselves. Some modern authors, including James Joyce, Ezra Pound[①], and T. S. Eliot often used specialized allusions, which are rarely understood by common readers. The works of Shakespeare are often sources of allusions.

典故是一种修辞，间接或隐蔽地提到一个事件、人物、地点、神话或者文学作品。因为典故并没有清楚地标识出来，所以读者需要具有丰富的知识才能自己进行联系。一些现代作家，例如詹姆斯·乔伊斯、埃兹拉·庞德和 T. S. 艾略特经常使用普通读者很难理解的特殊典故。莎士比亚的作品经常是典故的来源。

---

① Ezra Pound (1885—1972) was an American poet, best known as one of the most important representatives of Imaginism.

Ambiguity（复义性）

In 1930, the pioneer of New Criticism, William Empson (1906—1984) published his book *Seven Types of Ambiguity*, which is one of the most influential critical works of the 20th century. Since then, the term ambiguity has been widely used in criticism to mean that a word or expression is used to signify two or more distinct descriptive senses or to express two or more feelings or attitudes. In a word, ambiguity means multiple interpretations.

在1930年，新批评的先锋，威廉·燕卜荪（1906—1984）出版了《复义七型》，这是20世纪最有影响的批评作品之一。自此，复义性就在评论界广泛使用，指一个单词或表述被用来暗指两个或者更多的含义，或者用来表达两种或更多的情感或态度。总而言之，复义性就是指多种解释。

American Realism（美国现实主义）

As a literary movement, realism initiated in France in the 19th century and is often associated with the French novelists—Gustave Flaubert and Balzac. In American literature, realism encompasses the period of time from the Civil War to the turn of last century (1865—1918). It is a reaction against romanticism and attempts to present real life without romantic subjectivity. So according to Sir Paul Harvey[1], realism was "a loosely used term meaning truth to the observed facts of life"[2]. Its representatives are William Dean Howells[3],

---

[1] Sir Paul Harvey (1869—1948) was a British diplomat and editor of literary reference works.

[2] Sir Paul Harvey, *The Oxford Companion to English Literature*, 1930. extracted from Katherine Paterson, *Read For Your Life* #16, Kindle Edition, p. 4.

[3] William Dean Howells (1837—1920) was an American realist writer and literary critic, known as the "The Dean of American Letters". *Christmas Every Day* and *The Rise of Silas Lapham* are his notable works.

Henry James①, Mark Twain②, O Henry③and so on.

现实主义是 19 世纪起始于法国的文学运动，经常与法国小说家古斯塔夫·福楼拜、巴尔扎克相联系。在美国文学中，现实主义始于内战时期，结束于 20 世纪初（1865—1918）。现实主义是对浪漫主义做出的反应，试图不带有任何浪漫主观性来描述现实生活。所以根据保罗·哈维所说，现实主义就是"一个泛指真实呈现所观察到的现实生活的术语"。其代表人物有威廉·迪恩·豪威尔斯、亨利·詹姆斯、马克·吐温、欧·亨利等。

Angry Young Men（愤怒的青年）

"Angry young men", considered to be derived from Leslie Paul's *Angry Young Man* published in 1951, was first coined by the Royal Court Theatre's press agent to describe John Osborne④'s *Look Back in Anger* (1956). It is used to refer to a group of working-and-middle-class British young writers and critics in the 1950s who were dissatisfied with some political and social phenomena and criticized the problems. John Osborne and Kingsley Amis⑤are leading members of the group.

"愤怒的青年"被认为来源于莱斯利·保罗 1951 年出版的《愤怒的青年》，最初是由皇家宫廷剧院的报社用来描述约翰·奥斯本的《愤怒的回顾》（1956）。现用来指在 20 世纪 50 年代一群工人和中层

---

① Henry James (1843—1916) was an American writer famous for *Daisy Miller* (1879), *The Portrait of a Lady* (1881) and *The Ambassadors* (1903). He was considered as one of the founders and leaders of realism.

② Mark Twain (1835—1910) was an American writer, best known for *The Adventure of Tom Sawyer* (1876) and *Adventure of Huckleberry Finn* (1885).

③ O Henry (1862—1910) was an American short story writer best known for his witticism, wordplay, and unexpected endings in his short stories.

④ John Osborne (1929—1994) was an English writer, whose *Look Back in Anger* earned him reputation.

⑤ Kingsley Amis (1922—1995) was an English novelist, poet and critic, whose *Lucky Jim* (1954) is one of representative works of Angry Young Men.

阶级的英国年轻作家和批评家，他们对一些政治和社会现象很不满意并对其进行批评。约翰·奥斯本和金斯利·艾米斯是其领袖。

Antihero（反英雄）

An antihero, as a term opposed to hero first used in 1714, is a protagonist in literature, theatre and film who lacks traditional heroic qualities such as courage, sacrifice, competence and morality. Antiheroes are often lazy, mean, weak and incompetent, but are not actually evil. They are sympathetic but indifferent to politics. In the 19th century, the antihero was very popular and became an established form of social criticism. In the early 20th century, many writers created many antiheroes in their works, such as, Franz Kafka's *The Metamorphosis* (1915) and Jean-Paul Sartre's *La Nausée* (1938).

反英雄，作为一个与"英雄"相对的术语，最先在 1714 年使用，是指在文学、戏剧和影视中缺少传统的英雄品质，例如勇敢、牺牲、能力和美德。反英雄们往往是懒惰的、吝啬的、虚弱的、力不胜任的，但是事实上他们本质不坏。他们富有同情心但是对政治冷漠。在 19 世纪，反英雄受到热捧并成为社会批评的既定形式。在 20 世纪初，很多作家在其作品中塑造了个性鲜明的反英雄，例如弗兰兹·卡夫卡的《变形记》（1915）以及让－保罗·萨特的《恶心》（1938）。

Antithesis（对偶）

According to *The Columbia Encyclopedia*, published by Columbia University Press in 2000, antithesis is "a figure of speech involving a seeming contradiction of ideas, words, clauses, or sentences within a balanced grammatical structure. Parallelism of expression serves to emphasize opposition of ideas". Alexander Pope (1688—1744) and other poets cultivated antithesis in the 18th century to make readers better understand what they wanted to express. Samuel Johnson①once said "Marriage has many pains, but celibacy has no pleasures"②, which obviously employs antithesis.

根据哥伦比亚大学在 2000 年出版的《哥伦比亚百科全书（第六版）》，对偶是 "一种修辞方式，在对应的语法结构中包含了观点、词语、从句或者句子表面上的矛盾。并行性表达是为了强调观点的相对"。亚历山大·蒲柏（1688—1744）和其他的诗人在 18 世纪为了使读者能更好地理解他们想要表达的意思而原创了对偶。塞缪尔·约翰逊曾说到 "婚姻多痛苦，单身无乐趣"，这句话就很明显使用了对偶。

Aphorism（格言）

An aphorism is a concise and pointed statement which tells us a general truth, principle or precept in a fact tone. An aphorist often gives a sentence or two to artful integrity. Let's take Oscar Wilde's aphorism as an example: "one's real life is often the life one does not lead." In our life, we are often confronted with aphorisms. For example: "A bird in the hand is worth two in the bush." "Birds of a feather flock together."

格言就是简洁明了的一句话，它以一种事实的口吻告诉我们一个普遍的道理、原则或者训诫。格言家经常给出的格言是一两句有巧妙完整性的句子。让我们来看一下奥斯卡·王尔德的格言 "一个人真正的生活就是他从来没有过过的生活。" 在我们生活中，我们经常能看到格言。例如："一鸟在手，胜过二鸟在林。""物以类聚、人以群分。"

Apollonian and Dionysian（日神式思维与酒神式思维）

According to ancient Greek mythology, Apollo and Dionysus are Zeus's

---

① Samuel Johnson (1709—1784) was an English poet, essayist, critic, and biographer considered as a prominent figure in the 18th century.

② Samuel Johnson, *The History of Rasselas, Prince of Abyssinia*, Chapter 26. http://www.gutenberg.org/files/652/652 - h/652 - h. htm.

two sons. Apollo is the god of sun who represents reason and form, while Dionysus is the god of wine who represents ecstasy and chaos. Inspired by the mythology, Friedrich Nietzsche (1844—1900) put forward his philosophical and literary dichotomy in *The Birth of Tragedy* (1872). He thinks that Apollonian means the unique individuality and all types of form and structure are Apollonian, while Dionysian, opposed to Apollonian, means giving up individuality and all forms of enthusiasm and ecstasy are Dionysian. The true tragedy consists of the tension between the Apollonian and the Dionysian. Without the Apollonian, the Dionysian lacks the form and structure to make a coherent piece of art, and without the Dionysian, the Apollonian lacks the necessary vitality and passion. During the "long sixties" (1958—1974), Dionysian was an influential term in America.

根据古希腊神话，阿波罗与狄奥尼索斯都是宙斯的儿子。阿波罗是太阳神，代表着理性与形式，而狄奥尼索斯是酒神，代表着疯狂和混乱。受到了神话的启发，弗里德里希·尼采（1844—1900）在《悲剧的诞生》（1872）提出了哲学和文学的两分法。他认为日神式思维意味着个人主义，所有类型的形式与结构都是日神式思维，而酒神式思维与日神式思维相反，它意味着抛弃个人主义，所有形式的热情与疯狂都是酒神式思维。真正的悲剧是由日神式思维和酒神式思维之间的张力组成的。没有日神式思维，酒神式思维缺乏形式与结构，不能成为连贯的艺术作品；没有酒神式思维，日神式思维缺少必要的生气与激情。在"漫长的六十年代"（1958—1974），酒神式思维成为美国颇具影响力的词汇。

Archetypal Criticism（原型批评）

Archetypal criticism has been used much as a literary criticism since the publication of Maud Bodkin's *Archetypal Patterns in Poetry* in 1934. It derives from Carl Jung's "collective unconscious" (a kind of universal psyche) and prevailed in western countries in the 1950s, when New Criticism began to decline.

It argues that cultural and psychological myths determine a literary work's meaning. Mythology is reckoned as "the textbook of the archetypes" by Jung.

Northrop Frye (1912—1991), a Canadian literary critic, is one of the most eminent founders of the criticism. His *The Anatomy of Criticism* published in 1957 elaborately interprets mythological archetypal criticism. In addition, G. Wilson Knight (1897—1985), Robert Graves (1895—1985), Philip Wheelwright (1901—1970), and Joseph Campbell (1904—1987) are also notable representatives.

自 1934 年莫德·鲍德金的《诗中的原型模式》出版，原型批评理论就一直作为文学批评理论而被使用。它起源于卡尔·荣格的"集体无意识"（一种普遍的心理）并且在新批评理论开始衰落的 20 世纪 50 年代在西方国家盛行。

它认为文化和心理神话决定了一个文学作品的意义。荣格认为神话传说是"原型的教科书"。

诺思洛普·弗莱（1912—1991），加拿大文学批评家，是该理论最为杰出的创始人之一。他在 1957 年出版的《批评的剖析》详尽地解释了神话原型批评。除此之外，威尔逊·奈特（1897—1985），罗伯特·格雷夫斯（1895—1985），菲利普·维尔莱特（1901—1970），还有约瑟夫·坎贝尔（1904—1987）都是杰出的代表人物。

Aristotelian Criticism（亚里士多德批评主义）

Aristotle, as a great Greek philosopher, was famous for *Poetics* produced around 335 or 330 B. C. It mainly discussed tragedy and epic. So his doctrine and theories about tragedy and the tragic hero can be found in it.

In Aristotle's opinion, plot is more important than character in a tragedy. He summarizes six elementary aspects of tragic poetry: dianoia (thought), melos (music), opsis (spectacle), mythos (story or plot), lexis (diction), and ethos (character).

In contrast to Platonic Criticism, Aristotelian Criticism lays more attention to literary analysis of the work itself.

亚里士多德，是一位伟大的希腊哲学家，因在公元前335年或者公元前330年出版的《诗学》而闻名。该书主要讨论悲剧和史诗，所以他关于悲剧以及悲剧英雄的观点和理论在该书中都得以体现。

依亚里士多德所见，在悲剧中情节要比人物更重要。他总结了悲剧诗歌的六个主要方面：思想、韵律、场面、情节、措辞以及人物。

与柏拉图批评主义相比，亚里士多德批评主义更注重文本本身的文学分析。

Assonance（半韵）

Assonance is a figure of repetition: two or more neighboring words repeat the resemble or similar vowel sounds but start with different consonants, as in "Men sell the wedding bell", "lake" and "fate".

As a literary device, it is used to achieve emphasis, cohesion and musical effect in a short part of a text.

Assonance is so similar to rhyme that many people are confused. What differentiates assonance from rhyme is that rhyme usually is both similar vowel and consonant sounds, as in "lake" and "fake".

半韵是一种重复：相邻的两个或者更多的单词有着一样或者相似的元音发音，但是以不同的辅音开头，例如"Men sell the wedding bell"以及"lake 和 fate"。

半韵是一种文学方法，是为了对文中的一个小片段进行强调从而达到连贯和优美的效果。

半韵与韵律很相似，所以很多人会弄混。半韵与韵律的不同在于韵律通常包含的是元音与辅音都相似的发音，例如"lake 和 fake"。

Augustan Age（奥古斯都时代或拉丁文学全盛时代）

Augustan Age originally referred to the age of the Roman emperor Augustus, from 27 B. C. to 14 A. D. , during which three immortal Latin poets Virgil①, Ovid②, and Horace③created great literary works. Augustus Age marked the golden age of Latin literature.

The first half of the eighteenth century (more specifically, the period after the Restoration era to the death of Alexander Pope) in English literature was also called Augustan Age, because many famous writers, such as Alexander Pope (1688—1744), Johnathan Swift (1667—1745), John Dryden (1631—1700) and Joseph Addison (1672—1719) self-consciously imitated the Augustan writers (mentioned in the first paragraph) to achieve harmony, precision and urbanity in their poems.

奥古斯都时代本来是指罗马帝王奥古斯都统治时期，从公元前 27 年到公元 14 年，在此期间，三位永垂不朽的拉丁诗人维吉尔、奥维德和贺拉斯创作了伟大的文学作品。奥古斯都时代标志着拉丁文学的黄金期。

18 世纪上半叶（更准确地说，就是复辟时期之后直到亚历山大·蒲柏去世为止）在英国文学中也被称为奥古斯都时代。因为，很多著名的作家，例如亚历山大·蒲柏（1688—1744）、乔纳森·斯威夫特（1667—1745）、约翰·德莱顿（1631—1700）以及约瑟夫·爱迪生

---

① Virgil (70 B. C. —19 B. C.) was an ancient Roman poet of the Augustan period, best known for *Eclogues*, *Georgics*, and *Aeneid*.

② Ovid (43 B. C. —17/18 A. D.) was an ancient Roman poet of the Augustan period, notable for *Metamorphoses*.

③ Horace (65 B. C. —8 B. C.) was a leading poet during the Augustan period, famous for *Arts Poetica*.

（1672—1719）自觉地模仿奥古斯都时期的作家（第一段提到的）以达到诗歌的和谐、准确以及优雅。

Automatic Writing（自动书写）

Automatic writing, also called freewriting, is a form of writing advocated by surrealist Andre Breton[①]in the early 20th century. During the process of automatic writing, the writer writes something unconsciously. That is, the hands form the message or information, but the writer is unaware of what will be written down. The writer writes whatever words come to mind. It is considered to be an excellent tool for generating creative ideas.

自动书写，也被称为自由书写，是一种写作方式，由超现实主义者安德烈·布勒东在 20 世纪初倡导。在自动书写过程中，作者无意识地进行写作。也就是说，手用来书写文字或信息，但是作者对写的东西并无意识，作者会写出任何头脑中出现的单词。自动书写被认为是产生创造性观点的极好工具。

Avant-garde（先锋）

Avant-garde, a phrase loaned from French, means "advanced guard". It has military origin, meaning the front part of an army. But now, it refers to the group of people who have surprising, progressive, innovative and creative ideas especially in the fields of art, literature, culture, etc.

In 1845, Gabriel-Désiré Laverdant first used the phrase in reference to art and literature. The avant-garde breaks the old rules and boundaries, explores new things, and advocates radical social reforms.

先锋，是从法语来的外来词，意思是"先进的士兵"。它起源于

---

① Andre Breton (1896—1966) was a French writer and the founder of Surrealism, whose *Surrealist Manifesto* (1924) was a notable book.

军队，意思是队伍的前面部分。但是现在，它用来指那些在艺术、文学、文化等领域有着惊人、先进、革新和创新想法的人们。

在 1845 年，加布里埃尔·德西雷·拉韦尔第一次使用该词来指艺术与文学。先锋们打破陈规，探索新事物并倡导激进的社会变革。

B

Ballad（民谣）

ZA ballad, as a form of short narrative folk song, is derived from Europe in the late Middle Ages. Later, ballads were transmitted orally to America, Australia and North Africa, and enjoyed great popularity. Traditional ballads were collected and printed until the 18th century. For example, Thomas Percy①'s *Reliques of Ancient English Poetry* (1765) and Francis James Child②'s *English and Scottish Popular Ballads* (1882—1898). Wystan Hugh Auden③, Bertolt Brecht (1898—1956), and Elizabeth Bishop (1911—1979) are representatives of modern literary ballads.

A ballad stanza is a four-line stanza, known as a quatrain, which is the most common stanza form.

民谣，作为简短的民歌叙事方式在中世纪末期起源于欧洲。随后以口头形式传播到美国、澳大利亚和北非并大受欢迎。直到 18 世纪，

---

① Thomas Percy (1729—1811) was a bishop and editor, whose *Reliques of Ancient English Poetry* (1765) was the first of the great ballad collections.

② Francis James Child (1825—1896) was an American scholar and educator, notable for his collection of ballads.

③ Wystan Hugh Auden (1907—1973) was an Anglo-American poet, whose poetry is famous for stylistic achievement.

传统的民谣才被收集整理并打印出来。例如托马斯·珀西的《英国古诗拾遗》（1765）和弗朗西斯·詹姆斯·蔡尔德的《英格兰与苏格兰民谣集》（1882—1898）。威斯坦·休·奥登（1907—1973）、贝尔托特·布莱希特（1898—1956）、伊丽莎白·毕肖普（1911—1979）是现代民谣的代表人物。

民谣诗是一种四行诗，是最普通的诗歌形式。

Baroque（巴洛克风格作品）

"Baroque" was originally used to derogatorily describe the 17th-century artistic style（lyrical, exaggerated and luxuriant style）which is different from the Renaissance style. But now it descriptively refers to a style of sculpture, architecture, painting, literature, music and theater that began in Rome, Italy at the beginning of the 17th century and then spread to Germany and other European countries.

In literature it refers to the verse or prose with an elaborately formal and magniloquent style. Milton's *Paradise Lost*（1667）is one example. John Donne's metaphysical poems are sometimes considered as baroque.

"巴洛克"最开始是用来贬低17世纪与文艺复兴风格截然不同的艺术风格（热情奔放、浮夸和奢华的风格）。现在是用来描述17世纪开始出现在意大利的罗马，然后传到德国和其他欧洲国家的雕刻、建筑、绘画、文学、音乐和歌剧中的风格。

在文学中它指具有精致庄重和富丽堂皇的风格的诗歌或散文。弥尔顿的《失乐园》（1667）就是其中的例子。约翰·邓恩的玄学派诗歌有时也被认为是具有巴洛克风格。

Bathos（顿降法）

Bathos is a literary term, which was first used by Alexander Pope in his essay *Peri Bathous* or *The Art of Sinking in Poetry* in 1727 to mock the abuse of figures of speech by bad writers.

Bathos refers to an abrupt and often unsuccessful juxtaposition of the elevated and the commonplace, producing a ridiculous effect. It can be used both intentionally to create humorous effects and accidentally by unskilled writers or poets.

Martin Price writes that "Swift and Pope use bathos constantly to dramatize the collapse of mind in the very activities in which it takes pride"[1].

顿降法是一个文学术语，由亚历山大·蒲柏在 1727 年的散文《诗歌沉降艺术》中第一次使用，以嘲讽那些拙劣的作家对于语言修辞的滥用。

顿降法是指高尚与平庸事物的突然且失败的并举，从而产生一种荒谬的效果。它可以为制造幽默的效果故意使用，也可以是拙劣的作家或诗人的无意而为。

马丁·普莱斯写道："斯威夫特和蒲柏不断地使用顿降法把本来引以为豪的思维活动的突然崩溃戏剧化"。

Beast Fable（动物寓言）

The beast fable, as a form of allegorical writing, is often a short story or poem in which animals speak and act like human beings to dramatize human faults. It is created to reflect the people's real world for pedagogic purpose. The great ancient Greek writer Aesop is famous for his beast fables and is considered one of the best-known writers who have greatly contributed to Western literature.

Hollywood's films also take the beast fable as a central genre, for example *Kong Fu Panda*, *Simba* and so on.

---

[1] David Mikics, *A New Handbook of Literary Terms*, New Haven: Yale Univeristy Press, 2007, p. 37.

动物寓言，作为一种寓言写作形式，通常是短故事或者诗歌。在寓言中动物们像人类一样说话、做事，以把人类的缺点戏剧化。动物寓言的创作就是为了反映人类的真实世界以达到教育的目的。伟大的古希腊作家伊索因为动物寓言而出名，被认为是对西方文学做出巨大贡献的著名作家之一。

好莱坞的电影也把动物寓言作为一种主要的形式，例如《功夫熊猫》、《狮子王》等。

Beats or Beat Generation（垮掉一代）

After the Second World War, that is, in the 1950s and 1960s, influenced much by the Eastern philosophy and religion, a group of American writers and artists came to maturity. They rejected the conventional social values, espoused anarchism, communal living, homosexuality, alcoholism and drugs to rebel against the materialistic society, and appealed for unfettered self-realization.

It was a controversial subculture in America at that time, gaining both praises and condemnations. A number of notable writers are included in the group: Allen Ginsberg[1], Jack Kerouac[2] and William Burroughs[3]. Allen Ginsberg read his long poem *Howl* publicly in 1955 (in fact the poem was published formally in 1956 and then was forbidden for its "sensuality"), which symbolized the formation of Beat Generation. *Howl* and Jack Kerouac's *On the Road* are considered as the *Bible* for Beat Generation.

第二次世界大战后，也就是在 20 世纪 50 年代和 60 年代，由于受

---

[1] Allen Ginsberg (1926—1997) was an American poet, known as the author of *Howl*. He was one of the leaders of the Beat Generation.

[2] Jack Kerouac (1922—1969) was an American writer, best known for *On the Road* (1957). He was a primary figure of the Beat Generation.

[3] William Burroughs (1914—1997) was an American Beat Generation writer, best known for his novel *Naked Lunch* (1959).

到东方哲学和宗教的影响，一群美国作家和艺术家开始走向成熟。他们摒弃传统的社会价值观，支持无政府主义、群居、同性恋、酗酒和吸毒来反抗物欲横流的社会，并渴望毫无约束的自我实现。

在当时，这是美国一个饱受争议的非主流文化，毁誉参半。很多知名作家都属于这一群体：艾伦·金斯堡、杰克·凯鲁亚克以及威廉·巴勒斯。艾伦·金斯堡在 1955 年公开阅读自己的长诗《嚎叫》（事实上该诗在 1956 年正式出版，却因为"淫乱"而被禁），这标志着垮掉的一代的形成。《嚎叫》和杰克·凯鲁亚克的《在路上》被认为是垮掉的一代的《圣经》。

Belles-lettres（纯文学）

Belles-lettres is a French word, meaning "beautiful letters". It is used to describe a type of literary writing, which focuses on aesthetics, originality of its style and tone, rather than on content and its ideas. Innovative word use, sophisticated writing style, and beautiful expressions are some of belles-lettres' features.

In contrast to scholarly and academic writing, belles-lettres doesn't stick to patterns or conventions. Therefore, it is a visual feast and an aesthetic enjoyment to read such works.

Belles-lettres 是一个法语词，意思是"优美的文字"。现在用它来形容一种写作方式：注重于美学、写作风格与格调的原创性，而不是内容和观点。创新单词的使用、熟练的创作风格以及优美的表达都是该类文学的特征。

与学术和理论写作相比，纯文学并不循规蹈矩。因此，读这类作品是一个视觉的盛宴和美的享受。

Bildungsroman（成长小说）

The term "bildungsroman" is derived from German, meaning "novel of

coming-of-age story". In the latter half of the 18th century, the Bildungsroman became a special type of novel used in English literature. It mainly deals
with a character's growth from childhood to adulthood, gaining both moral
and psychological maturity and the conflicts between the character's self-ful-
fillment and his or her social reality. Johann Wolfgang von Goethe[1]'s *Wilhelm
Meister's Apprenticeship* (1795—1796) is a classic example of the genre.

该词来源于德语，意思是"成长小说"。在 18 世纪后半期，成长
小说成为英语文学中使用的特殊的小说形式。它主要讲述人物从孩童
到成年的成长过程，获得道德与心理上的成熟以及人物的自我实现与
社会现实之间的矛盾冲突。约翰·沃尔夫冈·冯·歌德的《威廉·麦
斯特的学习时代》（1795—96）是该类型小说的经典范例。

Biography（传记）

Biography refers to a full description of a particular person's life, including his or her character, social background, education, work and death,
as well as his or her experiences and activities.

The most famous surviving biography is the *Parallel Lives of Greek and
Roman Notables* written by Plutarch (46 A. P. —120 A. D.).

Autobiography is a biography written by the writer about himself or herself. The first fully developed and influential autobiography is St. Augustine's
Confessions, written in the 4th century.

传记是指对于特定人物的一生进行详尽地描写，包括他或她的性
格、社会背景、教育、工作和死亡，同时还有他或她的经历和活动。

流传至今、最负盛名的传记是由普鲁塔克（公元 46 年—公元 120
年）所写的关于希腊和罗马名人的《希腊罗马名人列传》。

---

① Johann Wolfgang von Goethe (1749—1832) was a German writer, critic and statesman, considered as one of the giants of world literature. His *The Sorrows of Young Werther* (1774) made him world
famous.

自传是作者写的关于自己的传记。第一部详尽描述且影响力深远的自传是圣·奥古斯丁在公元四世纪写的《忏悔录》。

Black Arts Movement（黑人艺术运动）

Black Arts Movement, as the cultural branch of the Black Power Movement, is one of the most important times in African-American literature. It happened in 1960s, when America was facing both social and political turbulence. It advocated black solidarity and black pride, and encouraged black people to establish their own publishing houses, magazines and art institutions.

Larry Neal proclaimed in his essay *The Black Arts Movement* (1968): "Black Arts Movement is the aesthetic and spiritual sister of the Black Power Concept. As such, it envisions an art that speaks directly to the needs and aspirations of Black America."[1]

Stokely Carmichael (1941—1998) and Malcolm X (1925—1965) were its spokesmen. In addition, Nikki Giovanni (1943—), Sonia Sanchez (1934—), Maya Angelou (1928—2014), Hoyt W. Fuller (1923—1981), and Rosa Guy (1922—2012) were also famous writers involved in the movement.

黑人艺术运动，作为黑人权力运动的文化分支，是美国黑人文学的重要时期之一。它发生在 20 世纪 60 年代，当时美国正面临着社会和政治动乱。它倡导黑人团结和黑人自尊并鼓励黑人建立自己的出版社、杂志和艺术机构。

拉里·尼尔在其评论《黑人艺术运动》(1968) 中说道："黑人艺术是黑人权力概念的美学与精神姊妹。因此它构想出一种可以直接表

---

① Larry Neal, *The Black Arts Movement*, http://nationalhumanitiescenter.org/pds/maai3/community/text8/blackartsmovement.pdf.

达美国黑人的需求和渴望的艺术。"

斯托克利·卡迈克尔（1941—1998）和马尔科姆·艾克斯（1925—1965）是其代言人。除此之外，尼基·乔瓦尼（1943—）、索尼娅·桑切斯（1934—）、玛雅·安吉罗（1928—2014）、霍伊特·福勒（1923—1981）以及罗莎·盖伊（1922—2012）是参与该运动的著名作家。

Black Mountain College and Black Mountain Poets（黑山学院与黑山派诗人）

Black Mountain College was located in Black Mountain, North Carolina and was as an experimental institution from 1933 to 1956. It believed that arts were significant to human understanding and laid emphasis on art education and practice.

Black Mountain poets were a group of poets drawn to the college to study or to teach and most of them became American avant-garde in 1950s. Charles Olson (1910—1970), Robert Duncan (1919—1988), Denise Levertov (1923—1997), Jonathan Williams (1929—2008), and Robert Creeley (1926—2005) are the best known representative poets of the school. They refused the poetic tradition advocated by T. S. Eliot, and emulated the freer style of William Carlos Williams (1883—1963). Their poems were published in Black Mountain Review (1954—1957) established by Creeley and Olson. *Projective Verse* (1950) written by Charles Olson was their manifesto, so they were also called "projectivist poets".

黑山学院坐落在卡罗莱纳州北部的黑山，从 1933 年到 1956 年期间是一所实验机构。它相信艺术对于人类的理解力至关重要，并强调艺术教育与实践的重要性。

黑山派诗人是一群到该学院学习或者教书的诗人，并且他们很多人都成为了美国 20 世纪 50 年代的先锋派。查尔斯·奥尔森（1910—

1970）、罗伯特·邓肯（1919—1988）、丹妮斯·莱维托芙（1923—1997）、乔纳森·威廉姆斯（1929—2008）、罗伯特·克里利（1926—2005）他们都是黑山派代表诗人。他们拒绝 T. S. 艾略特所倡导的诗歌传统，模仿威廉·卡洛斯·威廉姆斯（1883—1963）更为自由的诗歌风格。他们的诗发表在由克里利和奥尔森创立的《黑山评论》（1954—1957）上。由查尔斯·奥尔森完成的《投射诗》（1950）是黑山派诗人的宣言，所以他们也被称为"投射派诗人"。

Black Comedy or Black Humor（黑色幽默）

Black comedy or black humor was a modern literary trend that emerged in America in 1960s. It often used farce and satire to describe a "taboo", such as death, disease, or warfare to make people understand that individuals are helpless victims of fate. It prevails in Modern American literature.

As a matter of fact, though Andre Breton, a surrealist, published *Anthology of Black Humor* in 1945, the term "black humor" didn't come into common use until 1960s. Joseph Heller's *Catch-22* (1961) is reckoned as the most typical work of the school. In addition, Kurt Vonnegut's *Slaughterhouse Five* (1969) and Thomas Pynchon *Gravity's Rainbow* (1973) are also notable works.

黑色喜剧或者黑色幽默是 20 世纪 60 年代在美国兴起的一个现代主义文学流派。它经常使用滑稽剧和讽刺来描写"禁忌"，例如死亡、疾病或者战争，以此来让人们明白个人就是无助的命运牺牲品。它在美国现代文学中盛行。

事实上，虽然超现实主义者安德烈·布勒东在 1945 年出版了《黑色幽默选集》，但是"黑色幽默"这个词直到 20 世纪 60 年代才普遍使用。约瑟夫·海勒的《第二十二条军规》（1961）被认为是该流派最典型的作品。除此之外，库尔特·冯内古特的《第五号屠宰场》（1969）以及托马斯·品钦的《万有引力之虹》也值得一提。

Blank Verse（无韵诗）

Blank verse refers to the poetry comprised of unrhymed lines in regular meter, usually iambic pentameter, which makes it different from free verse. It emerged in Italy and was widely used during the Renaissance. It has been considered by Jay Parini（1948—）as "probably the most common and influential form that English poetry has taken since the 16th century"[1]. It is Christopher Marlowe that first made full use of blank verse and made it the standard for many English writers, including Shakespeare and Milton. Yeats, Pound and Frost also preferred the form. Though it began to decline when Modernism arrived in the 20th century, its role in poetry is undisputed.

无韵诗是指不押韵的格律诗，通常是五音步抑扬格，这也是它与自由诗的不同所在。它出现于意大利，在文艺复兴期间被广泛应用。杰伊·帕里尼（1948—）认为它"很可能是自16世纪以来最普遍、最有影响力的英语诗歌形式"。克里斯托弗·马洛最先使用无韵诗，并使其成为很多英国作家的写作标准，甚至包括莎士比亚和弥尔顿。叶芝、庞德和弗罗斯特都非常喜爱这种诗歌形式。虽然到20世纪现代主义出现的时候它开始衰落，但是其在诗歌界的作用毋庸置疑。

Bloomsbury Group（布鲁姆斯伯里文化圈）

The Bloomsbury Group, also called "Bloomsberries", referred to a group of well-educated and talented intellectuals of the upper middle class. From 1904, some writers and artists began to meet regularly at the Gorden Square home of Thomby Stephen in Bloomsbury, London to indulge in free conversations about arts, literature and philosophy.

---

[1] Jay Parini, *The Wadsworth Anthology of Poetry*, Cengage Learning, 2005, p. 655.

They refused the traditional Victorian ideas and shared similar ideas and values. They held supportive attitudes toward gay rights, women's rights, open marriages, and so on. "In short, they were determined to reinvent society, at least within their own circle."[①] The group existed for more than twenty years, but it never became a school. Among them, E. M. Forster (1879—1970), Lytton Strachey (1880—1932) and Virginia Woolf (1882—1941) were the most famous writers in the group.

布鲁姆斯伯里文化圈，也被称为"布鲁姆斯伯里人"，是指一群受到良好教育、才华过人的中产阶级上层知识分子。从 1904 年开始，一些作家和艺术家开始定期在坐落于伦敦布鲁姆斯伯里戈登广场的托比·斯蒂芬的家里会面，自由地讨论艺术、文学和哲学。

他们拒绝传统的维多利亚观点。他们有着相似的观点和价值观，对同性恋权益、女人权益、开放婚姻等持支持态度。"简而言之，他们下定决心要彻底改造社会，至少改造他们自己的圈子。"该圈子持续了二十多年，但并没有成为一个流派。其中，爱德华·摩根·福斯特（1879—1970）、利顿·斯特雷奇（1880—1932）、弗吉尼亚·伍尔夫（1882—1941）是该圈子的最出名的作家。

Bluestockings（蓝袜子）

There is a story about the origin of bluestockings: Benjiamin Stillingfleet (1702—1771), a translator and publisher, was not rich enough to wear silk stockings, so everyday he just wore blue stockings to attend the gatherings led by Elizabeth Montagu (1720—1800), who was the founder of Blue Stockings Society and was later called "the Queen of the Bluestockings".

---

① O'Neil, *Patrick M. Great World Writers: Twentieth Century*, Cavendish Square Publishing, 2004.

Today, in English, the term "bluestockings" refers to the educated, literary and intellectual women and men involved in the mid-18th-century Blue Stockings Society. They gathered informally and talked about literature, art and fashion, which was a revolutionary activity as opposed to traditional women's activities.

有个故事是关于蓝袜子起源的：翻译家兼出版商的本杰明·斯蒂林弗利特（1702—1771）并不富裕，买不起丝袜，所以每天他都穿着蓝色的长袜参加由伊丽莎白·蒙塔古（1720—1800）举办的聚会。蒙塔古就是蓝袜子集会的创始人，后来被称为"蓝袜子王后"。

现在，在英语中，bluestockings 这个单词是指参加了 18 世纪中期的蓝袜子集会且受过教育、对文学感兴趣、有知识的女性或者男性。他们非正式地聚在一起，讨论文学、艺术和时尚，这与传统的女性活动相比是一个具有革命意义的活动。

Bombast（浮夸的言语）

Bombast is a word with a pejorative meaning. It refers to the pompous, boasting and pretentious speech or writing which sounds significant but is actually disproportionate and meaningless. In poetry and drama, bombast is often spoken by a hero or heroine for ridiculous effects. For example, in *Midsummer Night's Dream*, Bottom often uses bombast, which is a humorous indication of his arrogant stupidity and ignorance.

该词一个贬义词，它是指浮华、高傲、做作的语言或者写作，听起来很重要但是事实上不合理且毫无意义。在诗歌和戏剧中，为了达到讽刺的效果，主人公经常使用浮夸的言语。例如在《仲夏夜之梦》中，博顿经常使用浮夸的言语，这恰恰是他高傲的愚蠢与无知的幽默暗示。

Bovarysme（包法利主义）

Bovarysme derives from Emma Bovary, the protagonist of Gustave Flaubert（1821—1880）'s debut novel *Madame Bovary*（1856）. In the novel, Emma is dissatisfied with her marriage with doctor Bovary and imagines herself as a heroine in a romance, trying to escape from everyday realities. She has a few adulterous affairs to search for "true love", but commits suicide in desperation at last. Flaubert once said "Life is such a hideous business that the only way to tolerate it is to avoid it... by living in Art."[①] Thus, Bovarysme, to some extent, refers to an escapist attitude toward life.

包法利主义来源于居斯塔夫·福楼拜（1821—1880）的处女作《包法利夫人》（1856）中的女主人公爱玛·包法利。在该小说中，爱玛对自己与包法利医生的婚姻不满足，把自己想象成浪漫爱情故事的女主人公以此逃避现实生活。她为了寻找"真爱"几次出轨，结果在绝望中自杀。福楼拜曾说过："生活就是丑恶的交易，唯一忍受生活的方式就是通过生活在艺术之中来躲避它。"因此，包法利主义从某种意义上来说就是指对生活所持的逃避态度。

Bowdlerization （恶意删除）

The word originated from Thomas Bowdler（1754—1825）, an English editor and physician, who was famous for publishing *The Family Shakespeare*, a bowdlerized version of Williams Shakespeare's works. He removed some parts in Shakespeare's original works that were offensive for 19th-century children and women to read.

Bowdlerization refers to the removal of some parts considered offensive or vulgar from a book, movie, play, etc. Today, the word is often used in a pejorative sense by editors and scholars to indicate an inferior quality literary work.

该词来源于英国编辑兼医生的托马斯·鲍德勒（1754—1825），

---

① Frederick Brown, *Flaubert*: *A Biography*, Harvard University Press, 2007, p. 353.

他因为出版了《家庭版莎士比亚集》而出名，这是一个对威廉·莎士比亚作品进行删减的版本。他把莎士比亚原著中的对于 19 世纪的妇女和儿童不太适宜读的部分进行了删减。

该词是指把一些被认为冒犯或者粗俗的部分丛书、电影、戏剧等中删掉。现在该单词经常被编辑和学者用来形容拙劣的文学作品。

Burns Stanza or Standard Habbie（彭斯诗节或者哈比标准）

Burns stanza is named after Robert Burns（1759—1796），a famous Scottish poet，who used the stanza in about fifty poems. But it was not invented by him but by Habbie Simpson（1550—1620）. So it was known as "Standard Habbie" before Burns. Burns Stanza consists of six lines with an "aaabab" rhyme pattern. A great deal of Burns's works，including "To a Mouse"，"To a Louse"，"To a Haggis"，etc. used the stanza.

The following is the first part of Burns's "To a Louse"

To a Louse

On Seeing One on a lady's Bonnet，at Church

Ha！ Whaur ye gaun，ye crowlin ferlie？

Your impudence protects you sairly；

I canna say but ye strunt rarely，

Owre gauze and lace；

Tho'. faith！ I fear ye dine but sparely

On sic a place.

（Modern English Translation）

Ha！ Where are you going，you crawling wonder？

Your impudence protects you sorely；

I can not say but you swagger rarely，

Over gauze and lace；

Though faith！ I fear you dine but sparingly

On such a place.

彭斯诗节是以伟大的苏格兰诗人罗伯特·彭斯（1759—1796）命名，他在大概五十多首诗中使用该诗节。但发明者并不是他，而是哈比·辛普森（1550—1620），所以在彭斯之前也被叫做"哈比标准"。彭斯诗节由以"aaabab"为韵律的六行诗组成。彭斯的很多作品，例如《致老鼠》、《致虱子》、《致哈吉斯》等都是使用了彭斯诗节。

以下是《致虱子》中的第一部分：

《致虱子》

在教堂里看到一位女士帽子上的一个虱子有感

哈，往哪儿跑，你这爬虫？

仗着大胆乱动，

摇摇摆摆上了帽缝，

进出纱巾和花边，

我敢说没什么可供吃用，

在那等地点。

译者——王佐良

Burlesque（滑稽讽刺作品）

In literature, burlesque, as a form of satire, refers to a literary work which employs a variety of techniques (mainly by imitating the manner or the subject matter of a serious literary genre) to cause laughter. It is "an incongruous imitation". There are two primary species of burlesque: "High Burlesque" and "Low Burlesque". Parodies and mock epics (or heroic-comical poems) are high burlesques, while the Hudibrastic poems and travesties are low burlesques.

Alexander Pope's *The Rape of the Lock* (1714) is a mock epic and Samuel Butler's *Hudibras* (1663) is a Hudibrastic poem, both of which are representative works of burlesque.

在文学中，滑稽讽刺作品，作为一种讽刺形式，是指使用大量技巧（主要是通过模仿一个严肃文学作品的方式或题材）来引起大笑。它就是"一个不相称的模仿性作品"。它有两种主要的形式：升格嘲讽作品和降格嘲讽作品。戏谑模仿和模拟史诗（或者也叫英雄滑稽诗）都属于升格嘲讽作品，而休迪布拉斯式滑稽诗和效颦作品都是降格嘲讽作品。

亚历山大·蒲柏的《夺发记》（1714）是模拟史诗，塞缪尔·巴特勒的《休迪布拉斯》（1663）就是休迪布拉斯式滑稽诗，它们都是滑稽讽刺作品的代表。

Byronic Hero（拜伦式英雄）

Byronic Hero was named after Byron（1788—1824）, a leading poet in the Romantic movement. From 1813 to 1816, he published six epics later called "Oriental Tales" by a joint name. In them, he created rebellious, struggling, arrogant, stubborn, pessimist and melancholic heroes, who rose against state power, social rules and religious morality but couldn't find a right way out. Such types of people are Byronic Heroes.

拜伦式英雄以浪漫主义运动有名的诗人拜伦（1788—1824）命名。从1813年到1816年，他出版了六部长诗，后来被统称为"东方叙事诗"。在诗中，他塑造了叛逆奋争、高傲固执，悲观忧郁的英雄人物，他们与国家强权、社会秩序、宗教道德抗争，却找不到正确的出路。这样的人就是拜伦式英雄。

C

Cacophony (杂音)

The term "cacophony" originated from Greek, meaning "bad sound". In literature, cacophony, the opposite of euphony, refers to some strident, unpleasant and jarring sounds combined in writing. In poetry, it is sometimes used by poets intentionally to let readers sense the situation and add emotional depth to the moment. The following tongue twister is an example of cacophony: "She sells seashells down by the seashore."

该词来源于希腊语，意思是"糟糕的声音"。在文学中，杂音与谐音恰恰相反，是指在写作中的某些尖锐、讨厌和刺耳的声音。在诗歌中，诗人有时故意使用杂音为了让读者能亲临其境并能增添情感共鸣。下面的绕口令便是杂音的一例子："She sells seashells down by the seashore."（她在海边卖贝壳。）

Canon (佳作集)

Canon is a term used to refer to a collection of literary works which have gained a status of authority and are widely respected and read. Scholars think that the works in a canon are the most influential of a special time or place.

Thus, canon serves as a guide for reading.

佳作集是指已经获得权威地位并且被广泛尊重与阅读的文学作品集。学者们认为佳作集中的作品是某个时期或者地区的最具影响力的作品。因此，佳作集是最好的阅读资料。

Calvinism（加尔文主义）

Calvinism refers to a branch of Reformed tradition in Protestantism. It is a movement first called "Calvinism" by Lutherans. It was named after John Calvin because of his great influences and important role in the confessional and ecclesiastical debates throughout the 17th century.

There are 5 major points of Calvinism, which are known as T. U. L. I. P. —Total Depravity（Original Sin）, Unconditional Election（God's Election）, Limited Atonement（Particular Redemption）, Irresistible Grace（Effectual Calling）, and Perseverance of the Saints.

Influential Calvinists include: Martin Bucer（1491—1551）, Heinrich Bullinger（1504—1575）, Thomas Cranmer（1489—1556）, John Knox（1505—1572）and many twentieth-century Calvinists.

加尔文主义是新教在改革过程的一个分支。该运动被路德会教友称为"加尔文主义"。它是以约翰·加尔文命名的，因为他在 17 世纪忏悔和神职辩论中的巨大影响和重要作用。

加尔文主义有五个要点，也就是 T. U. L. I. P——人性完全堕落（原罪）、无条件的拣选（上帝的选择）、有限的赎罪（特定的救赎）、不可抗拒的恩典（有效的呼召）以及圣徒永蒙保守。

影响力较大的加尔文主义者包括：马丁·布瑟（1491—1551）、海因里希·布林格（1504—1575）、托马斯·克兰默（1489—1446）、约翰·诺克斯（1505—1572），还有很多 20 世纪的加尔文主义者。

Captivity Narratives（囚禁故事）

Shortly after the publication of Mary Rowlandson's *The Sovereignty and*

Goodness of God in 1682, it instantly became a bestseller and the captivity narrative became a popular narrative in American and even world literature. Captivity narratives are stories with captures, suffering, rescues and escape. Such narratives often include a theme that the captive is first forced to live an alien, incompatible and undesirable life and finally attains salvation through faith.

玛丽·罗兰森的《神的主权与仁慈》在 1682 年出版后不久就成了畅销书，囚禁故事也成为了美国甚至世界文学中非常受欢迎的叙述形式。囚禁故事就是写了囚禁、苦难、拯救与逃离的故事。这种故事经常包含着一个主题：被困人被迫过着一种另类、矛盾、讨厌的生活，最后因为自己的信念而获得拯救。

Caricature（讽刺漫画）

The word is derived from the Italian "caricare", meaning "to exaggerate or load". Therefore, caricature refers to an exaggerated and satirical drawing or description of a person's character in either a visual or literary form to create a more striking impression of the original portrait. Some of earliest caricature can be found in Leonardo da Vinci's (1452—1519) works. However, it is Annibale Carracci (1560—1609) who made caricature as an independent art form. Thus he was considered the inventor.

According to Carracci, the caricaturist and the classical artist have the same task: "Both see the lasting truth beneath the surface of mere outward appearance. Both try to help nature accomplish its plan. The one may strive to visualize the perfect form and to realize it in his work, the other to grasp the perfect deformity, and thus reveal the very essence of a personality. A good caricature, like every work of art, is more true to life than the reality itself"[1].

----

[1] E. H. Gombrich, and E. Kris, *Caricature.* Middlesex, England: King Penguin, 1940, pp. 11 – 12.

　　该单词来源于意大利语"caricare"，意思是"夸张或者加载"。因此讽刺漫画是指以图画或者书面形式对一个人的性格进行讽刺夸张的描绘或描写来加深对原肖像的印象。在里奥纳多·达·芬奇（1452—1519）的作品中能看到早期的讽刺漫画。然而，阿尼巴尔·卡拉奇（1560—1609）才是使讽刺漫画成为一种独立的艺术形式的创始人。

　　根据卡拉奇所说，讽刺漫画家与传统的艺术家有着共同的任务："两者都是透过外表看深层实质，都呈现了自然。只不过一个是通过作品中的完美形式而实现，而另一个是抓住了畸形美来揭露个性的本质。好的讽刺漫画，就像艺术品一样，要比现实更为真实"。

Caroline Age（卡罗拉时代）

In Latin, the word "Carolus" is used for Charles. Caroline Age, also known as Cavalier Age, refers to the reign of Charles I of England between 1625 and 1649. The supporters of Charles I, called Cavaliers were in conflict with the Parliament supporters, known as Roundheads, which led to a Civil War (1642—1651). With the end of the Civil War, the Caroline Age also ended. In the period, Richard Lovelace (1617—1657), Thomas Crew (1595—1640), and Sir John Suckling (1609—1641) were the notable poets. John Milton (1608—1674) began to write and finished his early works, such as *Of Education* (1644), *Aeropagitica* (1644), *The Masque Comus* (1634) and *Lycidas* (1637). Thomas Browne (1605—1682) was one of the major writers. During this period, George Herbert (1593—1633) and John Donne (1572—1631) continued to write their metaphysical poems.

　　在拉丁语中，Carolus 用来指查理。卡罗拉时代，也被称为"保王党时代"，是指英国查理一世的统治时期，即从 1625 年到 1649 年。支持查理一世的人被称为"保王党"，他们与支持议会的被称为"圆颅党"的人发生冲突，引起内战（1642—1651）。在内战快结束的时候，卡罗拉时代结束。理查德·洛夫莱斯（1617—1657）、托马斯·克鲁（1595—1640）以及约翰·萨克林（1609—1641）是该时期著名的诗人。约翰·弥尔顿（1608—1674）开始在此期间写作并完成前期作品，例如《论教育》（1644）、《论出版自由》（1644）、《酒神之假面舞会》（1634）以及《利西达斯》（1637）。托马斯·布朗（1605—1682）是主要作家之一。除此之外，乔治·赫伯特（1593—1633）以及约翰·邓恩（1572—1631）在此期间继续创作他们的玄学派诗歌。

Carpe Diem（及时行乐）

Carpe Diem, translated from the Latin as "pluck or seize the day", means enjoying the pleasures of the moment without thinking about the future. It is derived from *Odes Book* I written by Horace (65 B. C. —8 B. C.) :

> "Dum loquimur, fugerit invida
>
> Aetas : carpe diem, quam minimum credula postero"
>
> (English Translation : While we're talking, envious time is fleeing : pluck the day, put no trust in the future.)

But it is Lord Byron (1788—1824) who first integrated the phrase into English. *To His Coy Mistress* written by Andrew Marvell (1621—1678) is a typical poem with the theme of "carpe diem".

> To His Coy Mistress
>
> Had we but world enough and time,
>
> This coyness, lady, were no crime.
>
> We would sit down, and think which way
>
> To walk, and pass our long love's day.
>
> Thou by the Indian Ganges' side

Shouldst rubies find; I by the tide
Of Humber would complain. I would
Love you ten years before the flood,
And you should, if you please, refuse
Till the conversion of the Jews.
My vegetable love should grow
Vaster than empires and more slow;
An hundred years should go to praise
Thine eyes, and on thy forehead gaze;
Two hundred to adore each breast,
But thirty thousand to the rest;
An age at least to every part,
And the last age should show your heart.
For, lady, you deserve this state,
Nor would I love at lower rate.
But at my back I always hear
Time's wingèd chariot hurrying near;
And yonder all before us lie
Deserts of vast eternity.
Thy beauty shall no more be found;
Nor, in thy marble vault, shall sound
My echoing song; then worms shall try
That long-preserved virginity,
And your quaint honour turn to dust,
And into ashes all my lust;
The grave's a fine and private place,
But none, I think, do there embrace.
Now therefore, while the youthful hue

Sits on thy skin like morning dew,

And while thy willing soul transpires

At every pore with instant fires,

Now let us sport us while we may,

And now, like amorous birds of prey,

Rather at once our time devour

Than languish in his slow-chapped power.

Let us roll all our strength and all

Our sweetness up into one ball,

And tear our pleasures with rough strife

Through the iron gates of life:

Thus, though we cannot make our sun

Stand still, yet we will make him run.

Carpe Diem 从拉丁语中翻译过来是"抓住今天",意思是享受当下的快乐不去想将来。它从贺拉斯(公元前 65 年—公元前 8 年)颂歌第一卷而来:

"当我们谈话之时,妒忌的时间就在飞逝:抓住今天,管它未来如何。"

但是是拜伦男爵(1788—1824)将该词融入到英语当中。安德鲁·马韦尔(1621—1678)的《致他娇羞的女友》就是一个以"及时行乐"为主题的典型诗歌。

《致他娇羞的女友》

我们如有足够的天地和时间,

你这娇羞,小姐,就算不得什么罪愆。

我们可以坐下来,考虑向哪方

去散步,消磨这漫长的恋爱时光。

你可以在印度的恒河岸边

寻找红宝石，我可以在亨柏之畔

望潮哀叹。我可以在洪水

未到来之前十年，爱上了你，

你也可以拒绝，如果你高兴，

直到犹太人皈依基督正宗。

我的植物般的爱情可以发展，

发展得比那些帝国还辽阔，还缓慢。

我要用一百个年头来赞美

你的眼睛，凝视你的娥眉；

用二百年来膜拜你的酥胸，

其余部分要用三万个春冬。

每一部分至少要一个时代，

最后的时代才把你的心展开。

只有这样的气派，小姐，才配你，

我的爱的代价也不应比这还低。

但是在我的背后我总听到

时间的战车插翅飞奔，逼近了；

而在那前方，在我们的前面，却展现

一片永恒的沙漠，辽阔，无限。

在那里，再也找不到你的美，

在你的汉白玉的寝宫里再也不会

回荡着我的歌声；蛆虫们将要

染指于你长期保存的贞操，

你那古怪的荣誉将化作尘埃，

而我的情欲也将变成一堆灰。

坟墓固然是很隐蔽的去处，也很好，

但是我看谁也没在那儿拥抱。

因此啊，趁那青春的光彩还留驻

在你的玉肤，像那清晨的露珠，

趁你的灵魂从你全身的毛孔

还肯于喷吐热情，像烈火的汹涌，

让我们趁此可能的时机戏耍吧，

像一对食肉的猛兽一样嬉狎，

与其受时间慢慢的咀嚼而枯凋，

不如把我们的时间立刻吞掉。

让我们把我们全身的气力，把所有

我们的甜蜜的爱情揉成一球，

通过粗暴的厮打把我们的欢乐

从生活的两扇铁门中间扯过。

这样，我们虽不能使我们的太阳

停止不动，却能让他们奔忙。

译者——杨周翰

Catharsis（净化）

Catharsis stems from "katharsis", a medical Greek word, meaning "purification" or "cleansing". Aristotle in his *Poetics* states that tragedy "effects through pity and fear the proper catharsis of these emotions" (Chapter 6). Therefore, a catharsis is a discharge of one's emotion through which one can liberate themselves from anxiety and tension or feel refreshed and renewal afterwards. William Shakespeare's *Macbeth* is considered an example of catharsis.

净化来源于希腊医学词语"katharsis"，意思是"洗净"或者"清洁"。亚里士多德在《诗学》中说到悲剧"通过怜悯与恐惧来达到情感的适当净化效果"（第六章）。因此，净化就是一个人情感的发泄，以此他可以摆脱焦虑与紧张或者之后感觉到振作和重生。威廉·莎士比亚的《麦克白》被认为是净化的力作。

Celtic Revival（凯尔特复兴）

Celtic Revival, also known as Irish Literary Renaissance or the Irish Literary Revival, refers to a variety of movements and trends that happened in the 19th and 20th centuries because of the growing Irish nationalism and the efforts of some intellectuals' efforts.

The noted poets and writers, including William Butler Yeats (1865—1939), Lady Gregory (1852—1932), George William Russel (1867—1935), J. M. Synge (1871—1909) and Edward Martyn (1859—1923) stimulated by strong nationalist sentiments, went back to study traditional Irish literature carefully to create a national literature different from European literature and advocated the revival of traditional Celtic art-forms to create a distinct national literature. During the Celtic Revival, many great English poems, dramas and novels emerged.

凯尔特复兴，也被称为"爱尔兰文学文艺复兴"或者"爱尔兰文学复兴"，是指由于日益增长的爱尔兰民族主义以及很多知识分子的努力，在 19 世纪与 20 世纪之间发生的很多运动与趋势。

这些著名的诗人与作家，包括威廉·巴特勒·叶芝、格雷戈里夫人（1852—1932）、乔治·威廉·拉塞尔（1867—1935）、约翰·沁孤（1871—1909）以及爱德华·马丁（1859—1923）受到强烈的爱国主义情感的驱使，仔细研究传统的爱尔兰文学以创造出不同于欧洲国家文学的国学，并倡导对传统的凯尔特艺术形式复兴，以创造卓越的民族文学。在凯尔特文艺复兴期间，很多英语诗歌、歌剧和小说涌现。

Chivalric Romance or Medieval Romance（骑士传奇或中世纪传奇）

With the improvement of knights' social status in the late 11th century, chivalric romance appeared as a type of prose and verse in Europe. Chivalric Romance (or medieval romance) is a literary genre, which originated in

France in the 12th century and then spread to other countries, enjoying high popularity in the aristocratic circles of High Medieval and Early Modern Europe. It described the adventures of legendary knights who were brave, loyal and courteous, and mainly laid emphasis on courtly love, honor, courage and loyalty.

Miguel de Cervantes' *Don Quixote* was a notable work of the genre. In addition, there are some other examples: Chrétien de Troyes' *Lancelot*, the anonymous *Sir Gawain and the Greeen Knight* and Thomas Malory's *Le Morte Darthur* (1485).

在 11 世纪末由于骑士的社会地位的提升，骑士文学在欧洲以散文诗的形式出现。骑士传奇（或中世纪传奇）是一种文学形式，12 世纪起源于法国后传播到其他国家，在中世纪和早期现代欧洲的贵族阶层颇受喜爱。它主要描写勇敢、忠诚、谦恭的传奇骑士们的冒险，并强调宫廷之爱、荣誉、勇气和忠诚。

米格尔·德·塞万提斯的《堂吉诃德》就是该类型的名著。除此之外，还有克雷蒂安·德·特罗亚的《兰斯洛特爵士》、无名氏的《高文爵士与绿衣骑士》和托马斯·马洛礼的《亚瑟王之死》（1485）。

Classicism（古典主义）

Classicism, as a literary genre, originated and boomed in France in the 17th century, and then spread to Western European countries. It lasted for about two centuries. That is, not until Romanticism rose in the early 19th century did it begin to decline.

It holds that in the process of creation and practice, a writer should observe the rules and conventions derived from ancient Greek and Roman literary works. The rule of "Three Unities" first put forward by Aristotle in his *Poetics* was the basic theory in classicism. In English literature, John Dryden (1631—1700), Pope and Samuel Johnson (1709—1784) are notable representatives of the genre.

古典主义，作为一种文学思潮，17 世纪在法国开始兴起并繁荣，然后传到西欧其他国家。它持续两个世纪之久。也就是说，直到 19 世纪早期浪漫主义兴起的时候，它才开始慢慢衰落。

古典主义认为在创作和实践过程中，作家应该遵守源自古希腊和古罗马文学作品中的规则和惯例。最早由亚里士多德在其《诗学》中提到的"三一律"便是古典主义的基础理论。在英国文学中，约翰·德莱顿（1631—1700）、蒲柏和塞缪尔·约翰逊（1709—1784）就是该思潮著名的代表人物。

Cliche（陈词滥调）

The term cliche, stemming from French, refers to a word, an idea or a saying that has lost its original meaning and has become a stereotype because of overuse.

该词来源于法语，是指一个单词、一个观点或者一个说法由于过度使用而失去了它原有的意思成为了一种定式。

Climax (Literary)（高潮）

The word is a Greek word meaning "ladder". It refers to the peak of a conflict or tension. So it is also a turning point at which a crisis began to be resolved. It is one of the most important literary elements and a necessary part of an excellent plot.

该词是一个希腊词，意思是"梯子"。它是指一个冲突或者矛盾的最顶点。所以它也是危机开始消解的转折点。它是重要的文学因素之一，也是一个完美情节的必要部分。

Close Reading（细读）

Close reading as a method and technique in literary criticism is closely related to New Criticism. I. A. Richards（1893—1979）and his student William Empson（1906—1984）are the pioneers. It requires readers to read texts carefully and be truly involved with the texts，focusing not only on the structure，theme and thoughts but also on the words，language，figures and all striking features of the texts. Readers should be able to think about both small linguistic items and large issues thoroughly and methodically. Close reading is a necessary method of serious literary study.

细读作为文学评论的一种方法与技巧与新批评主义有着密切的联系。I. A. 瑞恰慈（1893—1979）和他的学生威廉·燕卜荪（1906—1984）是先驱。细读要求读者要认真阅读文本并且真正深入文本，不但要注意结构、主题、思想还要注意单词、语言、修辞等所有文本中显著的特征。读者应该能够彻底地、有方法地思考小的语言问题以及大问题。细读是严肃的文学研究中必要的方法。

Comedy（喜剧）

Comedy，coming from the Greek word komos，originally meant a genre of drama in ancient Greece. Then in medieval and Renaissance，it referred to a play in which the protagonist overcame difficulties and had a happy ending. At that time the comedy was not amusing，and some were even serious in tone. Only from the 19th century on did comedy have its present meaning：it is a genre of literature which uses coincidences，humorous languages，amusing behavior and other devices to create comic effects and entertain the audience. Comedy can be further divided into romantic comedy，satiric comedy，comedy of humors and comedy of manners.

喜剧这个词来源于希腊词汇"komos"，最开始是指古希腊的一种戏剧形式。然后到中世纪和文艺复兴时期，它是指主人公克服重重困难最后皆大欢喜的戏剧。当时的喜剧并不搞笑，有些甚至语气严肃。直到 19 世纪开始，喜剧才有了现在的意思：它是一种文学形式，使用巧合、幽默的语言、搞笑的行为与其他方法来营造搞笑的气氛，以此逗乐观众。喜剧还可以进一步分为浪漫喜剧、讽刺喜剧、幽默喜剧以及风俗喜剧。

Comedy of Humors（幽默喜剧）

It is a type of comedy in which characters have their own behavioral traits and humors and each represents a type of personality. The kind of comedy can be traced back to Aristophanes (446 B. C. —386 B. C.), but it is Ben Jonson who popularized the comedy at the end of the 16th century. Jonson's *Volpone* (1605—1606) and *Every Man in His Humor* (1598) are examples of the genre.

幽默喜剧是一种喜剧类型，其中的人物都有自己的行为特点和幽默，每个人物代表了一种性格类型。这类喜剧可以追溯到阿里斯托芬（公元前446年—公元前386年），但是直到16世纪末，本·琼森才使该种喜剧广受欢迎。本·琼森《福尔蓬奈》（1605—1606）以及《人人高兴》（1598）都属于该类喜剧。

Comedy of Manners（风俗喜剧）

Comedy of manners is an ironic form of drama focusing on the manners, attitudes and conventions of a particular social group in a fashionable and "highly sophisticated" society. In England, William Shakespeare (1564—1616) might be considered as the pioneer of the genre and his *Much Ado about Nothing* (1600) was the first comedy of manners. It flourished during the Restoration period, so it is a synonym for "Restoration comedy"① .

William Wycherley's (1640—1715) *The Country Wife* (1675) and

---

① George Henry Nettleton, *British Dramatists from Dryden to Sheridan*, University of Notre Dame, p. 149.

William Congreve's （1670—1729） *The Way of the World* （1700） were masterpieces of the genre. In the late of 18th century, Oliver Goldsmith （1730—1774）（*She Stoops to Conquer*, 1773）, Richard Brinsley Sheridan （1751—1816）（*The Rivals*, 1775; *The School for Scandal*, 1777）and Oscar Wilde （1854—1900）　（*The Importance of Being Earnest*, 1895）revived the form.

　　风俗喜剧是一种戏剧的讽刺形式，主要描写在一个时尚、"非常精致"的社会里一个特定社会群体的习俗、态度和传统。在英国，威廉·莎士比亚可以被认为是该类喜剧的先锋，他的《无事生非》（1600）是第一部风俗喜剧。但是风俗喜剧在复辟时期繁荣，因此它也是"复辟喜剧"的同义词。

　　威廉·威彻利（1640—1715）的《乡下女人》（1675）和威廉·康格里夫（1670—1729）的《如此世道》（1700）是该类喜剧的名作。在 18 世纪末期，奥利弗·歌德史密斯（1730—1774）（《屈身求爱》，1773）、理查德·布林斯利·谢里丹（1751—1816）（《情敌》，1775；《造谣学校》，1777）以及奥斯卡·王尔德（1854—1900）（《不可儿戏》，1895）使该形式复兴。

Conceit（奇特的比喻）

Conceit, as a figure of speech, is considered as an extended metaphor. It means that a writer draws a comparison between two completely unrelated things in a clever way and tries to stimulate readers' imagination to uncover the similarity between the two different things. Therefore, a conceit is often surprising.

　　It can be divided into two types: metaphysical conceit and Petrarchan conceit.

Metaphysical conceit was developed by metaphysical poets in the 17th century. John Donne （1572—1631）and Andrew Marvell （1621—1678） were the most notable poets who considered metaphysical conceits as unconventional and intellectually challenging metaphors. Let's experience the metaphysical conceit in John Donne's poem *A Valediction*：*Forbidding Mourning*.

A Valediction：Forbidding Mourning
If they be two，they are two so
As stiff twin compasses are two；
Thy soul，the fixed foot，makes no show
To move，but doth，if the other do.
And though it in the center sit，
Yet，when the other far doth roam，
It leans and hearkens after it，
And grows erect，as that comes home.

Such wilt thou be to me，who must，
Like the other foot，obliquely run；
Thy firmness makes my circle just，
And makes me end where I begun

Petrarchan conceit was first used by Petrarch，an Italian poet in the 14th century and then by some Elizabethan imitators. It grows from the tradition of courtly love and uses hyperbole to compare the agony of lost love and the unpitying mistress.

奇特的比喻是一种修辞方法，被认为是延展的比喻。它是指作家用巧妙的方法把两个完全没关系的事物进行对比，激发读者的想象力来揭示这两个不同事物之间的相似性。因此奇特的比喻通常是令人惊讶的。

奇特的比喻有两种类型：玄学奇喻与彼特拉克比喻。

玄学奇喻是由 17 世纪的玄学派诗人发展而来。约翰·邓恩（1572—1631）与安德鲁·马维尔（1621—1678）便是最出名的玄学派诗人，他们认为玄学比喻是非传统并且极具智商挑战的比喻。让我们在约翰·邓恩的诗《告别辞：莫悲伤》中体会一下玄学比喻。

《告别辞：莫悲伤》

即便我俩的灵魂不是一体，

也会像圆规的两脚那样若即若离；

你的灵魂，那只固定的脚，

看似不动，实则会随另一只而移。

尽管它稳坐中央镇守，

但是倘使另一只真要去远游，

也会斜着身凝神倾听，

待君归来时，才又直身相候。

你对我正是这般，我定要

倾身围着你转，就像另外那只脚，

你的坚定成就了我的圆满

使我抵达终点时又重回起点报到。

译者——覃学岚

彼特拉克比喻首先由 14 世纪意大利诗人彼特拉克使用，随后被伊丽莎白时期的效仿者使用。它起源于宫廷爱情的传统，使用夸张来把失恋的痛苦与毫无同情心的女士进行对比。

Confessional Poetry（自白派诗歌）

Confessional poetry, a type of poetic style, emerged in America in the late 1950s and early 1960s. It focused on the exploration of the inner world and frankly revealed intimate experiences, personal problems, trauma, even mental illness, sexuality, suicide. It was a rebellion against the New Criticism and sometimes was classified as Postmodernism.

Robert Lowell （1917—1977, *Life Studies*, 1959）, Allen Ginsberg （1926—1997, *Howl*, 1956）, Sylvia Plath （1932—1963, *Ariel* 1965）, John Berryman （1914—1972, *Dream Songs*, 1964）, Anne Sexton （1928—1974, *To Bedlam and Part Way Back*, 1960）, and W. D. Snodgrass （*Heart's Needle*, 1969） are representative writers of the school and their high suicide rate （Berryman, Sexton, and Plath all committed suicide） also shocked the world.

自白派诗歌是一种诗歌形式，20世纪50年代末60年代初在美国兴起。它注重内心世界的探索，坦白地描写私人经历、个人问题、心灵创伤甚至是精神疾病、性、自杀等。它是对新批评的反抗，有时被归类为后现代主义。

罗伯特·洛威尔（1917—1977）（《生活研究》1959）、艾伦·金斯堡（1926—1997）（《嚎叫》1956）、西尔维娅·普拉斯（1932—1963）（《阿丽尔》1965）、约翰·贝里曼（1914—1972）（《梦歌》1964）、安妮·塞克斯顿（1928—1974）（《去拜蒂厄姆精神病院中途返回》1960）、W. D. 斯诺德格拉斯（1926—）（《心头的针》1969）都是该派的代表作家，他们的高自杀率也使世人震惊（贝里曼、塞克斯顿和普拉斯都是自杀）。

Concrete Poetry （具象诗）

Concrete poetry, sometimes used as visual poetry, was first coined in the 1950s. It is a kind of poetry, in which letter arrangements instead of conventional elements （such as the meaning of words, rhythm, rhyme and so on） are used to convey the meaning of a poem.

Augusto de Campos （1931—） and his brother Haroldo de Campos （1929—2003） were founders of the Concrete poetry movement in Brazil. George Herbert's "Easter Wings" and "The Altar" are notable works of the genre.

具象诗，有时也被称为图像有形诗，是在 20 世纪 50 年代首次使用的。在具象诗中，使用字母排列而不是传统的因素（例如词意、韵律、韵脚等）来传达诗的意义。

奥古斯都·德·坎波斯（1931—）和其哥哥哈罗尔德·德·坎波斯（1929—2003）就是巴西具象诗运动的创始人。乔治·赫伯特《复活节之双翼》和《祭坛》是该类型诗的著名代表作。

Courtly Love（宫廷之爱）

Courtly Love, also called "Chivalry Love" or "fine love" in Medieval France, began in the southern France in the late 11th century and then spread throughout France and finally into England, Germany and other European countries. It allowed knights and ladies to show their admiration regardless of their marital state or status but meanwhile laid emphasis on nobility, chastity, fidelity and chivalry, which was a challenge to traditional love.

Gaston Paris (1839—1903) popularized the term "courtly love" in 1883, and since then the term has been commonly accepted. In *The Legend of King Arthur*, the love between Guinevere (the queen) and Sir Lancelot is a notable example of courtly love.

宫廷之爱，在中世纪的法国也被称为"骑士之爱"或者"高尚之爱"，11 世纪末期兴起于法国南部，然后在整个法国传开，最终发展到英国、德国和其他的欧洲国家。它允许骑士和女主人之间表达爱意，不管他们的婚姻状态或者地位，但是与此同时强调高尚、纯洁、忠诚和骑士气概，这对于传统的爱是一种挑战。

加斯顿·帕里斯（1839—1903）在 1883 年使该词普及，并自此被普遍接受。在《亚瑟王传奇》中，王后格尼维尔与兰斯洛之间的爱就是典型的宫廷之爱。

Critical Realism（批判现实主义）

Critical Realism refers to a literary trend that came into being in the mid

19th century and flourished in the forties and in the beginning of fifties in Europe.

The critical realists criticized capitalistic society and its systems from a democratic viewpoint. They attacked the ruling classes satirically and showed profound sympathy to the ruled class. In critical realists' works, the hypocrisy and greed of the upper classes were shown to the readers relentlessly; meanwhile the honesty and kind-heartedness of the lower classes were described vividly. They appealed for the social reform rather than revolution to eradicate the social evils. They emphasized describing things in great detail and advocated perfection of novels.

Representative writers include Charles Dickens, William Makepeace Thackeray, Charlotte Bronte, Emily Bronte, Elizabeth Gaskell, Thomas Hardy and so on.

批判现实主义是指在 19 世纪中叶形成的一种文学形式，在 40 年代和 50 年代初在欧洲盛行。

批判现实主义者用民主视角批评资本主义社会和制度。他们讽刺地抨击统治阶级，并对被统治阶级深刻同情。在批判现实主义者的作品中，上层人的虚伪与贪婪被无情地展现在作者面前，同时，底层人的诚实与善良也被形象地描述。他们呼吁通过社会改革而不是革命来清除社会罪恶。他们强调叙事要详细，并倡导完善小说。

代表作家有查尔斯·狄更斯、威廉·梅克比斯·萨科雷、夏洛蒂·勃朗特、艾米丽·勃朗特、伊丽莎白·盖斯凯尔、托马斯·哈代等。

D

Dadaism（达达主义）

Dadaism, as an anti-art movement of the European avant-garde, began in Zurich, Switzerland during the World War I and spread to France, Germany and New York shortly thereafter. It rejected the traditional ways of art appreciation and introduced some new techniques and aesthetics, using all art forms including visual arts, literature, and theater to fight against barbarism, brutality in the war and demand for the freeing of the individual. It advocated nihilism. In New York, Marcel Duchamp (1887—1968) and Francis Picabia (1879—1953) were the leaders of the movement. It reached its peak in 1916 to the early 1920s and then it gave way to surrealism.

Though it didn't last for a long time, it had far-reaching influences on almost all the 20th-century schools of literature.

达达主义，作为欧洲先锋派的反艺术运动，在第一次世界大战期间起始于瑞士的苏黎世，很快就蔓延到法国、德国和纽约。它摒弃传统的审美方式，引入新的技术与美学，使用包括视觉艺术、文学以及戏剧在内的所有的艺术形式与战争中的野蛮与残暴相抗争，并要求个人的解放。它倡导的是虚无主义。在纽约，马塞尔·杜尚（1887—1968）与弗朗西斯·毕卡比亚（1879—1953）是该运动的领导人。该运动在 1916 年达到巅峰，一直持续到至 20 世纪 20 年代初，最后被超现实主义取代。

虽然该运动持续时间不长，但是影响深远，对几乎所有的 20 世纪的文学流派都有影响。

Dead Language（死语言）

Dead Language refers to a language that doesn't change and seems to be frozen. It is not used in daily discourse and communication and is learned just because of its cultural, linguistic or social significance. Latin, Sanskrit, and Ancient Greek are dead languages.

死语言是指一种没有任何改变，看似冻结的语言。在日常会话和交流中不使用，只是因为它的文化、语言或者社会重要性才被学习。拉丁语、梵语以及古希腊语都属于死语言。

Dead metaphor（死隐喻）

A dead metaphor, also known as a "frozen metaphor", is a figure of speech. It has been used so extensively and repetitively that it has lost its metaphoric power and effectiveness.

死隐喻，也被称为"冻结的隐喻"，是一种修辞方式。由于广泛和频繁地使用而失去了原本的比喻力和效果。

Decadence（颓废运动）

Decadence is an artistic and literary movement in 1890s that originated and flourished in France and spread to other European countries. It was mainly influenced by Romanticism and Naturalism and then was associated with symbolism and aesthetic movement. Artificiality, sexuality, perversity, ennui, death, annihilation and decay are the themes.

Baudelaire was considered by decadents as their inspiration and his *Flowers of Evil* (1857) was called the "Bible" of decadence. *The Yellow*

Book was reckoned as one of the chief books of decadent writing. J. K. Huysmans. (1848—1907) was seen as a significant representative of the movement, and his *A Rebours* (1884 translated as *Against Nature*) was called by Arthur Symons (1865—1945) "the breviary of the Decadence" Paul Verlaine (1844—1896) and Stéphane Mallarmé (1842—1898) were counted as decadents, while Oscar Wilde, Arthur Symons, and Ernest Dowson (1867—1900) are usually cited as the leading English decadents.

颓废运动是 19 世纪 90 年代的一场艺术与文学运动，它在法国起源并繁荣后传到其他的欧洲国家。它受到浪漫主义与自然主义的影响，然后与象征主义以及唯美主义思潮相结合。矫揉造作、性、任性、无聊、死亡、虚无以及衰败都是该运动的主题。

波德莱尔被颓废派认为是启发他们灵感的人，他的《恶之花》(1857) 被称为颓废派的"圣经"。《黄皮书》被认为是颓废派写作的主要杂志之一。乔里·卡尔·于斯曼 (1848—1907) 被认为是该运动的主要代表人物，他 1884 年的《逆天》被阿亚·西蒙斯 (1865—1945) 称为"颓废派的摘要"。保尔·魏尔伦 (1844—1896) 以及斯特凡·马拉梅 (1842—1898) 都属于颓废派成员。奥斯卡·王尔德、亚瑟·西蒙斯、厄内斯特·道森 (1867—1900) 是英国的颓废派代表。

De Casibus Tragedy（命运悲剧）

"De casibus tragedy" originated from Boccaccio's *De Casibus Virorum Illustrium* (*Fates of Famous Men*), which is about some famous people who fall from the heights of happiness to misfortune. It tells us that a person, however hard he fights, will inevitably be controlled by destiny. Thomas Sackville[1]'s *Mirror for Magistrates* (1559) also describes the tragedy.

---

[1] Thomas Sackville (1536—1608) was the first Earl of Dorset and Baron Buckhurst. He was an English poet and statesman.

命运悲剧来源于薄伽丘的《名人的命运》，主要讲述了一些名人从快乐的顶峰一下坠入到不幸的谷底的故事。它告诉了我们，无论一个人多么地努力，最终都不可避免地被命运所控。托马斯·萨克维尔（1536—1608）的《官员的镜子》（1559）就是写的这种悲剧。

Deconstruction（解构）

The term "deconstruction" was first used by Jacque Derrida[1]in his book *Of Grammatology* in 1967. Now it refers to a philosophical and literary movement which arose in the 1960s and focused on analyzing the relationship between text and meaning, in reaction to "Husserlian phenomenolgy, Saussurean and French structuralism, and Freudian and Lacanian psychoanalysis."[2] It gained popularity in the 1980s.

According to Barbara Johnson[3], "Deconstruction is not synonymous with 'destruction', however. It is in fact much closer to the original meaning of the word 'analysis' itself, which etymologically means 'to undo' —a virtual synonym for 'to de-construct' ... Ifanything is destroyed in a deconstructive reading, it is not the text, but the claim to unequivocal domination of one mode of signifying over another. A deconstructive reading is a reading which analyzes the specificity of a text's critical difference from itself."[4]

Thus, deconstruction means questioning almost all of the literary authorities and challenging traditional assumptions and analysis of texts. Deconstructionists hold that a text has no fixed explanation, and every reader

① Jacque Derrida (1930—2004) was a well-known French philosopher and the "founder" of deconstruction.

② Irena Makayrk, *Encyclopedia of Contemporary Literary Theory*, Toronto: University of Toronto Press, 1993, p. 25.

③ Barbara Johnson (1947—2009) was an American literary critic and professor of English and Comparative Literature in Harvard University.

④ Barbara Johnson, *The Critical Difference*. 1981, from *A Dictionary of Literary Terms and Literary Theory*, edited by J. A. Cuddon. London: Blackwell, 1991.

can have their own understandings of the text.

该词最先是由雅克·德里达在 1967 年《论文字学》中使用。现在是用来指在 20 世纪 60 年代崛起的哲学与文学运动，主要关注于分析文本与意思之间的关系，是对"胡塞尔的现象学、索绪尔与法国结构主义、弗洛伊德与拉康的精神分析做出的反应"。在 20 世纪 80 年代广受欢迎。

根据芭芭拉·约翰逊所说："解构不是破坏的同义词。事实上它与'分析'这个词的原始意义'解开'很相近——也是'解构的'的同义词……在解构阅读下，如果有遭到破坏之物，它一定不是文本，而是明确认为一种表意模式主宰另一种表意模式的主张。解构阅读就是一种分析一个文本截然不同于自身的异质性的阅读。"

因此，解构的意思是对几乎所有的文学权威进行质疑，挑战传统的想法和文本分析。解构主义者坚信任何一个文本都没有固定的解释，每个读者都有对文本自己的理解。

Decorum（合体）

The word "decorum" comes from Latin words decor and decorus, meaning appropriateness of behavior or conduct. As a term in literary criticism and a principle of classical rhetoric theory, it emphasizes propriety or fitness. That is, in a literary work, its words, its subject matter, its characters, its narrative styles should be matched to one another and suitable for the readers and the the given circumstance. The theory had its roots in Aristotle's (384 B. C. —322 B. C.) *Poetics* (335 B. C.) and Horace's (65 B. C. —8 B. C.) *Ars Poetica* (*The Art of Poetry*, 19 B. C. [①]), in which the importance of appropriate style in epic, tragedy, comedy, etc were dis-

---

① The date of the poem is uncertain. The date 19 B. C. is given by the *Oxford Companies to Classical Literature*, p. 74.

cussed.

Horace says, for example: "A comic subject is not susceptible of treatment in a tragic style, and similarly the banquet of Thyestes cannot be fitly described in the strains of everyday life or in those that approach the tone of comedy. Let each of these styles be kept to the role properly allotted to it."①

单词 "decorum" 来自拉丁语词汇 decor 和 decorus，意思是行为或者举止的适宜性。作为文学评论的术语和经典修辞理论的原则，它强调适宜性。也就是说，在文学作品中，其言语、主题、人物、叙事风格应该彼此匹配，并且与读者和给定的环境相适宜。该理论起源于亚里士多德（公元前 384 年—公元前 322 年）的《诗学》（公元前 335年）和贺拉斯（公元前 65 年—公元前 8 年）的《诗艺》（公元前 19年），两部作品探讨了史诗、悲剧、喜剧等的适宜风格的重要性。

例如贺拉斯说过："一部喜剧作品不适宜以悲剧的形式进行处理，同样地，吃人的筵席不适合描写成日常生活的状态或者以接近喜剧的语气来写。让每个风格都能保留适合自己的作用。"

Defamiliarization（陌生化）

Defamiliarization, also known as "estrangement", was first coined by Viktor Shklovsky②in 1917 in his *Art as Device* in opposition to Russian symbolists' theories of art. As one of the concepts of Formalism, it is an artistic device of presenting common things in an unfamiliar or strange way to enhance the perception of the familiar and provide the audience with a fresh perspective. According to Shklovsky, Tolstoy's *Kholstomer* (1886) is a good example of defamiliarization.

---

① Horace. *On the Art of Poetry*. Translated by T. S. Dorsch. In: *Aristotle/Horace/Longinus*: *Classical Literary Criticism*. London: Penguin Books, 1965, p. 82 (corresponding to lines 81—106 in the Latin version).

② Victor Shklovsky (1893—1984) was a Russian and Soviet literary theorist, critic, writer, and pamphleteer. He was famous for being the founder of Russian Formalism.

陌生化，是由维克多·什克洛夫斯基在 1917 年《艺术手段》中反对俄罗斯象征主义艺术理论提出来的。作为形式主义的一个重要概念，它是用陌生的方式来呈现一些普通的事物，以此来加强对熟知事物的概念，给读者提供一个全新的视角。根据什克洛夫斯基，托尔斯泰的《霍尔斯托梅儿》（1886）是陌生化的一个范例。

Deism （自然神论）

The word "deism", derived from the Latin word for God: "Deus", refers to a religious movement which became popular with intellectuals during the age of Enlightenment, especially in Britain. Then via Voltaire's works, deism spread to France, Germany and the United States. Deists believe that God has created the universe but he is uncaring and uninvolved in the world, having no interaction with the beings in it. Therefore, deism is a natural religion and more rational, compared with Christianity.

单词 "deism" 来源于拉丁语词汇 "Deus"，意思是 "上帝"。它是指启蒙运动时期在文人中很受欢迎的宗教运动，尤其是在英国。后来通过伏尔泰的作品自然神论传到欧洲、德国和美国。自然神论者相信上帝创造了宇宙，但是他并不关注也不参与到世界的活动，与世界的人类毫无联系。因此自然神论与基督教相比是一种自然的、更加理性的宗教。

Denouement （结局）

Denouement refers to the final outcome or resolution of the story, which usually takes place after the climax of the plot. It's often where things are resolved and loose ends are tied up.

结局是指故事的最终结尾或者解决，通常发生在情节的高潮过后。常见的结局就是事情得以解决，结果水落石出。

Deuteragonist（配角）

Deuteragonist, a word from Greek, is the second important character after the protagonist in a story. The person can be either with or against the protagonist. Aristotle states in *Poetics*, "it was Aeschylus who first raised the number of the actors from one to two. He also curtailed the chorus and made the dialogue be the leading part". [1]

配角是一个希腊词汇，是指在故事中仅次于主角的第二重要人物。配角可以是和主角一伙的也可以是他的对手。亚里士多德在《诗学》中写到"是埃塞库罗斯最先把人物从一个增加到两个。他还削减了副歌，使对话成为了主体部分"。

Dialogic Criticism（对话批评）

Dialogic criticism, first coined by Soviet philosopher Mikhail Bakhtin (1895—1975) in his work *The Dialogic Imagination*, is a critical approach used to understand and interpret literary works. Bakhtin put forward "polyphony" and "heteroglossia" to analyze novels. According to Bakhtin, a novel contains numerous voices or perspectives; no one voice or perspective can monopolize the truth. Dialogic criticism mainly analyzes the interplay of these many voices.

对话批评，首先由苏联哲学家米哈伊尔·巴赫金（1895—1975）在其作品《对话想象》中提出，它是一种用来理解和解释文学作品的批评方法。巴赫金提出了"复调"和"杂语"来解释小说。根据巴赫金的理论，一篇小说包含很多声音或者视角：没有一个声音或者视角能操控真理。对话批评主要分析这些诸多声音的相互作用。

---

[1] Aristotle. *Poetics*. Perseus Digital Library, 2006.

Diction（措辞）

Diction means a writer's choice of words, phrases and style of expression, which makes the writer's distinctive and peculiar writing style. Diction is considered as the mark of quality writing, separating good writing from bad. Aristotle, in *Poetics*, states that "Diction comprises eight elements: Phoneme, Syllable, Conjunction, Connective, Noun, Verb, Inflection, and Utterance".①

措辞的意思是作者对于单词、词组和表达风格的选择，这就使作者有着独具一格的写作风格。措辞被认为是一部作品质量的衡量标准，能够区分优质作品与劣质作品。亚里士多德在《诗学》中说到"措辞是由八个因素组成：音位、音节、连词、关系词、名词、动词、音调变化和表达"。

Didactic Literature（教诲文学）

Didactic literature refers to a literary work which conveys a moral theme or other educational and instructive information to the audience.

It can be argued that every text in the early modern period had the potential to be viewed as didactic.②Alexander Pope's (1688—1744) *An Essay on Criticism* published in 1711 provides some advice on critics and criticism. It is a notable example of didactic writing.

教诲文学是指向读者传达道德主题或者其他教育和指导信息的文学作品。

可以说在现代时期早期，每个作品都可被看成是教诲文学。亚历山大·蒲柏（1688—1744）在 1711 年出版的《论批评》为批评和评

---

① Aristotle. *Poetics*. Perseus Digital Library, 2006.

② Natasha Glaisyer and Sara Pennell, *Introduction: Didactic Literature in England*, 1500—1800, Ashgate, 2003, p. 2.

论提供了很多意见。这是教诲写作的典型例子。

Différance（延异）

Différance, a French word, was first coined by Jacques Derrida (1930—2004) in 1963 in his essay *Cogito and the History of Madness.* In French, "diferrer" means both "to deffer" and "to differ", so "différance" refers to both different and deferred conditions. It is very difficult to define "differance", because "it is neither a word nor a concept". Derrida intentionally misspelled the word "difference" to emphasize that hearing a word does not give the complete picture or meaning of it.

According to Derrida, differance is the "hinge" between speech and writing, and between inner meaning and outer representation. As soon as there is meaning, there is difference.[①]Readers can have different understandings of a text because of their different experiences, moods and backgrounds. Therefore, no one meaning is better than the other.

延异是一个法语词，是由雅克·德里达在 1963 年的《我思与疯癫的历史》中首次使用。在法语中，"diferrer" 既有 "延迟" 的意思也有 "不同" 的意思，所以 "différance" 既指不同也指延迟的情况。很难对 "différance" 下定义，因为 "它既不是一个单词也不是一个概念"。德里达故意把 difference 拼错是为了强调听到的单词并不能给出整个画面或者单词的完整意思。

根据德里达所说，延异就是听力与写作之间的关键所在，是内部含义与外部所指的中枢。只要有意义，就一定有延异。读者因为不同的经历、情绪和背景对文章的理解也会不同，所以没有哪个意义要比别的好。

---

① Jacques Derrida, *Dissemination*, Barbara Johnson translated, London: Continuum, 2005. p. ix.

Digression（离题）

Digression is often employed by a writer intentionally as a stylistic or rhetoric device to create a diversion from the main point of the narrative to talk about some unrelated topics, explaining background information, describing a character's motivation and establishing suspense. Since Corax of Syracuse[1], digression was a part of an oration or composition in Classical rhetoric. Cicero (106 B. C. —43 B. C.) was a master of digression. [2] Jonathan Swift's (1667—1745) *A Tale of A Tub* (1704) and Laurence Sterne's (1713—1768) *Tristram Shandy* (1759—1767) are two examples of using digression in satirical works.

离题作为一种文体与修辞技巧经常被作者故意使用以达到从叙述的主题转换到谈论一些不相关的话题的效果，以此来解释背景知识，描述人物的动机，制造悬疑等。自从高乐斯开始，离题在古典修辞学中成为演说或者写作中的一部分。西塞罗（公元前 106 年—公元前 43 年）是使用离题的大师。乔纳森·斯威夫特（1667—1745）的《木桶的故事》（1704）以及劳伦斯·斯特恩（1713—1768）的《项狄传》（1759—1767）是在讽刺作品中使用离题的代表作。

Discourse（话语）

The term "discourse" comes from the Latin word "discursus", meaning "running to and fro" It is the great French philosopher and social theorist Michel Foucault (1926—1984) who made the term popular in Archeology of Knowledge & The Discourse on Language (1969). He gave us the definition of discourse: systems of thoughts composed of ideas, attitudes, and courses

---

[1] Corax lived in the 5th century B. C. and he was one of the founders of ancient Greek rhetoric.

[2] H. V. Canter. "Digressio in the Orations of Cicero", *The American Journal of Philology*, Johns Hopkins University Press, Vol. 52, No. 4, 1931, pp. 351 – 361.

of action, beliefs and practices that systematically construct the subjects and the worlds of which they speak. In recent decades, the term is often used in theoretical discussions and literary studies.

该词来自拉丁语词汇"discursus", 意思是"来回跑"。伟大的法国哲学家和社会理论学家米歇尔·福柯 (1926—1984) 在《知识考古学与语言话语》(1969) 中使该词被广为接受。他是这样定义的:话语就是由人们谈论话题和世界时的观点、态度以及行为、信念和实践过程构成的思维体系。在近几十年, 该词经常在理论讨论和文学研究中使用。

Distancing Effect (间离效果)

Distancing effect, also known " alienation effect or estrangement effect", is a technique used by a dramatist to prevent the audience from having an emotional involvement in the play. It was first coined by playwright Bertolt Brecht (1898—1956) in his essay on *Alienation Effects in Chinese Acting* (1936). According to him, the distancing effect "played in such a way that the audience was hindered from simply identifying itself with the characters in the play. Acceptance or rejection of their actions and utterances was meant to take place on a conscious plane, instead of, as hitherto, in the audience's subconscious". [1]

间离效果, 是由戏剧家使用来防止观众情感投入的一种手段。它是由剧作家贝尔托·布莱希特 (1898—1956) 在其 1936 年发表的论文《论中国戏剧表演的间离效果》中首次使用。根据他所说, 间离效果"是防止观众把自己认为成是戏剧中的人物。拒绝还是接受演员的演技和语言都是在观众的有意识情况下进行, 而不是在潜意识下进行的"。

---

[1] John Willett, ed. and trans. , *Brecht on Theatre*, New York: Hill and Wang, 1964, p.91.

Doggerel （打油诗）

Doggerel refers to a form of verse of inferior literary value which is loosely constructed and often irregular in rhythm and in rhyme for burlesque or comic effect. John Skelton, the 15th century English poet, was considered a genius of doggerel. Jonathan Swift (1667—1745), Samuel Butler (1835—1902) and Ogden Nash (1902—1971) also used doggerel in their English comic verses.

打油诗是指为了取得滑稽和搞笑的效果而结构松散，韵律与韵脚都不规则、文学价值较低的诗歌。15 世纪英国诗人约翰·斯凯尔顿被认为是打油诗的天才。乔纳森·斯威夫特（1667—1745）、塞缪尔·巴特勒（1835—1902）以及奥顿·纳什（1902—1971）在自己的英文滑稽诗歌中也使用打油诗。

Dramatic Monologue （戏剧独白）

Dramatic monologue is a literary genre in which a character expresses his or her own views to a reader or to an imaginary listener, making the reader or the listener better understand that character's feelings. But the listener's replies are not given in the work. The Victorian Age saw the peak of the dramatic monologue in English poetry. It was perfected by Robert Browning (1812—1889), whose poem *My Last Duchess* was a prominent practice of dramatic monologue.

In addition, Tennyson's *Ulysses* (1842) and T. S. Eliot's *The Love Song of J. Alfred Prufrock* (1917) are representative works of this type.

戏剧独白是一种文学形式，其中主人公向读者或者假想的听者表达自己的观点，使读者或者听者能够更好地理解主人公的情感。但是听者的回答在作品中并未给出。维多利亚时代是英语诗歌中戏剧独白的高峰时期。该类型是由罗伯特·布朗宁完善的，他的诗《我已故的公爵夫人》便是该类型诗歌的杰作。

除此之外，丁尼生的《尤利西斯》（1842）和 T. S. 艾略特的《阿尔弗雷德·普鲁弗洛克的情歌》（1917）都是戏剧独白的代表之作。

Dream Allegory（梦幻寓言诗）

Dream allegory, also known as "dream vision", is a literary device of poetry employed especially by poets in the Middle Ages. In a story, the protagonist falls asleep and comes across some adventures in his dream. With the help of a guide, the protagonist gets resolutions for his waking concerns. The genre was widely used from late Latin times until the 15th century in European countries. Chaucer's "dream visions" *Parliament of Foules*, *Book of the Duchess*, and *House of Fame* are representatives. In the era of Romanticism, it reemerged. For example, Keats's *Hyperion* (1818—1819), The Fall of *Hyperion* (1819), Shelley's *The Triumph of Life* (1822) and Lewis Carroll's Alice in Wonderland (1865). Dante's *Divine Comedy* (1307—1321) is considered the most developed form of the genre.

梦幻寓言诗，是一种在中世纪被诗人使用的诗歌文学方式。在故事中，主人公睡着了，在梦中经历了一些冒险。在向导的帮助下，主人公得到了睡觉之前一直担心的问题的解决方法。该文学类型在拉丁时代末期一直到 15 世纪在欧洲国家被广泛使用。乔叟的梦幻寓言诗《百鸟议会》《公爵之书》和《声誉之屋》是代表之作。在浪漫主义时期，该类诗又重新出现。例如济慈的《海伯利安》（1819）、《海伯利安的陨落》（1819）、雪莱的《生命的凯旋》以及路易斯·卡罗尔的《爱丽丝梦游仙境》（1865）。但丁的《神曲》（1307—1321）被认为是梦幻寓言诗的极致。

Dystopia（反面乌托邦）

Dystopia, an antonym of utopia, was first used by J. S. Mill in one of his Parliamentary Speeches in 1868. Now it is used to refer to the works that describes an imaginary and undesirable society in which ominous tendencies of our current social, political and technological orders are projected into a disastrous future culmination to draw readers' attention to real-world issues.

Aldous Huxley's *Brave New World* (1932), George Orwell's 1984 (1949), and Margaret Atwood's *The Handmaid's Tale* (1986) are representative works describing dystopia.

反面乌托邦是乌托邦的反义词，J. S. 米尔在 1868 年的一次国会演讲中首先使用。现在它用来描述想象且不受欢迎的社会，在这个社会中我们现在社会、政治和技术秩序中的不祥预兆会达到一个灾难性的顶峰，以此来让读者关注现实中的问题。

赫胥黎的《美丽新世界》（1932）、乔治·奥威尔的《1984》（1949）以及玛格丽特·阿特伍德的《女仆的故事》（1986）就是描写反面乌托邦的代表作。

E

Echo Verse（回声诗歌）

Echo verse is a writing device dating back to Ancient Greece. The last word or syllable in a line is echoed, usually with different spellings or meanings, as a response in the next line. It was popular during the Middle Ages and then revived in France, Italy and England in the 16th and 17th centuries. George Herbert's poem *Heaven* and Jonathan Swift's *A Gentle Echo on Woman* are the best-known examples.

回声诗歌是起源于古希腊的一种写作方法。每一行的最后一个单词或者音节在下一行中作为回应被重复，通常拼写或者意思不一样。在中世纪时期，回声诗歌很流行。在 16 世纪和 17 世纪时，法国、意大利和英国又开始复苏。乔治·赫伯特的诗歌《天堂》还有乔纳森·斯威夫特的《关于女人的温柔回声》是该类诗歌的范例。

Eclogue（牧歌）

Eclogue, also called "Bucolics", is a genre of poem on a pastoral subject depicting rural life, which is usually in the form of a dialogue between shepherds, depicting rural life. The Greek poet Theocritus (310 B. C.—250 B. C.) is considered as the inventor of the genre. The Roman poet Virgil (70

B. C. —19B. C.) wrote ten Eclogues published in approximately 39 B. C. , which made him famous. In Renaissance, Dante (1265—1321), Petrarch (1304—1374) and Boccaccio (1313—1375) revived the genre. Edmund Spenser's (1552—1599) *The Shepheardes Calender* (1579) is considered the first outstanding eclogue in English.

牧歌，是一种以描写农村生活的田园事物为主题的诗歌类型，通常是以放牧人之间的对话来描述田园生活。希腊诗人忒奥克里托斯（公元前310年—公元前250年）被认为是该类诗歌的创始人。罗马诗人维吉尔（公元前70年—公元前19年）在公元前39年左右发表了十篇牧歌而一举出名。在文艺复兴时期，但丁（1265—1321）、彼特拉克（1304—1374）以及薄伽丘（1313—1375）使该类诗歌复苏。埃德蒙·斯宾塞的《牧人月历》（1579）被认为是第一部杰出的英语牧歌。

Ecocriticism（生态批评）

The term "ecoriticism" was first coined by William Rueckert in his 1978 essay *Literature and Ecology: An Experiment in Ecocriticism.* In 1996, Cheryll Glotfelty defined ecocriticism as "the study of the relationship between literature and the physical environment". [1] He thinks "that human culture is connected to the physical world, affecting it and affected by it. Ecocriticism takes as its subject the interconnections between nature and culture... As a critical stance, it has one foot in literature and the other on the land; as a theoretical discourse, it negotiates between the human and the nonhuman". [2]

Ecocriticism started developing in America and England in the 1990s. Therefore, it is still a new area of study. Ecocritics are endeavoring to solve

---

① Cheryll Glotfelty. *The Ecocriticism Reader: Landmarks in Literary Ecology.* Athens: The University of Georgia Press, 1996, pp. xviii – xix.

② Ibid.

the complex problems between human beings and the world they live in.

该词首先是由威廉·鲁克特在 1978 年的论文《文学与生态：生态批评的试验》中提出来的。在 1996 年谢里尔·格洛特费尔蒂定义生态批评就是研究 "文学与自然环境之间的关系"。他认为 "人类文化是与物质世界联系在一起的，它影响着物质世界也受物质世界的影响。而生态批评则把自然与文化之间的联系作为研究主题……作为一种批评立场，它站在文学与自然的两个阵营；作为一种理论话语，它在人类与非人类之间斡旋"。

生态批评在 20 世纪 90 年代开始在美国和英国发展。因此，这还是一个比较新的研究领域。生态批评者正在致力于解决人类与人类居住的世界之间复杂的问题。

Ecofeminism （生态女性主义）

Ecofeminism, also called "ecological feminism", is an academic movement combining ecology and feminism. The word was first coined by Francoise D'Eaubonne, a French feminist, in her work *Le féminisme ou la mort* in 1974, which marked the beginning of ecofeminism. According to Mary Mellor,[1] "Ecofeminism is a movement that sees a connection between the exploitation and degradation of the natural world and the subordination and oppression of women. It emerged in the mid-1970s alongside second-wave feminism and the green movement. Ecofeminism brings together elements of the feminist and green movements, while at the same time offers a challenge to both. It takes from the green movement a concern about the impact of human activities on the non-human world and from feminism the view of humanity as gendered in ways that subordinate, exploit and oppress women"[2]. Rosemary Ruether

---

[1] Mary Mellor is a Social Science Professor at Northumbria University, Newcastle upon Tyne UK and Chair of its Sustainable Cities Research Institute. She has a longstanding interest in alternative, green and feminist economics.

[2] Mary Mellor. *Feminism & Ecology*. New York: New York University Press, 1997, p. 1.

(1936—), one founder of ecofeminism, advocated women to work hard to end the domination of nature while fighting for their own liberation.

生态女性主义，是把生态学与女性主义结合在一起的学术运动。该词最早是由法国女性主义者弗朗西丝娃·德奥波妮在 1974 年的《女性主义·毁灭》中使用，这标志着生态女性主义的开端。根据玛丽·梅勒，"生态女性主义是把对自然的开采破坏与对女人的统治压迫联系在一起，它随着第二次女性主义浪潮在 20 世纪 70 年代中期出现。生态女性主义把女性主义与绿色运动的元素相联系，与此同时对二者提出挑战。它有绿色运动中关于人类活动对于自然世界影响的担忧，也有女性主义中关于统治、剥削和压迫妇女的人道主义观点"。生态女性主义的创始人之一罗斯玛丽·路德（1936—）倡导女人们在为自己的自由斗争的同时要为结束自然的统治而努力。

Edwardian Era （爱德华时代）

Edwardian era, named after King Edward VII (1841—1910), refers to the period from 1901 to 1910 when the UK was reigned by Edward VII, and is sometimes extended to the beginning of WWI in 1914. It is considered as "a golden age" with great social and economic changes. Some famous English and Irish writers produced highbrow literary works during the period, among them James Barrie (1860—1937), Arnold Bennett (1867—1931), Joseph Conrad (1857—1924), Ford Maddox Ford (1837—1939), John Galsworthy (1867—1933), George Bernard Shaw (1856—1950), Thomas Hardy (1840—1928), Rudyard Kipling (1865—1936), J. M. Synge (1871—1909), Alfred Noyes (1880—1958), Arthur Symons (1865—1945), P. G. Wodehouse (1881—1975) and H. G. Wells (1866—1946).

爱德华时代，以国王爱德华七世（1841—1910）命名，是指从 1901 到 1910 年爱德华七世统治英国的时期，有时延伸到 1914 年第一次世界大战爆发时期。该时代被认为是有着巨大的社会与经济变革的"黄金时代"。一些著名的英国和爱尔兰作家在该时期出版了很多高雅的文学作品，其中有詹姆斯·巴里（1860—1937）、阿诺德·贝内特（1867—1931）、约瑟夫·康拉德（1857—1924）、福特·马多克斯·福特（1837—1939）、约翰·高尔斯华绥（1867—1933）、乔治·伯纳德·肖（1856—1950）、托马斯·哈代（1840—1928）、鲁德亚德·吉卜林（1865—1936）、约翰·沁孤（1871—1909）、阿尔弗雷德·诺伊斯（1880—1958）、阿瑟·西蒙斯（1865—1945）、佩勒斯·格伦维尔·伍德豪斯（1881—1975）以及赫伯特·乔治·威尔斯（1866—1946）。

Elegy（挽诗）

Elegy refers to a kind of poetry written in elegiac couplets (a poetic form consisting of a hexameter verse followed by a pentameter verse). Its principal themes are death, sorrow, war and love. Thomas Gray's (1716—1771) *Elegy Written in a Country Churchyard* and Lord Alfred Tennyson's (1809—1892) *In Memoriam* are notable elegies.

挽歌是指一种用挽联（一种五步格诗后面再跟有一个六步格诗的诗歌形式）的形式写下的诗歌。其重要的主题有死亡、悲痛、战争和爱情。托马斯·格雷（1716—1771）的《墓园挽诗》和阿尔弗雷德·丁尼生（1809—1892）的《缅怀》都是著名的挽歌。

Elizabethan Age（伊丽莎白时代）

Elizabethan Age, named after Elizabeth I (1533—1603), refers to the period from 1558 to 1603, during which Elizabeth I was Queen of England and Ireland. The Elizabethan Age saw a great rise in nationalism and flowering in literature and arts. World-famous play-writers such as Ben Jonson (1572—1637), Christopher Marlowe (1564—1593), and William Shakespeare (1564—1616) wrote immortal works in the Age. The well-known poet Edmund Spenser (1552—1599) and renowned philosopher Francis Bacon (1561—

1626) also lived in the era. The Renaissance in England coincided with the Age, so it is described as a golden age①in English history.

　　伊丽莎白时代是以伊丽莎白一世（1533—1603）命名，是指从1558 年到 1603 年伊丽莎白一世统治英国和爱尔兰的时期。伊丽莎白时代出现了高涨的爱国主义，它是文学与艺术的兴盛时期。闻名世界的剧作家本·琼森（1572—1637）、克里斯托弗·马洛（1564—1593）以及威廉·莎士比亚（1564—1616）在该时期创作了不朽的作品。著名的诗人埃德蒙·斯宾塞（1552—1599）以及哲学家弗朗西斯·培根（1561—1626）也都生活在该时代。英国的文艺复兴恰巧与该时期一致，所以它在英国史上被认为是黄金时代。

Elliptical poetry（晦涩诗）

Elliptical poetry is a literary term made popular by Stephen Burt in a 1998 review of Susan Wheeler's Smokes in *Boston Review*. Robert Penn Warren (1905—1989)② mentioned "elliptical" in his "Pure and Impure Poetry" (1943): "In a recent book, *The Idiom of Poetry* (1941), Frederick Pottle③has discussed the question of pure poetry. He distinguishes another type of pure poetry, in addition to the types already mentioned. He calls it 'Elliptical', and would include in it symbolist and metaphysical poetry (old and new) and some work by poets Collins, Blake, and Browning." Warren thought some poets "become impatient of this meaning [explicit statement of ideas in logical order] which seems superfluous, and perceive possibilities of

---

　　① C. S. Lewis. *English Literature in the Sixteenth Century* (*Excluding Drama*). New York: Oxford University Press, 1954, p. 1.

　　② Robert Penn Warren was an American poet, novelist, and literary critic and was one of the founders of New Criticism.

　　③ Frederick Pottle (1897—1987) was an American scholar and an expert in the study of James Boswell.

intensity through its elimination. "① "The prime characteristics of this kind of poetry is not the nature of its imagery but its obscurity. "②

晦涩诗是一个文学词汇，它是由史蒂芬·波特在 1998 年《波士顿评论》中对苏珊·维勒的《烟》进行评论时而被人熟知的。事实上，罗伯特·佩恩·沃伦在《论纯诗与非纯诗》（1943）中提到了"晦涩"，他写道："在最近的一本书《诗歌的习语》（1941）中，弗雷德里克·波特尔讨论了纯诗的问题。除了已经提到的诗歌类型之外，他还区分了另一种纯诗。他称之为'晦涩诗'。象征主义和玄学派（新的和旧的）诗歌还有柯林斯、布莱克以及布朗宁的一些作品都属于该类诗歌。"沃伦认为一些诗人"讨厌按照逻辑顺序清楚陈述自己的观点，认为这实在是多余，想要摆脱束缚来表达情感"，"这种诗的主要特征不是在于意象而是在于晦涩"。

Emblem（象征符号）

An emblem is a combination of texts and images, consisting of three components: a title, a picture and an explanatory text. The Italian Renaissance poet Andrea Alciato（1492—1550）was considered as the father of emblem literature and he was famous for his book *Emblemata*（1531）. Emblems were influenced much by ancient Greek and Roman myths and legends and became very popular in Italy and France in the 16th and 17th centuries. Edmund Spenser, Ben Johnson, Richard Crashaw③and George Herbert were influenced greatly by the emblem.

象征符号是内容与表象相结合，由题目、图片以及解释组成。意大利文艺复兴诗人安德烈亚·阿尔恰托（1492—1550）被认为是象征

---

① Edward Hirsch, *A Poet's Glossary*, Houghton Mifflin Harcourt, 2014, p. 200.

② Ibid.

③ Richard Crashaw（1613—1649）was an English poet, famous for being one of the figures associated with the metaphysical poets in 17th English literature.

符号文学之父，因为《象征符号》（1531）一书而出名。象征符号受到古希腊和古罗马的神话传说的影响很大，16、17 世纪在意大利和法国广受欢迎。埃德蒙·斯宾塞、本·琼森、理查德·克拉肖以及乔治·赫伯特都受到了象征符号的影响。

Enlightenment（启蒙运动）

Enlightenment was a progressive intellectual movement stretching from the late 17th to the late 18th century（more exactly, French Revolution in 1789）, which was also called "the Age of Reason" by Thomas Paine. It originated in England, with Thomas Hobbes（1588—1679）, John Locke（1632—1704）, Alexander Pope（1688—1744）, Jonathan Swift（1667—1745）as representatives, and then in the 18th century, it spread to European countries, in which French enlightenment was the most influential movement. Many outstanding thinkers, such as Voltaire, Montesquieu, Rousseau, Diderot, came to the fore.

Many thinkers and writers named the movement by themselves, they thought they were more enlightened than their compatriots and wanted to enlighten the whole world with modern philosophy. They attacked the dark medieval world-views and appealed for equality, reason and science because they believed that human reason was the key to solve social problems.

启蒙运动是从 17 世纪末到 18 世纪末（更准确地说是到 1789 年的法国革命）发生的一个进步的知识分子运动，它也被托马斯·佩恩称作"理性时代"。它兴起于英国，托马斯、霍布斯、约翰·洛克、亚历山大·蒲柏·乔纳森·斯威夫特是其代表人物，然后到 18 世纪蔓延到欧洲国家，尤以法国启蒙运动影响最为深远。很多杰出的思想家纷纷涌现出来，例如伏尔泰、孟德斯鸠、卢梭、狄德罗。

这是很多思想家和作家自己给这个运动命名的。他们认为他们要比同胞们更开明，想要用现代哲学使整个世界开化。他们批判黑暗的中世纪世界观，呼吁平等、理性和科学，并深信人的理性是解决社会问题的关键。

Epic（史诗）

An epic, as a grand literary genre, is a long oral narrative poem which describes a hero's deeds or historical events of cultural and historic significance. Epics were originally transmitted orally and then were reorganized and processed into written form. Among these are *Iliad* and *Odyssey*. There are also "literary epics", which were created by poets imitating the traditional form. Virgil's *Aeneid* and Milton's *Paradise Lost* (1667) are of the kind.

史诗，作为一种庄严的文学流派，是很长的口头叙事诗，主要描述有重要文化和历史意义的英雄事迹或者历史事件。史诗起初是口口相传的，然后经过整理加工成文字形式。《伊利亚特》和《奥德赛》便是此类史诗。还有一种"文学史诗"，是诗人通过模仿传统史诗形式进行创作的。维吉尔的《埃涅阿斯纪》和米尔顿的《失乐园》（1667）就是该种类型史诗。

Epic Simile（史诗式明喻）

Epic simile, also known as "Homeric simile", is a simile developing several lines to compare two objects. It is often used in epic poetry. Homer, Virgil, Dante, Milton and other epic poets often used epic simile in their works. *The Poetry of The Aeneid* (1965) written by Michael C. J. Putnam[1] discusses the epic similes in Virgil's *Aeneid*.

史诗式明喻，也被称作"荷马式明喻"是把两个事物进行比较的连续几行的明喻，通常在史诗中使用。荷马、维吉尔、但丁、弥尔顿

---

[1] Michael C. J. Putnam (1933—) is an American classicist specializing in Latin literature. He is famous for his publications about Virgil's *Aeneid*.

以及其他的史诗诗人经常在作品中使用史诗明喻。迈克尔·普特南所写的《埃涅阿斯纪中的诗》（1965）讨论的就是维吉尔《埃涅阿斯纪》中的史诗明喻。

Epigram（隽语）

The word "epigram" originally came from a Greek word "epigramma", meaning "to write on or inscription". In the Hellenistic period, the epigram became a literary device, referring to a pithy, witty, memorable and interesting statement. The Roman poet Martial[1]was a famous writer of epigrams. Then the epigram became a popular Renaissance literary genre, and in the 16th and 17th centuries, it flourished. The critic J. C. Scaliger[2]in his *Poetics* (1560) divided epigrams into four types: gall, vinegar, salt and honey (that is, an epigram can be bitterly angry, sour, salacious, or sweet). [3]

该词来源于希腊词"epigramma"，意思是"在上面写或者雕刻"。在希腊化时期，隽语成为一个文学手段，是指简短、诙谐、难忘、有趣的陈述。罗马诗人马休尔是一个著名的隽语作家。隽语后来成为流行的文艺复兴时期文学类型，在 16 世纪和 17 世纪处于兴盛期。批评家斯卡里格在《诗学》（1560）中将隽语分为四种类型：苦、酸、咸和甜（也就是说，隽语可以分为愤怒、厌烦、淫秽和愉快四种类型）。

Epigraph（引语）

The word "epigraph" comes from the Greek word "epigraphein", meaning "to write on". Epigraph is a literary device often putat the beginning of a text in the form of a quotation, a poem or a phrase. It can serve as a summary, an in-

---

① Martial (between 38 A. D. and 41 A. D. —between 102 A. D. and 104 A. D.), was a Roman poet famous for his twelve books of Epigrams.

② J. C. Scaliger (1484—1558) was an Italian scholar and physician.

③ David Mikics, *A New Handbook of Literary Terms*, Yale University Press, 2007, p. 106.

troduction or a preface to emphasize the theme or to attract the readers.

该词来自希腊词汇"epigraphein",意思是"在上面写"。引语是一种文学手段,经常由作者以引用、诗歌或者成语的方式放在文章的开头。可以用来做摘要、简介或者前言来强调主题或者吸引读者。

Epilogue (后记)

Epilogue is a literary device that is often placed at the end of a novel, a play, or any other literary piece to provide some additional information and bring closure to the work.

后记是一种文学手段,经常由作者放在小说、戏剧或者其他类型的文学作品末尾以提供额外的信息,为作品结尾。

Epistolary Novel (书信体小说)

Epistolary novel, as a genre of fiction, dates back to ancient Roman times. It refers to a novel written in the form of letters. It can let readers know the characters' thoughts and feelings without the writer's interference, which can bring strong sense of reality to readers. The epistolary novel gained prominence in the mid-eighteenth century, which is witnessed by the success of Samuel Richardson[①]'s *Pamela* (1740), *Clarissa* (1748) and *The History of Sir Charles Grandison* (1753).

书信体小说是一种小说形式,可以追溯到古罗马时期。它是指以书信体形式写作的小说。它可以在没有作者干预的情况下让读者了解人物的思想和情感,这为读者带来了很强的真实感。书信体小说在 18 世纪中期颇受欢迎,塞缪尔·理查森的《帕米拉》(1740)、《克拉丽莎》(1748)以及《查尔斯·格兰迪森爵士的历史》(1753)的成功就恰恰说明了这一点。

---

① Samuel Richardson (1689—1761) was an English writer famous for his epistolary novels in the 18th century.

Epitaph （墓志铭）

The word "epitaph" is derived from a Greek word "epitaphios", meaning "a funeral oration". Now, it refers to a statement written to be inscribed or an inscription on a gravestone, honoring a deceased person. Some writers, such as Oscar Wilde, Robert Frost and John Keats, have written their own epitaphs before their death. John Keats's epitaph is "Here lies one whose name was writ in water".

该词来源于希腊词汇 "epitaphios"，意思是 "葬礼上的演说"。现在它是指写下来的要进行铭刻的言语或者刻在墓碑上的碑文，以纪念死去之人。一些作家，例如奥斯卡·王尔德、罗伯特·弗罗斯特以及约翰·济慈都是在生前就已经写好自己的碑文。约翰·济慈的碑文是 "此处躺着的是名字写在水中的人"。

Epiphany （顿悟）

The word "epiphany" derives from the ancient Greek "epiphaneia" with the meaning of "manifestation, striking appearance". James Joyce (1882—1941), one of the most famous Irish novelists, popularized the secular usage of the word in his early draft of *A Portrait of the Artist as a Young Man* entitled *Stephen Hero* (published posthumously in 1944). The Joycean epiphany means "a sudden spiritual manifestation, whether from some object, scene, event, or memorable phase of the mind—the manifestation being out of proportion to the significance or strictly logical relevance of whatever produces it". [1]

Now the word can be used in any situation in which an ordinary object or scene is understood from a new and deeper perspective because of a sud-

---

[1] Morris Beja, *Epiphany in the Modern Novel.* Seattle: University of Washington Press, 1971, p. 18.

den and enlightening realization.

"顿悟"一词来源于古希腊单词"epiphaneia"，意思是"显现，突然的出现"。詹姆斯·乔伊斯（1882—1941），是最著名的爱尔兰小说家之一，他在《一个青年艺术家的画像》的初稿题名为《英雄斯蒂芬》（作者逝世后于 1944 年出版）中使该词普及。乔氏顿悟是指"突然的精神反应，要么来自某种物体、场景、事件或者思维的记忆片段——而该反应与激发它出现的事物没有任何严格意义上的关系"。

如今，凡是指因为突然和有启发作用的意识从全新、深层的角度来理解普通的事物或者情景都可以使用该词来形容。

Epithalamion or Epithalamium（喜歌）

Epithalamion originally referred to a wedding song sung by boys and girls outside the marital Chamber in ancient Greece. Sappho[1] is considered as the first poet to begin writing epithalamia. Inspired by Sappho, Catullus[2] wrote two famous epithalamia (his poems 61 and 62). Renaissance poets revived the tradition. For example, Edmund Spenser created *Epithalamion* (1595) for his bride, Elizabeth Boyle, which was influential for later poets. The genre declined during the Enlightenment.

喜歌最开始是指在古希腊婚礼上由童男童女在婚房外唱的歌曲。萨福被认为是第一个开始写喜歌的诗人。受到了萨福的启迪，卡图卢斯写了两首著名的喜歌（第 61 篇及第 62 篇诗歌）。文艺复兴时期诗人使该文化复苏。例如埃德蒙·斯宾塞为自己的新娘，伊丽莎白·博伊尔创作的《喜歌》（1595）影响颇大。喜歌在启蒙时期开始慢慢衰落。

---

[1] Sappho (610 B. C. —570 B. C.), Greek lyric poet famous for the beauty of her writing style.

[2] Catullus (84 B. C. —54 B. C.) was a Roman poet who wrote in the neotericstyle of poetry. Ovid, Horace, and Virgil were greatly influenced by him.

Epithet （绰号）

Epithet, as a literary term, refers to a descriptive word or phrase used to highlight a person or thing's characteristic so that listeners or readers can remember the person or thing easily. For example, in the name Alfred the Great, "the Great" is an epithet; in the name Richard the Lion-Hearted, "the Lion-Hearted" is an epithet. Homer used many epithets in his *Iliad* and *Odyssey*, such as "gray-eyed Athena" and "wine-dark sea" (Aegean Sea).

绰号作为文学术语是指为了让听者或者读者能够容易地记住某人或某事，而使用描述性词汇来强调该人或该物的特点。例如，在伟大的阿尔弗雷德中，"伟大的"就是一个绰号；狮心王查理中，"狮心王"就是一个绰号。荷马在《伊利亚特》和《奥德赛》中使用了大量的绰号，例如"灰眼雅典娜'以及"暗酒海"（指代爱琴海）。

Ethics （伦理学）

Ethics, also known as moral philosophy, is a branch of philosophy studying human character. That is, ethics tells us what is morally right and wrong. Some literary critics, such as William Hazlitt[1] and Matthew Arnold[2], concentrated on ethics in literary works.

伦理学，也叫道德哲学，是研究人类品格的哲学分支。也就是说，伦理学告诉我们什么是道德上的正确与错误。一些文学批评家，例如威廉·黑兹利特以及马修·阿诺德都关注文学作品中的伦理学。

Euhemerism （欧赫墨罗斯学说）

Euhemerism is named after a Greek writer Euhemerus who wrote a uto-

---

[1] William Hazlit (1778—1930) was an English writer famous for his humanistic essays and literary criticism.

[2] Matthew Arnold (1822—1888) was an English poet, essayist and literary critic of great repute.

pian work entitled *The Sacred Inscription* in the beginning of the 3rd century B. C. In it he put forward a theory known as Euhemerism that all the Greek gods and goddesses were originally real heroes in historical events, and they were worshiped after their deaths.

欧赫墨罗斯学说是以希腊作家欧赫墨罗斯命名的，他在公元前 3 世纪初完成了一本叫作《神圣的碑文》的乌托邦作品，其中他提出了一个被称为欧赫墨罗斯学说的理论：所有的希腊男神和女神起初都是历史事件中的真正英雄，他们死后才被信奉为神。

Euphuism（尤弗伊斯体或绮丽体）

In the 1580s, during the reign of Queen Elizabeth, an elegant literary style known as Euphuism became fashionable. Euphuism takes its name from the hero in the prose romances Euphues: *The Anatomy of Wit* (1578) and *Euphues and his England* (1580) written by John Lyly[①]. Euphuism deliberately and excessively used antitheses, alliterations and similes. Famous playwrights, such as Robert Greene[②]and William Shakespeare were greatly influenced by it.

在 16 世纪 80 年代，在伊丽莎白女王统治时期，一种文雅的被称为尤弗伊斯体的文学方式开始流行。尤弗伊斯体得名于约翰·利利写的散文传奇作品《尤弗伊斯：才智之剖析》（1578）以及《尤弗伊斯和他的英格兰》（1580）。尤弗伊斯体故意大量使用对偶、头韵和比喻。著名剧作家，罗伯特·格林以及威廉·莎士比亚都受到了尤弗伊斯体的很大影响。

---

① John Lyly (1553—1606) was an English prose writer and dramatist, best remembered for his prose romance *Euphues*.

② Robert Greene (1558—1592) was an English dramatist popular in his days.

Euphemism（委婉语）

Euphemism, as a literary device, refers to some indirect, polite or vague words or phrases which are used to take the place of those considered to be harsh, unpleasant, or offensive.

委婉语作为一种文学手段，是指为了代替那些被认为粗鲁、讨厌或者冒犯的词汇或短语而使用的一些间接、礼貌或者含糊的词汇或短语。

Expressionism（表现主义）

Expressionism, as an anti-traditional modernist and creative movement in literature and art, originated in Germany before the First World War and reached a peak in Berlin during the 1920s. It was influenced much by Symbolism, Fauvism and Cubism, laying emphasis on the expression of emotional experience and denying the objectivity of the real world by exaggerating and distorting it. It was a reflection of emotional chaos and the crisis of social culture.

Its effects can be seen in Arthur Miller's *Death of a Salesman* as well as in the theater of the absurd. Der Blaue Reiter（"The Blue Rider"）, Die Brücke（"The Bridge"）, Die Neue Sachlichkeit（"The New Objectivity"）and the Bauhaus School were groups of expressionist artists.

表现主义是一种反传统的现代主义和具有开创性的文学和艺术运动，在第一次世界大战前起始于德国，并于 20 世纪 20 年代在柏林达到顶峰。它受到了象征主义、野兽主义和立体主义的影响，强调了情感经历的表达，通过夸张和歪曲事实否认现实世界的客观性。它是当时情感混乱和社会文化危机的体现。

其效果在阿瑟·米勒的《销售员之死》以及荒诞派戏剧中得以体现。"青骑士派""桥社""新客观派"以及"包豪斯学派"都是表现主义艺术家。

Existentialism（存在主义）

"Existentialism", one of the most influential philosophical schools, came into being in Germany in 1920s; became popular in France after the Second World War and boomed in America in 1950s. The term was generally considered to be first coined by Nietzsche. It stressed individual personality, freedom and subjective experience in the meaningless world. "Existence precedes essence" is its motto.

Soren Kierkegaard (1813—1855), Arthur Schopenhauer (1788—1860), Karl Theodor Jaspers (1883—1969), Martin Heidegger (1889—1976) are usually called "precursors" of the trend.

"存在主义"是最有影响力的哲学流派之一，在20世纪20年代形成于德国，第二次世界大战后在法国流行，20世纪50年代在美国繁荣。该词普遍被认为是由尼采最先提出。它强调在无意义的世界中的个性、自由和主观经验。"存在先于本质"是其座右铭。

索伦·克尔凯郭尔（1813—1855）、亚瑟·叔本华（1788—1860）、卡尔·西奥多·雅斯贝尔斯（1883—1969）和马丁·海德格尔（1889—1976）可被看作该流派的"先驱"。

F

Fable（寓言）

The word "fable" is derived from the Latin "fabula", meaning "story". Fable, as one of the oldest literary genres, refers to a short story employing animals, plants or inanimate things as the main characters and ending with a moral lesson or didactic purpose. Aesop (620 B. C. —540 B. C.) was an ancient Greek fabulist and his *Aesop's Fables* is reckoned as the greatest fable in the world. Phaedrus (15 B. C. —50 A. D.) was another famous fabulist recognized as the source of the modern Aesop Fables.

该词来源于拉丁语词汇"fabula"，意思是"故事"。寓言作为最古老的文学类型之一，是指用动物、植物或者没有生命的事物作为主人公，而以道德教育或说教目的的结尾的短故事。伊索（公元前620年—公元前540年）是古希腊的寓言家，其《伊索寓言》被认为是最伟大寓言。裴德罗（公元前15年—公元50年）是另一个著名的寓言家，他被认为是现代伊索寓言的开始。

Fabliau（讽刺性寓言诗）

Fabliau（the plural form is "fabliaux"）was originally a French literary genre that flourished in the 13th century. Geoffrey Chaucer[①]started to employ fabliaux which had been much dead for over 100 years as a writing style in his well-known work, *The Canterbury Tales*. Larry Benson defines "fabliau" in his introduction to *The Riverside Chaucer* like this：

"A fabliau is a brief comic tale in verse, usually scurrilous and often scatological or obscene. The style is simple, vigorous, and straightforward；the time is the present, and the settings real, familiar places；the characters are ordinary sorts. . . the plots are realistically motivated tricks and ruses. The fabliaux thus present a lively image of everyday life among the middle and lower classes. Yet that representation only seems real. . . the plots, convincing though they seem, frequently involve incredible degrees of gullibility in the victims and of ingenuity and sexual appetite in the trickster-heroes and-heroines. "[②]

讽刺性寓言诗（复数形式是"fabliaux"）最开始是一种在 13 世纪繁荣的法国文学形式。杰弗雷·乔叟开始在其著名的《坎特伯雷故事集》中使用已销声匿迹 100 多年的讽刺性寓言诗。拉里·本森在《河畔的乔叟》的引言中是这样定义"讽刺性寓言诗"的：

"讽刺性寓言诗是以诗歌形式写的简短的滑稽故事，通常比较粗俗、下流、淫秽。该形式简单、奔放、直接；时态用一般现在时，背景都是真实、熟悉的场景，人物都是普通的类型，情节是比较现实的计谋和诡计。因此，讽刺性寓言诗展现的是中产阶级与下层阶级日常生活的生动形象。然而这只不过看似真实……情节，虽然好像很让人

---

① Geoffrey Chaucer（1343—1400），the most important writer of the Middle Ages, was considered as the "Father of English Literature".

② Larry Dean Benson, *The Riverside Chaucer*, Oxford University Press, 2008, p. 7.

信服，但是经常包括令人难以置信的上当者的被骗以及骗子男主人公和女主人公的足智多谋和情欲。"

Fairy Tale（神话）

Fairy tales, developing out of folktales, refer to fictional stories that involve fantastic magical beings such as giants, dwarves, fairies, witches and some other magical enchantments or transformations. Fairy tales have very similar plots, characters and endings. *Prince Charming*, *Puss in Boots* and *Cinderella* are examples of fairy tales.

神话从民间传说发展而来，是指包含了不切实际的魔幻的事物，例如巨人、矮人、仙女、巫婆还有其他的施展魔法或魔法变身等。神话有非常相似的情节、人物和结局。《白马王子》《穿靴子的猫》以及《灰姑娘》都属于神话。

Fancy and Imagination（设想与想象）

In the 18th century, fancy and imagination were used synonymously and could be used interchangeably. But during the Romantic period, especially after Samuel Taylor Coleridge①published *The Biographia Literaria* in 1817, the difference was recognized. According to Coleridge, fancy, inferior to imagination, is just a mechanical process of combing things together and a passive operation of mind, while imagination has a more "mysterious power" to create new things by fusing different ideas and impressions. Thus, the biggest distinction between "the two words is that the fancy combines, and imagination creates".

在 18 世纪，设想与想象被当成同义词使用并没有什么区别，可以

---

① Samuel Taylor Coleridge (1772—1834) was an English poet and founder of the Romantic Movement in England. He was also a member of Lake poets.

互换使用。但是在浪漫主义时期，尤其是在塞缪尔·泰勒·柯勒律治在1817年出版了《文学传记》之后，差异变得明显。根据柯勒律治所说，设想比想象低级，它只不过是把事物结合在一起的机械过程，思维的被动运行，而想象有着"更为神奇的力量"，可以把不同的想法和表达融合起来创造新的事物。因此，两词之间最大的区别在于"设想是结合而想象是创造"。

Fantasy（幻想）

Fantasy refers to a form of literary genre using supernatural or unreal elements in the plot, setting or theme. Such a kind of story often takes place in an imaginary or exaggerated world with some magical things or creatures. Therefore, fantasy has no specific relation with reality.

幻想是指在情节、背景或者主题中使用一些超自然或者不真实元素的文学形式。幻想经常发生在想象的或者夸张的世界里，里面有神奇的事物。因此，幻想与现实没有什么具体的联系。

Farce（闹剧）

Farce is a literary genre employing exaggeration, horseplay, nonsensical, humorous manner or deliberate absurdity in order to entertain the audience. It lays emphasis on plots and neglects characterization. People consider it to be inferior to comedy but it has succeeded enjoying its popularity in Western world till now.

闹剧是使用夸张、胡闹、废话、幽默的行为或者故意的荒谬而使人发笑的文学类型。它强调情节而忽视人物的刻画。人们认为它比喜剧低劣，但是到现在为止它在西方世界一直颇受欢迎。

Feminism（女性主义）

The word "feminism", derived from the French word "feminisme", was coined by Charles Fourier[1]and first used in English in the 1890s. [2] It now refers to the beliefs and ideas that women should have political, economic and social equality with men. Mary Woollstonecraft[3]is viewed as the founder of feminism and her *A Vindication of the Rights of Woman* (1792) is reckoned as the first great feminist work.

There are three waves in feminism.

The first-wave referred to the period from the end of the 19th century to the beginning of the 20th century. The word "first-wave" was coined by Martha Lear in *The New York Times Magazine* in 1968. During the period, feminists mainly fought for women's suffrage. Virginia Woolf's *A Room of Their Own* (1929) is considered the milestone of modern feminist criticism. She advocates that women should have their own room for writing, that is, women should endeavor to be financially and intellectually independent. Woolf also put forward the notion of female bisexuality. Another prestigious work is Simone de Beauvoir's *The Second Sex* (1949), which introduces the notion of "otherness" and is famous for "one is not born, but rather becomes, a woman". [4]It lays the groundwork for second-wave feminism.

The second-wave (1960s—1980s) began in the U. S. A. and then spread to other countries. The term "second-wave" was coined by Martha Lear. During the period, many famous works appeared, such as Kate Millet[5]'s *Sexual*

---

[1] Charles Fourier (1772—1837) was a famous French philosopher and an early socialist thinker associated with "utopian socialism".

[2] Ted Honderich, *The Oxford Companion to Philosophy*, Oxford: Oxford University Press, 1995, p. 29.

[3] Mary Wollstonecraft (1759—1797) was an English revolutionary thinker, writer and England's early feminist, best known for her advocacy for women's rights.

[4] Simone de Beauvoir, *The Second Sex*, translated by H. M. Parhsley, New York: Vintage Books, 1989, p. 267.

[5] Kate Millet (1934—) is an American feminist author, artist, and feminist. She has been described as one of the most influential Americans of the 20th century.

Politics (1969), Elaine Showalte[①]'s *A Literature of Their Own: British Women Novelists from Bronte to Lessing* (1977) and *The Madwoman in the Attic* (1979) written by Sandra Gilbert[②]and Susan Gubar[③]. All the works provide more mature theories for feminism, therefore, the second-wave feminism is highly theoretical.

The third-wave feminism (1990s—present) "is buoyed by the confidence of having more opportunities and less sexism".[④]Rebecca Walker[⑤]coined the term "third-wave feminism" in 1992. During the period, Nira Yuval-Davis[⑥]put forward the notion of "transversal politics" in *Gender and Nation* (1997), which is an important contribution to the third-wave feminism. According to Nira Yuval-Davis, "transversal politics" is different from "identity politics". "The idea is that each participant in the dialogue brings with her a rooting in her own membership and identity, but at the same time tries to shift in order to engage in exchange with women who have different membership and identity."[⑦] The third-wave feminism makes great progress both in politics and theory.

该词来源于法语的"feminisme",是由夏尔·傅里叶在19世纪90年代在英语中首次使用。现在是指认为女人与男人应该在政治、经济和社会上平等的信念和想法。玛丽·沃斯通克拉夫特被认为是女性主义的奠基人,她的《女权辩护》(1792)被认为是第一部伟大的女性

---

① Elaine Showalter (1941—) is an American writer, literary critic and feminist. She is the founder of gynocritics.

② Sandra Gilbert (1936—) is an American writer, literary critic and renowned poet.

③ Susan Gubar (1944—) is an American writer and distinguished Professor.

④ Jennifer Baumgardner & Amy Richards, *Manifesta: Young Women, Feminism, and the Future*, Macmillan, 2000, p. 83.

⑤ Rebecca Walker (1969—) is an American writer and works as a feminist.

⑥ Nira Yuval-Davis, born in Israel, is a Professor in Gender & Ethnic Studies at the University of Greenwich in London.

⑦ Nira Yuval-Davis, *Gender and Nation*, Sage Publications, 1997, pp. 130 – 131.

主义著作。

共有三波女性主义运动。

第一波是指从19世纪末到20世纪初的运动。"第一波"这个词是由玛莎·里尔在1968年的《纽约时报杂志》中首次提出。在此期间，女性主义者主要为了女人的选举权斗争。弗吉尼亚·伍尔夫的《一间自己的房间》（1929）被认为是现代女性主义批评的里程碑。她提倡妇女们应该有自己的写作房间，也就是说女人应该努力成为经济和思想独立的女人。伍尔夫还提出了女人雌雄共体的概念。另一本颇负盛名的作品是西蒙·德·波伏娃的《第二性》（1949），主要介绍了"他者"的概念，并且以"女人不是天生的，而是后来变成的"出名，它为第二波女性主义运动奠定了基础。

第二波女性主义运动（20世纪60年代到80年代）在美国开始然后扩展到其他国家。"第二波"这个词是由玛莎·里尔首次提出的。在此期间，出现了很多出名的作品，例如凯特·米丽特的《性政治》（1969）、伊莱恩·肖沃尔特的《她们自己的文学：从勃朗特到莱莘的英国女性小说家》（1977）以及桑德拉·吉尔伯特和苏珊·格巴合著的《阁楼上的疯女人》等。所有这些作品为女性主义提供了更为成熟的理论，因此第二波女性主义运动是高度理论性的。

第三波女性主义运动（20世纪90年代到现在）"有了更多的机遇和更少的性别歧视"。丽贝卡·沃克在1992年第一次使用了"第三波女性主义"。在此期间，伊瓦·戴维斯在《性别与民族》（1997）中提出了"纵横政治"的概念，这对第三波女性主义有着重要的贡献。根据她的说法，"纵横政治"与"认同政治"不同。"纵横政治是每个对话的参与者都会随身带有自己的成员资格与身份，但是同时努力转变以适应与那些有着不同成员资格与身份的人进行交流。"第三波女性主义在政治和理论上都取得巨大的进步。

Fiction（小说）

The word "fiction" is derived from the Latin "fictiō", meaning "a fashioning or feigning". Fiction refers to a type of literature that is created from imagination. The plots, characters and dialogue are made up by fiction writers. Romance, dramas, novels, short stories, novellas, science fiction, mystery stories belong to fiction.

该词来源于拉丁语"fictiō",意思是"捏造或者虚构"。小说就是指一种由想象而创造的文学形式。情节、人物和对话都是由小说作家编造出来的。传奇、戏剧、长篇小说、短篇小说、中篇小说、科幻小说、神话故事等都属于小说。

Figure of Speech（修辞格）

A figure of speech refers to a literary device, using a word or an expression that is different from its literal meaning for the purpose of emphasis, embellishment or clarification. There are many kinds of figures of speech: simile, metaphor, hyperbole, personification, synecdoche and so on. Figures of speech are often used in prose and poetry.

修辞格是指为了强调、润色或者澄清的目的，使用表达意义不同于字面意义的单词或者短语的文学手段。有很多种修辞格：明喻、暗喻、夸张、拟人、提喻等。修辞格经常在散文和诗歌中使用。

Fetishism（恋物癖）

The word "fetishism", derived from the Portuguese "feitiço" meaning "obsessive fascination", was coined by the French philosopher Charles de Brosses (1709—1777) in 1757. [1] Fetishism means "the hyperbolic, obsessive cherishing of a particular commodity as if it were a thing bearing great

---

① Donald Preziosi, *The Art of Art History: A Critical Anthology*, Oxford University Press, 2009, p. 109.

spiritual value". ①

There are two types of fetishism: sexual fetishism and commodity fetishism. According to Freud in his *Introductory Lectures on Psychoanalysis* (1916—1917), sexual fetishism means that a person gets sexual satisfaction primarily through the admiration of an object or an asexual body part. "Commodity fetishism" was coined by Karl Marx in *Capital: Critique of Political Economy* (1867), meaning that money is a fetish for many people but it stops people from seeing the exploitation in the economic society.

该词起源于葡萄牙语中的"feitiço",意思是"强烈的痴迷",它是由法国哲学家查理·布罗西斯(1709—1777)在1757年首次使用的。恋物癖意思是"对于普通物品的夸张、强烈的喜爱,就好像它是一件有着极大精神价值的东西一样"。

有两种类型的恋物癖:性恋物癖和商品恋物癖。根据弗洛依德在《精神分析引论》(1916—1917)中所说,性恋物癖就是指一个人主要通过对于某件物品或者身体非性器官的崇拜而得到性满足。"商品恋物癖"是由卡尔·马克思在《资本论:政治经济批评》(1867)中首次使用,是指很多人对于金钱有恋物癖,可是金钱却蒙蔽了人们的双眼,让他们看不到经济社会剥削的本质。

Fin de Siècle(世纪终点)

Fin de siècle is a French phrase meaning "the end of the century". When the literary term is used in a literary work, it refers to the years between 1880 and 1914, which is the end of an era (a period of degeneration) as well as the new beginning of another era (a period of hope). The years saw the decadence, extreme aestheticism, and despair in France as well as

---

① M. H. Abrams, *A Glossary of Literary Terms. Seventh Edition.* Boston: Heinle & Heinle, 1999, p. 120.

some social and scientific progress.

这是一个法语短语，意思是"世纪终点"。当在文学作品中使用该词时，它是指 1880 年到 1914 年期间，这是一个时代的结束（堕落的时期）也是另一个时代的全新开始（希望的时期）。该时期见证了法国的颓废、极端唯美主义以及绝望，也看到了一些社会和科学的进步。

Flashback（倒叙）

Flashback, as a literary device, refers to an interruption of the normal chronological order of events. Writers often use flashbacks to insert past events in the narratives of a prose, novel or poetry to provide background information or context.

倒叙，作为一种文学手段，是指对于事件正常的时间顺序进行打断。作家在散文、小说或者诗歌的叙述中经常使用倒叙插入过去的事件以提供背景信息或者语境。

Flat Character（扁平人物）

A flat character, also known as "static character", is a person who has only one, maybe two, personality characteristics. He or she is usually unchanged and only plays a supporting role to the main character as a minor character in a literary work. Mrs. Micawber in Charles Dickens's *David Copperfield* (1849—1850) is an example.

扁平人物，也被称为"静态人物"，是指只有一种或者两种个性特征的人。扁平人物通常都是一成不变的，在文学作品中作为次要人物对主人公起着支撑作用。在查理·狄更斯的《大卫·科波菲尔》中的米考伯夫人便是扁平人物的例子。

Fleshly School （肉欲诗派）

Robert Buchanan①first used the term "Fleshly School" in *The Contemporary Review* （October 1871） under the pseudonym "Thomas Maitland" as a fierce attack on the Pre-Raphaelites school like Dante Gabriel Rossetti②, William Morris③and Algernon Swinburne④for their immorality and sensuality.

罗伯特·布坎南在《现代评论》（1871 年 10 月） 以笔名托马斯·梅特兰德首次用 "肉欲诗派" 针对前拉斐尔派如但丁·加百利·罗塞蒂、威廉·莫里斯以及阿尔杰农·斯温伯恩等诗人的不道德和好色而进行猛烈的攻击。

Foil （配角）

Foil is character in a literary work who contrasts with the protagonist to highlight the characteristics and qualities of the protagonist.

配角是文学作品中的与主人公相对的人物，用来强调主人公的品格和品质。

Folklore （民间传说）

The term "folklore" was first coined by the English antiquarian William Thomas in 1846 to describe the traditions, beliefs and expressions of a culture, subculture, or group all over the world, including jokes, legends, myths, oral history, fairy tales, stories, superstition, proverbs and so on.

---

① Robert Buchanan （1841—1901） was an English novelist, poet and playwright. He is best known for his attack on Pre-Raphaelites.

② Dante Gabriel Rossetti （1828—1882） was an English painter and poet. He was one of the founders of Pre-Raphaelite Brotherhood.

③ William Morris （1834—1896） was an English poet, novelist, translator and socialist activist associated with the Pre-Raphaelite Brotherhood and the English Arts and Crafts Movement.

④ Algernon Swinburne （1837—1909） was an English critic and one of the most accomplished lyric poets of the Victorian age.

It is handed down orally from generation to generation. "Surely no other discipline is more concerned with linking us to the cultural heritage from the past than folklore; no other discipline is more concerned with revealing the interrelationships of different cultural expressions than folklore; and no other discipline is so concerned with discovering what it is to be human. "[1] As the heart of all cultures, it connects people to their past and binds people together.

"民间传说"一词是由英国古文物研究者威廉·托马斯在 1846 年首次提出的,用来描述全世界的一种文化、亚文化或者群体的传统、信念和表达,包括笑话、传说、神话、口头历史、童话、故事、迷信、谚语等。它是通过口头方式代代相传的。"没有哪个学科能像民间传说这样关注把我们与过去的文化遗产联系起来;没有哪个学科能像民间传说这样关注揭露不同文化表达方式之间的关系;没有哪个学科能像民间传说这样关注于揭示人类的样子"。作为所有文化的核心,它把人们与过去相连,将人们凝聚在一起。

Formalism (形式主义)

Formalism, as literary criticism, emerged in Russia and Poland during the 1910s. The establishment of two organizations (the Society for the Study of Poetic Language founded in 1916 and the Moscow Linguistic Circle founded in 1915) marked the formal beginning of formalism in Russia. Russian formalists advocate the study of "literariness" and think that the text itself in a literary work should be the focus instead of the author's life or social class. So formalism concentrates on literary form and technical devices to the exclusion of its background and social values. "Defamiliarization" put for-

---

[1] William A. Wilson. "The Deeper Necessity: Folklore and the Humanities". *Journal of American Folklore*, 1988, p. 101.

ward by Vicktor Shklovsky (1893—1984) is the most important concept of the school. Viktor Shklovsky, Yuri Tynyanov①, Boris Eichenbaum②, Roman Jakobson③, and Grigory Vinokur④are influential scholars of the school. Formalism ended in 1930s because of Stalin's opposition. But it has great influence on Western literary criticism, especially structuralism.

形式主义，作为文学批评理论，在 20 世纪 10 年代出现在俄罗斯和波兰。两个组织（建于 1916 年的诗歌语言研究会和建于 1915 年的莫斯科语言学会）的建立标志着俄罗斯形式主义的正式开始。俄罗斯形式主义者提倡"文学性"研究，并认为文学作品的文本应该是研究的重点而不是作家的生活或者社会阶级。所以，形式主义关注的是文学形式和技术手段，而不包括背景和社会价值。由维克多·什克洛夫斯基（1893—1984）提出的"陌生化"是该学派的重要概念。维克多·什克洛夫斯基、尤里·图尼阿诺夫、鲍里斯·艾肯鲍姆、罗曼·雅各布森、格里高利·维诺库尔都是该学派颇具影响力的学者。形式主义在 20 世纪 30 年代由于斯大林的反对而结束。但是它对于西方文论的影响很深远，尤其是对结构主义的影响。

Frankfurt School（法兰克福学派）

Frankfurt School is a philosophical school associated with the Institute for Social Research which was founded by a group of intellectuals in the University of Frankfurt in Germany in 1923 with the donation by Felix Weil. Max

---

① Yuri Tynianov (1894—1943) was a Russian and Soviet famous writer, translator, scholar and literary critic, best known as an important member of the Russian Formalist school.

② Boris Eichenbaum (1886—1959) was a Russian and Soviet literary scholar and representative of Russian Formalism.

③ Roman Jakobson (1896—1982) was a Russian thinker, linguist and pioneer of structural analysis. He was one of the founders of Moscow Linguist Circle.

④ Grigory Vinokur (1896—1947) was a Russian linguist and literary critic.

Horkheimer[①], Theodor Adorno (1903—1969), Leo Lowenthal (1900—1993), Erich Fromm (1900—1980), Herbert Marcuse (1898—1979), and Walter Benjamin (1892—1940) were famous members of the school. They developed western Marxism and applied Neo-Marxism to social matters.

法兰克福学派是一个哲学流派，它与"社会研究中心"有关，该中心是在菲利克斯·韦尔资助下由一群知识分子于 1923 年在德国的法兰克福大学建立的。麦克斯·霍克海默、西奥多·阿多诺（1903—1969）、里奥·洛文塔尔（1900—1993）、埃里希·弗罗姆（1900—1980）、赫伯特·马尔库塞（1898—1979）、瓦尔特·本雅明（1892—1940）都是该派的著名成员。他们发展了西方马克思主义并且用新马克思主义解决社会问题。

Free Verse（自由诗体）

Free verse is an open form of poetry, originated by some French poets of the late 19th century to free themselves from traditional rules on rhythm and meter patterns. That is, poets are able to follow the rhythm of natural speech without any restriction to create poetry.

The most representative work of free verse is Walt Whitman[②]'s *Leavers of Grass*.

自由诗体是一种开放的诗歌形式，是 19 世纪末法国诗人为了从传统的对节奏和韵律的束缚中解脱出来而发起的。也就是说，诗人可以没有任何限制地根据自己自然的说话节奏进行诗歌创作。

自由诗体最具代表性的作品是沃尔特·惠特曼的《草叶集》。

---

① Max Horkheimer (1895—1973) was a German sociologist and philosopher best known as a memeber of the Frankfurt School.

② Walt Whitman (1819—1892) was an American poet, essayist and journalist, known as the "father of Free Verse".

Futurism （未来主义）

Futurism was an avant-garde art movement that emerged in Italy in 1909. The term was coined by Filippo Tommaso Marinetti①in *Founding and Manifesto of Futurism* published in the Paris newspaper *Le Figaro* on February 20, 1909. Futurists loved machines, speed, energy and technology, all of which they took as their inspiration. They enjoyed the changes and vitality of the modern world. But at the same time, they also supported wars and favored the growth of Fascism. Gino Severini②and Umberto Boccioni③were representative futurists. Futurism ended with the death of Marinetti in 1944.

Futurism was influential to the later artistic movements, such as Vorticism, Dadaism and Surrealism. ④

未来主义是 1909 年在意大利开始盛行的先锋艺术运动。该词是由菲利波·托马索·马里内蒂在 1909 年二月法国报纸《费加罗报》上发表《未来主义宣言》中提出的。未来主义者喜欢机械、速度、能源和技术，他们把这些当成自己的灵感。他们也喜欢现代世界的变化和活力。但是与此同时，他们支持战争，支持法西斯主义的发展。吉诺·塞维里尼以及翁贝托·波丘尼都是典型的未来主义者。未来主义随着马里内蒂在 1944 年去世而结束。

未来主义对于以后的艺术运动，例如漩涡派、达达主义以及超现实主义影响颇深。

---

① Filippo Tommaso Marinetti （1876—1944) was an Italian novelist, poet and the founder of Futurism.

② Gino Severini （1883—1966) was an influential Italian painter best known as member of Futurism.

③ Umberto Boccioni （1882—1916) was a famous Italian painter, sculptor and theorist of Futurism.

④ M. H. Abrams, *A Glossary of Literary Terms*. Seventh Edition. Boston: Heinle & Heinle, 1999, p. 129.

G

Gallows Humor（绞刑架幽默）

Gallows humor refers to describing some terrifying, painful, disgusting or life-threatening issues in a light, humorous or satirical manner.

绞刑架幽默是指用轻松、幽默或者讽刺的方式来描写一些恐怖、痛苦、恶心或者危及生命的事情。

Gender Studies（性别研究）

Gender studies, as a successor to feminist literary study, is an interdisciplinary field starting in the 1970s which is concerned with the study of gender and the interactions of gender with other social categorizations, including race, sexuality, religion, class, ethnicity, nationality etc. That is, gender studies mainly studies gender norms, gender identities and gender relations from intersectional perspectives. Over the decades, gender studies has grown rapidly and brought about diverse national and regional developments.

性别研究，作为女性主义文学研究的继承者，是在 20 世纪 70 年代兴起的一个跨学科领域，主要是研究性别还有性别与其他社会类别之间的关系，例如种族、性、民族、宗教、阶级、民族、国家等。也就是说，性别研究主要用跨学科角度研究性别标准、性别身份和性别关系。在过去的几十年，性别研究已经日益壮大，并且带来了民族和区域发展。

Genetic Fallacy（起源谬见）

Genetic fallacy is a logical fallacy which occurs due to irrelevance. That is, a claim for or against an idea is only based on the source or origin, rather than the current meaning or scenario. For example "It will rain today because my teacher said so".

起源谬见是因为不相关性而发生的一种逻辑错误。也就是说，对于某种观点的赞同或是反对仅仅基于来源或者起源，而不是基于当前的意思或者情境。例如，"今天会下雨，因为我的老师这么说的"。

Genre（类别）

Genre is a literary term coming from Latin "genus", meaning "kind" or "sort". It refers to the category of art, literature or music based on form, style, content or other criteria. Generally speaking, literature has five main genres: poetry, drama, prose, fiction and non-fiction. We are also familiar with epic, tragedy, comedy, lyric, romance, satire and elegy.

该词来源于拉丁语"genus"，意思是"种类"或者"类别"。它是指根据形式、风格、内容或者其他的标准对艺术、文学或者音乐等进行的分类。总的说来，文学有五种主要类别：诗歌、戏剧、散文、小说以及纪实文学。除此之外，我们还很熟悉的类别有史诗、悲剧、喜剧、抒情诗、传奇、讽刺以及挽歌。

Georgian Poetry（乔治诗集）

Georgian Poetry refers to five anthologies of poetry which were edited by

Sir Edward Marsh①and published by Harold Monro②during the early ten years（between 1912 and 1922）of George V's reign（1910—1936）of the United Kingdom. The Georgians were a group of poets, including William Henry Davies（1831—1921）, Edmund Blunden（1896—1974）, Hilaire Belloc（1870—1953）, Ralph Hodgson（1871—1962）, Rupert Brooke（1887—1915）, Wilfred Wilson Gibson（1878—1962）, Robert Graves（1895—1985）, Walter de la Mare（1873—1956）, Siegfried Sassoon（1886—1967）, D. H. Lawrence（1885—1930）etc.

乔治诗集是指在乔治五世统治英国期间（1910—1936）的早期十年间（1912—1922）由爱德华·马什主编由哈罗德·门罗出版的五部诗集。乔治时代诗人包括威廉·亨利·戴维斯（1831—1921）、埃德蒙·布伦登（1896—1974）、希莱尔·贝洛克（1870—1953）、拉尔夫·霍奇森（1871—1962）、鲁伯特·布鲁克（1887—1915）、威尔弗雷德·威尔森·吉布森（1878—1962）、罗伯特·格雷夫斯（1895—1985）、华特·德·拉·迈尔（1873—1956）、西格里夫·萨松（1886—1967）、戴·赫·劳伦斯（1885—1930）等。

Georgic（农事诗）

The word "georgic" is derived from the Greek "georgein", meaning "agricultural things". A georgic is a poem focusing on agriculture, rural affairs and people involved in labor. The Latin poet Virgil wrote four books of poems called *Georgics* in 29 B. C. , which described the human struggle with the forces of nature and were reckoned as Virgil's second major work.

该词来源于希腊词汇"georgein"，意思是"农事"。农事诗是主

---

① Sir Edward Marsh（1872—1953）was a British scholar, translator, art collector, civil servant and editor who was best known as the sponsor and friend of the Georgian poets.

② Harold Monro（1879—1932）was a British poet and the founder of the Poetry Bookshop in Bloomsbury. He did a lot for the development of Great War poetry.

要写农业、农事和农民的诗歌。拉丁诗人维吉尔在公元前 29 年写了四本名为《农事诗》的诗歌，主要描写了人类与自然之间的斗争，并且被认为是维吉尔的第二个主要著作。

Golden Age（黄金时代）

According to Greek mythology and legend, "Golden Age" refers to the time in the 5th century B. C. in classical Greece, when literature, drama, art, politics and philosophy were booming. There were five ages in all experienced by man: Golden Age, Silver, Bronze, Heroic and Iron (the present), which are followed by a decline. The Golden Age lies at the highest point when new developments happen quickly and new ideas flood. By extension, "Golden Age" can be applied to a period of primordial peace, harmony, stability, and prosperity.

根据希腊神话和传说，"黄金时代"是指古希腊公元前 5 世纪的时候，当时文学、戏剧、艺术、政治和哲学非常繁荣。人类共经历五个时代：黄金时代、白银时代、青铜时代、英雄时代和铁器时代（就是现在），时代在慢慢衰落。黄金时代是最高点，当时，新发展层出不穷，新观点如潮涌入。通过延伸，"黄金时代"可用来指原始意义上的和平、和谐、稳定和繁荣。

Goliardic verse（畅怀诗）

Goliardic verse, as a type of medieval satirical poetry, is attributed to Goliards who were wandering scholars, students and jesters in the 12th-c and 13th-c England, Germany and France. Goliard verse was mainly written in Latin in the form of mockery directed at the Church and the Pope. The underlying theme is carpe diem. Hugh Primas (1090—1160) and Walter of Chatillon①were

---

① Walter of Chatillon was a 12th – Century French writer best known for his Latin epic *Alexandreis*.

representative poets of the genre. [1]*Carmina Burana*, published by Joseph Andrews Schmeller in Germany in 1847, was considered as the most notable collection of Goliardic verse.

畅怀诗,作为中世纪的讽刺诗,主要是由 12 世纪和 13 世纪的英国、德国和法国的流浪学者、学生和小丑等游吟诗人所写。畅怀诗主要是将矛头直指教会和主教用拉丁文写的诗歌。"及时行乐"是其潜在的主题。休·普莱玛斯(1090—1160)、沃特·查提龙是该类诗歌的代表诗人。由约瑟夫·安德鲁斯·施梅勒在 1847 年出版的《布兰诗歌》被认为是最著名的畅怀诗歌集。

Gothic Novel(哥特式小说)

In 1764, Horace Walpole's novel *The Castle of Otranto* with the subtitle of "A Gothic Story" (in its second edition) was published, which established the mode of Gothic novel and marked its beginning.

The genre often employed ghosts, death, horror, haunted houses, mystery, misfortune and other supernatural phenomena to cause nightmarish terrors. In the 1790s, there appeared two branches: horrible Gothic Novels and sentimental Gothic novels. The latter ones discarded the use of horrible effects, making the stories more logical.

Gothic novels were more mature in the 19th century. Representative novels were Emily Bronte's *Wuthering Heights* (1847), Mary Shelley's *Frankenstein* (1818), Isaac Mitchelland's *The Asylum* (1804), Matthew Lewis's *The Monk* (1795) and Edgar Allan Poe's *The Fall of the House of Usher* (1839).

在 1764 年,霍勒斯·沃波尔的《奥特兰托城堡》出版了,在第

---

[1] Alex Preminger, O. B. Hardison, *The Princeton Handbook of Poetic Terms*, Princeton University Press, 2014, p. 85.

二版中还带了一个副标题——"一个哥特式故事"，它为哥特式小说建立了模式，象征着哥特式小说的产生。

该类小说经常使用鬼魂、死亡、恐怖、鬼屋、神秘、不幸和其他的超自然现象来引起噩梦般的恐惧。在 18 世纪 90 年代，出现了两个分支：恐怖型哥特小说和感伤型哥特小说。后者不再使用恐怖效果，故事变得更具有逻辑性。

哥特小说在 19 世纪较为成熟。代表作品有艾米丽·勃朗特的《呼啸山庄》（1847）、玛丽·雪莱的《弗兰肯斯坦》（1818）、伊萨克·米契尔的《庇护所》（1804），马修·刘易斯的《僧人》（1795）以及埃德加·爱伦·坡的《厄舍古屋的倒塌》（1839）。

Graveyard Poets（墓园派诗人）

"Graveyard poets", also called "Churchyard Poets" or "the Boneyard Boys", were a group of eighteenth-century poets whose poems were characterized by the themes of human mortality, bereavement, grave and similar things. They belonged to one branch of sentimentalism.

Thomas Gray's "Elegy Written in a Country Churchyard" （1751） is reckoned as the most famous production of the movement.

Graveyard poets were precursors of the Gothic genre and had great influence on the rise and development of romanticism.

"墓园派诗人" 也被称为 "教堂诗人" 或者 "墓地青年"，是一群 18 世纪的诗人，他们的诗以死亡、丧亲、墓地及类似的事情为主题。他们属于感伤主义的分支。

托马斯·格雷的《墓园挽歌》（1751）被认为是该运动最杰出的作品。

墓园派诗人是哥特式小说的先驱，并对浪漫主义的兴起和发展有深远的影响。

Grotesque（怪诞）

The word "grotesque" derives from the Italian word "grotte-caves", where painting from the reign of Augustus were discovered during the excavations of Rome at the end of the 15th century.①Initially, the word was only adopted in visual arts, but in the beginning of the 18th century, it was used as a literary term, meaning "the managing of the uncanny by the comic".② Grotesque combines ugliness and ornament, the bizarre and the ridiculous for ironic effect.

该词起源于意大利词汇"grotte-caves"，指的是在公元 15 世纪末发掘罗马的时候中发现了奥古斯都统治时期的壁画的洞穴。最开始，该词只适用于视觉艺术，但是到了 18 世纪早期，开始作为文学术语而被使用，意思是"通过喜剧形式处理怪异的事情"。怪诞为了达到讽刺效果将丑陋与美好、奇怪与荒谬结合在一起。

Grundyism（注重规矩）

The term originated from a character named Mrs Grundy in Thomas Morton③'s play *Speed the Plough* (1798). Mrs Grundy is a priggish person who follows closely to the line of convention. So grundyism means narrow conventionalism.

该词来源于托马斯·莫顿的《加快耕耘》（1798）中的一个叫格兰迪的人物名字。格兰迪夫人是一个死板，严格遵守习惯的人。所以该词的意思是严格的注重规矩的意思。

---

① Maria Haar, *The Phenomenon of the Grotesque in Modern Southern Fiction: Some Aspects of Its Form and Function*, Almqvist & Wiksell International, 1983, p. 1.

② Michael Steig, "Defining the Grotesque: An Attempt at Synthesis", *Journal of Aesthetics and Art Criticism*, 1970, p. 259.

③ Thomas Marton (1764—1838) was an English playwight.

H

Hagiography（圣徒传记）

Hagiography is a type of biography that studies the lives and miracles of the saints, ecclesiastical leaders and other people with sacred power. In modern literature, hagiography is seldom used.

圣徒传记是一种描写和研究圣人、神职领袖和其他有圣权的人的生活和事迹的传记。在现代文学中，圣徒传记很少被使用。

Hamartia（悲剧的弱点）

The word "hamartia" is derived from Greek "hamartanein", meaning "to err". It is a concept introduced by Aristotle in the *Poetics* to describe a protagonist's mistake or error in judgment that leads to the tragic downfall in a tragedy. Hamartia is often used in literary works to create a powerful plot, for example, Othello's jealousy in *Othello* and Hamlet's irresolution in *Hamlet*.

该词来源于希腊语"hamartanein"，意思是"犯错"。它是由亚里士多德在《诗学》中提出的，用来描写悲剧中的主人公在判断上的错误导致了悲剧性的毁灭。在文学作品中经常使用悲剧的弱点来建构强大的情节，例如《奥赛罗》中奥赛罗的妒忌以及《哈姆雷特》中哈姆雷特的犹豫不决。

Harlem Renaissance（哈莱姆文艺复兴）

Harlem Renaissance, first known as the "New Negro Movement", was a literary and cultural movement that spanned from 1918 through the middle of the 1930s' Depression. Between 1919 and 1926, many African-Americans, including some radical black intellectuals, immigrated from rural places to urban centers in northern cities, especially around Harlem, which resulted in Harlem Renaissance. James Weldon Johnson used "flowering of Negro literature" to refer to Harlem Renaissance, because during the period a group of African-American writers, artists and musicians began to reevaluate their own creative ability, advocated to build a new image of African Americans, and produced many unprecedented works with particular styles. Thus, African-Americans' creativity improved greatly.

Langston Hughes's *Not Without Laughter* (1931), George S. Schuyler's *Black No More* (1931), Arna Bontemps' *Black Thunder* (1936) are representative works of the genre.

哈莱姆文艺复兴，也叫"新黑人运动"，是从 1918 年一直延续到 20 世纪 30 年代中期的一次文学、文化运动。在 1919 年到 1926 年期间，很多非洲裔美国人，包括一些激进的黑人知识分子，从农村移居到北部城市的中心区，尤其是哈莱姆地区，这也就促成了哈莱姆文艺复兴。詹姆士·威尔顿·约翰逊用"黑人文学兴盛期"来指代哈莱姆文艺复兴，因为在此期间很多美国黑人作家、艺术家和音乐家开始重新评价自己的创作力，倡导建立新的黑人形象，并创作了很多前所未有、独具风格的作品。因此，黑人的创造力得到大幅度提升。

兰斯顿·休斯的《并非没有笑声》（1931）、乔治·斯凯勒的《再也不黑》（1931）阿那·邦当的《黑色雷电》（1936）是该类文学的代表作。

Hebraism （希伯来精神）

Generally speaking, Hebraism refers to the usage and characteristics of the Hebrew language, or to the Jewish people, their culture, ideology or faith. According to Matthew Arnold[1], Hebraism emphasizes faith, and Hellenism stresses knowledge. Our world moves between Hebraism and Hellenism, both of which arise out of the wants of human nature and address themselves to satisfy those wants. [2]

总的说来，希伯拉精神是指希伯来语言的用法和特征，或者指希伯来人，以及他们的文化、思想意识或者信仰。根据马修·阿诺德所说，希伯来精神强调信仰，而希腊文化强调知识。我们的世界就是在希伯来精神和希腊文化之间运动，它们都是源于人性的需求，并满足这些需求。

Hellenistic Age （希腊化时代）

Hellenistic Age refers to the period from the death of Alexander the Great in 323 B. C. to the rise of the Roman Empire in 31 B. C. . During this period, Greek language became the official language of the Hellenistic world and Greek culture and civilization spread quickly to the Mediterranean and Southwest Asia; the mixed culture produced a hybrid civilization and art underwent dramatic changes... All in all, Hellenism Age saw great advances in philosophy, science, art and literature.

希腊化时代是指从亚历山大大帝在公元前 323 年去世时一直到公元前 31 年罗马帝国兴起的这段时间。在该时期，希腊语成为了希腊化

---

[1] Matthew Arnold (1822—1888) was an English Victorian poet and literary critic, best known for his book *Culture and Anarchy* (1867).

[2] Mattew Arnold, *Culture and Anarchy*, Chapter 4, http：//faculty. gvc. edu/ssnyder/Hum101/hebraism_ and_ hellenism. htm.

世界的官方语言；希腊文化和文明迅速传播到地中海地区和西南亚；混合的文化产生了混合的文明；艺术经历了翻天覆地的变化……总而言之，希腊化时代见证了哲学、科学、艺术和文化上的巨大进步。

Hemingway Code Hero（海明威式英雄或硬汉）

Earnest Hemingway, a famous American novelist, created many impressive characters-soldiers, bullfighters, hunters and fishermen, who had to fight against violence, failure and death. Such kind of hero is called Hemingway Code Hero or Code Hero. The concept of death shaped their concept of life: death can't be avoided, so they do their best to enjoy all kinds of physical pleasures or take the most they can from life.

They share some common traits: ①they are courageous enough to have "beautiful adventures", ②they are so honest and loyal that they always keep their words, ③they have strong willpower, able to bear any pain and face death with dignity, ④they never show emotions and don't talk about what they believe in, ⑤They don't talk too much and they are men of action, ⑥they admit the truth of Nada (Spanish, "nothing").

Santiago in *The Old Man and The Sea* is a representative code hero, and his "A man can be destroyed but not defeated" has become a motto for many fighting men.

厄内斯特·海明威，是著名的美国小说家，塑造了很多令人印象深刻的人物——士兵、斗牛士、猎人和渔夫，他们与暴力、失败和死亡斗争。这些人物形象被称作"海明威式英雄或硬汉"死亡的概念体现了他们的生活理念：死亡难以避免，所以他们尽力享受各种各样的身体快乐，或者尽可能地从生活中获取最多的东西。

他们有着共同的特点：①他们很勇敢，敢于进行"美丽的冒险"，②他们诚实、真诚，总能信守诺言，③他们意志坚强，能够忍受任何疼痛并有尊严地面对死亡，④他们从来不把情感外露，不谈论自己深信的东西，⑤他们言语不多，他们是行动的巨人，⑥他们承认虚无。

《老人与海》中的桑提亚哥便是典型的硬汉，他的"人可以被毁灭，但不能被打败"成为很多奋斗中人的座右铭。

Heroic Couplet（英雄双行体）

Heroic couplet, a major English verse-form for poetry, is commonly used in epic and narrative poetry. Geoffrey Chaucer was a precursor. In his *Legend of Good Women* and *Canterbury Tales*, he applied iambic pentameters rhyming in pairs: aa, bb, cc, and so on, which was later known as heroic couplets.

It was perfected by John Dryden in the 17th century, became predominant in English poetry in the 18th century and began to decline in importance in the early 19th century. It was preferred especially by Alexander Pope.

英雄双行体是一种主要的英语诗歌形式，通常在史诗和叙事型诗歌中使用。杰弗雷·乔叟是该形式的先驱者。他在《贤妇传奇》和《坎特伯雷故事集》中使用了五音步抑扬格，以 aa，bb，cc 等形式进行押韵，这就是后来的英雄双行体。

它是由约翰·德莱顿在 17 世纪加以完善，在 18 世纪英语诗歌中占主导地位，在 19 世纪早期开始衰落。它受到了亚历山大·蒲柏的青睐。

Heroic Drama（英雄剧）

Heroic drama is a type of play popular in Restoration England during the 1660s and 1670s. The leading examples of heroic dramas were John Dryden's *Conquest of Granada* (1670) and *Aureng-Zebe* (1675). According to Dryden, heroic drama is distinguished by its heroic verse (closed couplets in iambic pentameter), grand matter and powerful hero.

英雄剧是在 17 世纪 60 年代和 70 年代在英国复辟时期流行的一种戏剧形式。约翰·德莱顿的《征服格拉纳达》（1670）以及《奥伦·泽比》（1675）是英雄剧的两个典范。根据德莱顿所说，英雄剧是要有自己的英雄诗歌体（以五音步抑扬格双行体结尾）、伟大的事件以及强大的主人公。

High Comedy（高雅喜剧）

High comedy is a type of comedy which deals with the life and problems of the genteel society. It is characterized by witty and sophisticated dialogue, biting satire and a complicated plot.

高雅喜剧是一种主要针对上流社会的生活和问题的一种喜剧，以诙谐熟练的语言、尖酸刻薄的讽刺以及错综复杂的情节为特点。

Higher Criticism（高等考证或高等批评）

Higher criticism, also known as "historical criticism", is a type of literary criticism which studies literary works especially biblical texts in order to understand something about the historical context. Higher criticism emerged in Germany in the late 18th century. In the 19th century, George Eliot's translations of Strauss[①]'s *Life of Jesus* (1846) and Feuerbach[②]'s *The Essence of Christianity* (1854) popularized higher criticism in England. In the early 20th century, it declined.

高等考证，也称作"历史批评主义"，是一种文学批评方式，主要是为了了解历史背景而对文学作品尤其是圣经文本进行研究。高等考证在 18 世纪末出现于德国。在 19 世纪，乔治·艾略特翻译了斯特劳斯的《耶稣传》（1864）以及费尔巴哈的《基督教的本质》（1854），

---

① David Strauss (1808—1874) was a German-Protestant philosopher, theologian and writer.

② Ludwig Feuerbach (1804—1872) was an influential German philosopher and moralist best noted for *The Essence of Christianity*.

使高等考证在英国颇受欢迎。在 20 世纪初，高等考证衰落。

Historical Fiction（历史小说）

Historical fiction is a literary genre in which historical events or figures are set as the theme to reflect the customs and mentality of the period as well as to explore the relationship between personal fortunes and social conflicts. The protagonists and the events are more or less based on historical facts, but sometimes a little imagined.

Historical fiction is written to enlighten and educate readers.

Walter Scott[①], Honoré de Balzac[②] and James Fenimore Cooper[③], whose works laid its foundation, are notable pioneers of the genre.

历史小说是一种文学形式，它以历史事件和人物作为题材以揭示那个时期的风俗以及人的思想情况，同时也探索着人的命运与社会冲突之间的关系。主人公和事件多多少少都是根据历史事实而来的，有时会有些虚构。

历史小说的创作是为了给读者以启示和教育。

沃尔特·司各特、奥诺雷·德·巴尔扎克和詹姆斯·费尼莫尔·库柏是该类小说的开拓者，他们的作品历史小说的奠定了基础。

Historicism（历史主义）

Historicism, as a kind of literary criticism, explores how a literary work is influenced by its historical, social, political and cultural circumstances

---

① Walter Scott (1771—1832) was a Scottish poet, playwright and one of the greatest historical novelists. *Waverley* (1814), *Rob Roy* (1817), *Ivanhoe* (1819), *Quentin Durward* (1823) are his representative works.

② Honoré de Balzac (1799—1850) was a French novelist, best known for his *La Comédie humaine* (*The Human Comedy*). He was reckoned as "the father of the naturalist novels".

③ James Fenimore Cooper (1789—1851) was the first major American novelist. His historical romances of frontier adventure known as the *Leatherstocking Tales* are influential.

instead of examining the text itself.

历史主义，作为一种文学批评方法，主要探讨文学作品如何受其创作的历史、社会、政治和文化背景的影响，而不是只研究文本自身。

Homily（布道）

The term "homily" is derived from the Greek word "homilia", meaning "have a communication with a person". As a literary term, it refers to a commentary given by a priest after a scripture has been read in order to teach a moral lesson or encourage those who hear it.

该词来源于希腊词汇"homilia"，意思是"与人交流"。作为文学词汇，它是指在读完经文之后由牧师进行解说以进行道德教育或者鼓励那些听者。

Horatian Satire（贺拉斯式讽刺）

The term "Horatian satire" is named after the classical Roman poet Horace who created influential works about Western culture. Horatian satire is gentle, witty and humorous. Its aim is to make readers laugh at the characters as well as themselves. Jane Austen's *Pride and Prejudice* (1813) and Oscar Wilde's *The Importance of Being Earnest* (1895) are models of Horatian satire.

该词以经典罗马诗人贺拉斯命名，他曾创作了对西方文化颇具影响力的著作。贺拉斯式讽刺很温和、睿智并幽默。其目的就是为了让读者在嘲笑人物的同时还嘲笑自己。简·奥斯汀的《傲慢与偏见》（1813）以及奥斯卡·王尔德的《不可儿戏》（1895）堪称贺拉斯式讽刺的典范之作。

Humanism（人文主义）

Humanism is an intellectual movement of the Renaissance and the mainstream ideology in Europe during the Renaissance. It came into being because of the new rising bourgeois class's fight against Feudalism and religion.

It centers on human beings' value and relies on science to understand the world. It abandons the creative method of symbolism prevailing in Middle Ages and utilizes realism to describe real life. Patrarch （1304—1374） is reckoned as the "Father of Humanism".

人文主义是文艺复兴时期的知识分子运动也是当时欧洲的主要思想体系。它是由于新兴的资产阶级与封建主义、宗教进行斗争而产生的。

它强调以人为本，依靠科学来理解世界。它摒弃了在中世纪盛行的象征主义创作方式，使用现实主义来描述现实生活。彼特拉克（1304—1374）被认为是"人文主义"之父。

Hymn （赞美诗）

The term "hymn" comes from Greek "humnos", meaning "a song of praise". According to Austin C. Lovelace[1], "Hymns are the voice of the people—first of all as prayers or praise to God, second as teaching of the faith and admonishing each other". [2]

该词来源于希腊语"humnos"，意思是"赞歌"。根据奥斯丁·洛夫雷斯所说，"赞美诗首先是指祈祷者或者赞扬上帝的声音，然后是宗教教义以及相互告诫"。

Hyperbole （夸张法）

Hyperbole is a figure of speech which uses deliberate exaggeration for emphatic effects.

---

[1] Austin C. Lovelace （1919—2010） was famous as an American church musicians, composer, organist, clinician, and choir director. He was called "the Dean of American Church Music".

[2] Austin C. Lovelace, "Interview with Austin C. Lovelace", *HYMN Magazine*, October 2004, pp. 16 – 17.

夸张法是为了达到强调效果而故意使用夸张言语的修辞方法。

Hyperbaton（倒装法）

Hyperbaton is a rhetorical device which puts words in an unexpected order in a sentence for the sake of emphasis, creating a different sentence structure and suggesting the same meaning.

倒装法是指为了起到强调作用将单词放在句子中意想不到的位置，使句子结构有所不同而句意不变的一种修辞方法。

I

Iambic Pentameter（五音步抑扬格）

Iamb is a metrical foot with two syllables, an unstressed syllable followed by a stressed syllable, or a short syllable followed by a long syllable. Iambic pentameter refers to a line consisting of five feet (five pairs of syllables), each of which is an iamb. Iambic pentameter usually appears in English-language poetry. William Shakespeare preferred to use it in his sonnets and plays.

抑扬格是有两个音节的音律，一个轻音后又一个重音，或者一个短音后又一个长音。五音步抑扬格是指由五个音律（五对音节）组成的一行，每个音律都是一个抑扬格。五音步抑扬格经常出现在英语诗歌中。威廉·莎士比亚在其十四行诗和戏剧中对此格青睐有加。

Idyll（田园诗）

The term refers to a kind of poem describing natural objects, pastoral scenes or a happy life in the rural area. It was first used by Greek poet Theocritus[①]in his short pastoral poems, *Idylls*.

该词是指描写自然景物、田园风貌或者农村的幸福生活的诗歌。首先由希腊诗人忒俄克里托斯在田园短诗《田园诗》中使用。

---

① Theocritus (310 B. C. ? —260 B. C. ?) was a Greek poet and the creator of bucolic poetry of the 3rd century B. C.

Imagery（意象）

Imagery is a literary term for the vivid language used by poets to appeal to readers' five senses: sound, sight, touch, smell and taste. Through imagery, readers can have better understanding of the authors' writings and deep impressions.

意象是一个文学术语，用来形容诗人为激发读者的五种官能：听、看、摸、闻和尝所使用的栩栩如生的语言。通过意象，读者可以对作品有更好的理解及更深的印象。

Imagism（意象主义）

Imagism was a 20th-century literary movement whose program was formulated by Ezra Pound（1885—1972）in about 1912. As the most influential movement in English poetry since Pre-Raphaelites, it opposed the overuse of sentiment and artifice which were common in Romantic and Victorian poetry. Instead, it emphasized the use of precise images, succinct words, and the rhythm composed by the musical phrase rather than the metronome.

Ezra Pound's *In a Station of the Metro*（1913）is a typical imagist poem. Besides, Amy Lowell[1], Hilda Doolittle[2], Richard Aldington[3], and F. S. Flint[4] were very prominent imagists.

意象主义是20世纪的文学运动，由埃兹拉·庞德在1912年建立了基本的模式。它是自前拉斐尔派开始影响力最大的英语诗歌运动，它反对在浪漫主义和维多利亚诗歌中常见的情感和技巧的过多使用，强调使

---

[1] Amy Lowell（1874—1925）was an American imagist poet with great achievement.

[2] Hilda Doolittle（1886—1961）was an American avant-garde poet and novelist, best known for her works in Imagism.

[3] Richard Aldington（1892—1962）was an English writer, notable as a founding poet of the Imagist Movement. His representative novel is *Death of a Hero*（1929）.

[4] F. S. Flint（1885—1960）was an English poet and member of the Imagist Movement.

用精准的意象、简洁的言语和有乐感的而不是节拍的诗韵。

埃兹拉·庞德的《在地铁车站》（1913）是典型的意象派诗歌。除此之外，艾米·洛威尔、希尔达·杜利特尔、理查德·阿尔丁顿和弗兰克·斯图亚特·弗林特都是非常杰出的意象主义者。

Impersonality（非个人化）

Impersonality is a great literary criticism put forward by T. S. Eliot (1888—1965) in his *Tradition and the Individual Talent* (1917). According to Eliot, "poetry is not a turning loose of emotion, but an escape from emotion; it is not the expression of personality, but an escape from personality. But, of course, only those who have personality and emotions know what it means to want to escape from these things". [1] That is, emotion is impersonal and it has nothing to do with poetry. Good criticism is directed at the form and structure of poetry instead of the poet. The theory lays a foundation for the new criticism.

非个人化是由托马斯·斯特尔纳斯·艾略特（1888—1965）在《传统与个人才能》（1917）中提出的伟大的文学批评理论。根据艾略特所说，"诗歌不是放纵情感，而是逃避情感；诗歌不是表达个性，而是逃避个性。但是，当然了，只有有个性和情感之人才知道想要逃避这些意味着什么"。也就是说，情感是非个性化的，它与诗歌没有关系。好的批评直指诗歌的形式与结构而非诗人。该理论为新批评奠定了基础。

Implied Author and Implied Reader（隐含作者与隐含读者）

Wayne Booth [2] introduced the concept of "implied author" in his *The*

---

① T. S. Eliot, "*Tradition and the Individual Talent*", Ⅱ *The Sacred Wood*, 1922 http: //www. english. illinois. edu/maps/poets/a_ f/eliot/tradition. htm.

② Wayne Booth (1921—2005) was an American literary critic and professor at the University of Chicago.

Rhetoric of Fiction published in 1961. He writes. "It is only as I read that I become the self whose beliefs must coincide with the author's. Regardless of my real beliefs and practices, I must subordinate any mind and heart to the book if I am to enjoy it to the full. The author creates, in short, an image of himself and another image of his reader; he makes his reader, as he makes his second self, and the most successful reading is one in which the created selves, author and reader, can find complete agreement. "① Thus, implied author is the real author's "second self" assumed by readers from various indicators in the text, which may be different from the real author's personality.

Wolfgang Iser (1926—2007) discussed "implied reader" in *The Implied Reader* (1974) *and The Act of Reading: A Theory of Aesthetic Response* (1976, trans. 1978). "The concept of the implied reader is therefore a textual structure anticipating the presence of a recipient, without necessarily defining him: this concept prestructures the role to be assumed by each recipient, and this holds true even when texts deliberately appear to ignore their possible recipient or actively exclude him. "② Thus, the "implied reader" is the recipient for whom the author intends to write, who is not the same as a real reader but is preconceived by the author. The theories of implied author and implied reader emphasize the objectivity of literary criticism, and contribute greatly to the development of narration theory.

韦恩·布斯（1921—2005）在 1961 年出版的《小说修辞学》中介绍了"隐含作者"这一概念。他写道："只有当我阅读的时候，我才成为那个与作者的信念一致的自我。不管真正的信念和实际情况如何，如果想要完全地融入文本，我必须屈从于文本中的观点和想法。

---

① Wayne Booth, *The Rhetoric of Fiction*, University of Chicago Press, 1961, p. 138.

② Wolfgang Iser, *The Act of Reading: A Theory of Aesthetic Response*. Baltimore: Johns Hopkins University Press, 1978, p. 145.

简而言之，作者塑造了自己的形象和读者的形象；他塑造了第二个自我的同时塑造了读者，最成功的阅读就是所塑造的作者和读者意见完全一致。"因此，隐含作者是读者通过文本的不同暗示而想象出来的作者的第二个自我，他很可能与真正作者的个性大相径庭。

沃尔夫冈·伊瑟尔（1926—2007）在《隐含读者》（1974）以及《阅读行为：美学反映理论》（1976，翻译本 1978）中讨论了"隐含读者"。"隐含读者就是指文本结构所预设但并未明确规定的接受者：该概念预设每个接受者所要承担的角色，即使文本故意忽视或者极力排斥可能的接受者，该概念同样适用。"因此，"隐含读者"就是作者的写作对象，与真正的读者不同，只是作者预想出来的。隐含作者与隐含读者强调文学批评的客观性，为叙事理论做出了重要贡献。

Impressionism（印象主义）

Impressionism is a literary writing manner in which the author intends to capture a feeling or sensory impression rather than to represent an accurate depiction or objective reality. Just as Sarah F. Paulk (1937—) in *The Aesthetics of Impressionism: Studies in Art and Literature* writes: "The (Impressionistic) novelists eliminated plot... the Impressionistic novel attempts to capture the perceiving mind in action. "[1] Stephen Crane[2], Joseph Conrad[3] and Virginia Woolf[4] are considered as the typical impressionists.

---

[1] Sarah F. Paulk, *The Aesthetics of Impressionism: Studies in Art and Literature*, Ann Arbor: University Microfilms International, 1979, p. 161.

[2] Stephen Crane (1871—1900) was an American realistic writer, noted for his novels *Maggie: A Girl of the Streets* (1893) and *The Red Badge of Courage* (1895), which were reckoned as the examples of American Naturalism and Impressionism.

[3] Joseph Conrad (1857—1924) was a British writer, best known for his novels *Heart of Darkness* and *Lord Jim*.

[4] Virginia Woolf (1882—1941) was an English writer, feminist, and modernist, best remembered for her novels *To the Lighthouse* and *Mrs. Dalloway*.

印象主义是一种文学写作形式，作者试图抓住一种感觉或者感官上的印象而不是进行准确描写或者呈现客观现实。正如萨拉·保尔克（1937—）在《印象主义美学：艺术与文学研究》中写道："印象主义小说家忽略情节……印象主义小说试图抓住行为中的感知思维。"斯蒂芬·克莱恩、约瑟夫·康拉德、弗吉尼亚·伍尔夫被认为是典型的印象主义者。

Intentional Fallacy and Affective Fallacy（意图谬误与情感谬误）

The term "intentional fallacy" was first coined by W. K. Wimsatt and Monroe Beardsley in 1946 in their essay *The Intentional Fallacy*. Intentional fallacy is an error of reading which tries to interpret a literary work based on the writer's intention, emotion, attitude, circumstance and so on.

The term "affective fallacy" was also put forward by Wimsatt and Bearsley in 1949. Affective fallacy is an error of reading which studies a literary work by reference to the reader's response.

Intentional fallacy and affective fallacy are important terms in New Criticism.

"意图谬误"一词是由维姆萨特和比尔兹利在 1946 年名为《意图谬误》的论文中首次使用。意图谬误是指根据作者的意图、情感、态度、生活背景等来研究文学作品的一种阅读错误。

"情感谬误"一词也是由维姆萨特和比尔兹利在 1949 年提出的。情感谬误是指根据读者的反映而研究文学作品的一种阅读错误。

意图谬误与情感谬误都是新批评中重要的术语。

Interior Monologue（内心独白）

Interior monologue, as a literary term, can often be used interchangeably with stream of consciousness. In interior monologue, a protagonist's thoughts and interior life are exposed to the reader or audience.

内心独白是一个文学术语，经常与意识流互换使用。在内心独白中，主人公的思想和内心世界被暴露给读者或者观众。

Interlude（幕间插曲）

According to Nicholas Davis, interlude is "the most convenient label for all those shortish late-medieval and early Tudor-plays, mainly preserved for us in printed editions, which we have grown used to regarding as comparable and to differentiating in our minds from other groupings of plays". [1] Now, it refers to a short play performed between courses at a banquet. John Heywood (1497—1580) was a great interlude writer best known for his *The Play of the Wether* (1533) and *The Play Called the Four PP.* (1544).

根据尼古拉斯·大卫所说，幕间插曲是"所有中世纪后期及都铎王朝早期以印刷版存留下来的简短戏剧的最方便统称，我们习惯用它与其他戏剧进行比较和区分"。现在，它是指宴会期间表演的短剧。约翰·海伍德（1497—1580）便是伟大的幕间插曲作家，以《天气的戏剧》（1533）和《四P戏剧》（1544）而闻名。

Irony（反讽）

Irony is a a rhetoric device in which the literal meaning is different from the actual meaning. There are three categories of irony such as verbal irony, dramatic irony and situational irony.

Verbal irony is when one says something but means something else.

Dramatic irony is when the audience knows something that the characters in the story don't know.

Situational irony is when the actual outcome is different from the expec-

---

[1] Nicholas Davis, *Meanings of the Word "Interlude": A Discussion*, Medieval English Theater, 1984, pp. 5 - 6.

ted outcome.

反讽是指字面意思与实际意思相反的修辞方法。有三种反讽，例如言语反讽、戏剧反讽和情境反讽。

言语反讽是指一个人说了什么事却意指其他。

戏剧反讽是指观众知道故事中的人物并不知道的事。

情境反讽是指真实的结果与预料的结果截然不同。

J

Jacobean Era（雅各布时代）

The word "Jacobean" comes from the Hebrew name Jacob, which is the original form of James. So Jacobean era refers to the period during which King James I (1603—1625) ruled England. The era saw flourishing and subtle changes in arts, architecture and literature. Jacobean drama was often filled with sex, evil, crimes and violence, such as *The White Devil* (1612) written by John Webster (1580—1634), *The Changeling* (1622) written by Thomas Middleton (1580—1627) and William Rowley (1585—1626), *King Lear* and *Macbeth* written by Shakespeare.

In addition, Ben Johnson[1], George Chapman[2], Thomas Browne[3], Francis Bacon[4], Francis Beaumont[5] were great writers of the age.

---

[1] Ben Johnson (1572—1637) was an English actor and playwright best known for his comedies *Every Man in His Humour* (1598) and *Volpone* (1605).

[2] George Chapman (1559—1634) was an English playwright, poet and translator best remembered for his translation of *Homer's Iliad* and *Odyssey*.

[3] Thomas Browne (1605—1682) was a famous physician and writer.

[4] Francis Bacon (1561—1626) was an English prominent philosopher, author and thinker best known for his empiricism.

[5] Francis Beaumont (1584—1616) was a Jacobean poet best famous for his collaboration with John Fletcher.

"Jacobean" 一词来源于希伯来名字雅各布（Jacob），这也是詹姆士（James）的最初形式。所以雅各布时代是指在詹姆士一世（1603—1625）统治英国的时期。该时期见证了在艺术、建筑和文学中的繁荣和微妙变化。雅各布时代戏剧经常充斥着性、罪恶、犯罪和暴力，例如约翰·韦伯斯特（1580—1634）的《白色恶魔》、托马斯·米德尔顿（1580—1627）与威廉·劳利（1585—1626）合著的《变节者》、莎士比亚的《李尔王》和《麦克白》。

除此之外，本·琼森、乔治·查普曼、托马斯·布朗、弗朗西斯·培根、弗朗西斯·博蒙特都是该时代伟大的作家。

Jazz Age（爵士时代）

Jazz Age, first coined by American writer F. Scott Fitzgerald (1896—1940), refers to the period of the 1920s and 1930s (it began after World War I and ended with the Great Depression), when Jazz music and dance became popular, particularly in America where society was experiencing prosperity and change.

It is considered as the second Renaissance in American literature. Fitzgerald's *The Great Gatsby* is the most representative work of the age. He described the age as such: "It was an age of miracles, it was an age of art, it was an age of excess, and it was an age of satire."[1]

爵士时代，是由美国作家司各特·菲茨杰拉德（1896—1940）首先使用，是指在 20 世纪 20 年代和 20 世纪 30 年代期间（始于第一次世界大战后，结束于大萧条），当时爵士音乐和舞蹈开始流行，特别是在美国，社会正经历着繁荣与变革。

它被认为是美国文学的第二次文艺复兴。菲茨杰拉德的《了不起的

---

[1] Fitzgerald, *Echoes of the Jazz Age*, 1931. https://pdcrodas.webs.ull.es/anglo/ScottFitzgeraldEchoesOfTheJazzAge.pdf.

盖茨比》是该时期最典型的代表作品。他是这样描述这个时代的："这是一个奇迹的时代，一个艺术的时代，一个挥金如土的时代，也是一个充满嘲讽的时代。"

Jeremiad（哀歌）

The term "Jeremiad" is named after Jeremiah, a Biblical prophet in the *Old Testament*, *the Book of Jeremiah* and *the Book of Lamentations*. In the 7th century B. C., Jeremiah ascribed the destruction of Israel to God's punishment because of its violation of the contract with the God.

Broadly speaking, a literary work in which the writer bitterly denunciates the condition of the society and attributes the misfortune as a penalty, sometimes can be called as a jeremiad.

该词是以《旧约：耶利米书》以及《旧约：耶利米哀歌》中的圣经先知耶利米来命名。在公元前 7 世纪，耶利米把以色列的灭亡归因于上帝的惩罚，因为它违背了与上帝的契约。

广义来讲，作者无情地谴责社会状况并将此不幸归结为惩罚的作品都可被称为哀歌。

Juvenalian satire（朱维诺式讽刺）

The term "Juvenalian satire" is named after Juvenal who was a Roman satirist active in the late 1st and early 2nd centuries. Juvenalian satire is harsh, abrasive and indignant. Its aim is to attack individuals and to criticize the society. Jonathan Swift[①]'s *Gulliver's Travels* (1726) is considered as the model of Juvenalian satire.

该词以活跃于 1 世纪末 2 世纪初的罗马讽刺家朱维诺命名。朱维

---

① Jonathan Swift (1667—1745) was an Anglo-Irish poet and satirist whose *Gulliver's Travels* (1726) was very famous.

诺式讽刺是尖酸、刻薄、愤慨的。其目的就是为了攻击个人和批评社会。乔纳森·斯威夫特的《格列佛游记》（1726）被认为是朱维诺式讽刺的典范之作。

K

Kenning （比喻复合辞）

Kenning, as a poetic device, is often associated with Anglo-Saxon, Old Norse and Old Icelandic poetry. It consists of two（often hyphenated）words describing an object or activity through metaphors. For example "whale-road" is used for the sea; "story-keeper" for book, "web-maker" for spider. A Kenning poem is a puzzle poem consisting of several lines of kennings to describe an object.

比喻复合辞，作为一种诗歌手法，经常与盎格鲁－撒克逊、古挪威以及古冰岛诗歌联系在一起。它是由两个词（经常是加连字符的）组成，通过比喻来形容一个物体或活动。例如"鲸鱼之路"用来指大海，"故事收藏者"指书籍，"织网者"指蜘蛛。比喻复合辞诗歌是由好几行比喻复合辞组成来描写一件事物的谜语诗。

Kunstlerroman （艺术家成长小说）

Kunstlerroman, also called "the artist novel", is a subgenre of Bildungsroman. It refers to a novel telling about a character's youth and his or her development into a poet, musician or painter. Johann Wolfgang von

Goethe's *The Apprenticeship of Wilhelm Meister* （1795—1796）, Samuel Butler[①]'s *The Way of All Flesh* （1903） and James Joyce[②]'s *A Portrait of the Artist as a Young Man* （1916） are examples of the genre.

　　艺术家成长小说是成长小说的一个分支。它是指讲述人物年轻时代及成为诗人、音乐家或者画家的成长过程的小说。约翰·沃尔夫冈·冯·歌德的《威廉·麦斯特的学习时代》（1795—1796）、塞缪尔·巴特勒的《众生之路》（1903）以及詹姆斯·乔伊斯的《一个青年艺术家的画像》（1916）都是该类小说的范例。

---

　　① Samuel Butler （1835—1902） was an English writer famous for his satire *Erewhon* （1872） and *The Way of All Flesh* （1903）.

　　② James Joyce （1882—1941） was an Irish writer noted for *Ulysses* （1922） and *Finnegans Wake* （1939）.

L

Lai Breton or Breton Lai（布里多尼籁歌）

The term "lai" is derived from the Celtic word "laid" meaning "song". A Breton lai is a short rhymed tale telling about adventures, battle, chivalry and love, involving supernatural elements and Celtic faeries. It became popular in France and England in the Middle Ages. The French lais composed by Marie de France in 1170s are thought to be the earliest Breton lais. Geoffrey Chaucer's *The Franklin's Tale* (from *The Canterbury Tales*) is considered as an example of Breton Lai.

该词"lai"起源于凯尔特词汇"laid"意思是"歌曲"。布里多尼籁歌是一种简短押韵的神话故事，主要讲述冒险、战争、骑士风度及爱情，包含许多超自然的元素以及凯尔特仙女等。该类故事在中世纪时期的法国和英国颇受欢迎。由玛丽·德·法兰西在12世纪70年代所写的籁歌被认为是最早的布里多尼籁歌。杰弗雷·乔叟的《富兰克林的故事》（出自《坎特伯雷故事集》）被认为是布里多尼籁歌的范例。

Lake Poets（湖畔派诗人）

At the beginning of the 19th century, William Wordsworth[1], Samuel

---

① William Wordsworth (1770—1850) was one of the founders of British Romantic poet best known for *Lyrical Ballads* (1798) in collaboration with Coleridge.

Taylor Coleridge①and Robert Southey②became known as the "Lake poets", because they lived in and got inspiration from the Lake District in the northwest of England. In 1817, Francis Jeffrey (1773—1850) derogatorily referred to them as the "Lake school" in *The Edinburgh Review*. George Gordon Byron③also called them "Lakers" mockingly. The Lake poets are reckoned as Romantic poets.

在 19 世纪早期，威廉·华兹华斯、塞缪尔·泰勒·柯勒律治以及罗伯特·骚塞成为"湖畔派诗人"，因为他们在英国西北部的湖畔地区居住并从此地获得写作灵感。在 1817 年，弗兰西斯·杰弗里在《爱丁堡评论》中贬低地称他们为"湖畔派"。乔治·拜伦也嘲笑他们为"湖人"。湖畔派诗人也是浪漫主义诗人。

Lament（挽歌）

A lament is a type of music, poem or song expressing grief, sadness, sorrow or regret for a loss, departure or death.

挽歌就是一种音乐、诗歌或者歌曲，来表达对损失、别离或者死亡的悲痛、伤心、惋惜或者遗憾之情。

Lampoon（讽刺文）

Lampoon is a satirical type of writing which sharply makes fun of a person or thing.

讽刺文是尖锐的嘲讽某人或某事的讽刺写作。

---

① Samuel Taylor Coleridge (1772—1834) was one of the leaders in British Romantic Movement. He was famous for his poems *The Rime of the Ancient Mariner* and *Kubla Khan*.

② Robert Southey (1774—1843) was a prolific writer and one of the leaders in British Romantic Movement.

③ George Gordon Byron (1788—1824), also known as Lord Byron, was one of the greatest British poets best noted for his poems *Don Juan* (1819—1824), *Childe Harold's Pilgrimage* (1812—1818) and *She Walks in Beauty* (1814).

Legend（传说）

The term "legend" is derived from the Latin word "legere" which means "to read". A legend is a story about a particular person and his/her deeds which are mentioned in history and have existed in reality. But there is no evidence for the details in the legends. So to some extent, legends are made up but different from myth which is based on completely supernatural stories.

该词来源于拉丁词"legere"意思是"读"。传说就是关于在历史中提到、现实中真实存在的某人及其事件的故事。但是传说中的细节并无迹可寻。所以从某种程度上来说，传说是编造出来的，却与完全根据超自然的故事而编造的神话传说不同。

Light Verse（谐趣诗）

Light verse, as a type of brief and humorous poetry written to amuse and entertain, flourished in the late 19th century. It can be on serious subjects using simple language. Samuel Butler's *Hudibras* (1663), Alexander Pope's *The Rape of the Lock* (1712—1714), and W. S. Gilbert①'s *Bab Ballads* (1869) are examples of light verse.

谐趣诗是一种简短幽默为了使人发笑的诗歌，在 19 世纪末期开始繁荣。它可以使用简单的语言来描写严肃的事物。塞缪尔·巴特勒的《休迪布拉斯》（1663）、亚历山大·蒲柏的《夺发记》（1712—1714）以及威廉·施文克·吉尔伯特的《巴布民谣》都是谐趣诗的范例。

Literature of the Absurd（荒诞派文学）

Literature of the absurd, originating in France after the Second World

---

① W. S. Gilbert (1836—1911) was a leading dramatist and poet in England. He was famous for his collaboration with Sir Arthur Sullivan in comic operas.

War, is one of the most important literary genres of post-modernist literature. It refers to a number of works which hold that human existence is absurd
and meaningless in an incomprehensible world and can only be represented
in absurd works.

The literature dominated the western theatrical circles for about twenty
years and began to decline in 1970s. Its philosophical background is existentialism and its roots are in the movement of expressionism and surrealism. Samuel Beckett (1906—1989) is the most influential and notable writer
of the genre. His *Waiting for Godot* (1954) and *Endgame* (1958) are representative works.

荒诞派文学在第二次世界大战后起源于法国，是后现代主义文学
重要的文学流派之一。一些作品认为在这个荒诞的世界，人类生存也
是荒诞、无意义的，并且只能在荒诞的作品中才能将其展现出来，它
们就属于该类文学。

荒诞派文学统治西方剧坛长达二十年之久，在 20 世纪 70 年代开
始衰落。它的文学基础是存在主义，起源于表现主义和超现实主义运
动。塞缪尔·贝克特（1906—1989）是该派最有影响力、最著名的作
家，他的《等待戈多》（1954）和《结局》（1958）是代表作品。

Litotes（曲言法）

Litotes is a figure of speech which consists of an intentional understatement using negative (often double negatives) to express the affirmative. For
example people often use "not bad" for "good", "not a little" for "very".

曲言法是一种修辞方法，用否定（经常是双重否定）来表达肯定
意思的故意低调陈述。例如人们常用"不坏"代替"好"、"不是一点
点"代替"非常"。

Liturgical Drama（宗教剧）

Liturgical drama, as a type of play in the Middle Ages, is based on the stories in the *Bible*. The plays were acted in church by Mass, sometimes as part of rituals carrying religious significance.

宗教剧是中世纪时期的一种戏剧，讲述《圣经》中的故事。宗教剧在教堂中由宗教团体演出，有时是宗教仪式的一部分，有重要的宗教意义。

Local Colorism（地方色彩）

Local colorism, as a literary trend, came into prominence in the late 1860s and declined in the turn of the 20th century. It was applied to literature which presented and interpreted settings, dialects, customs, costumes and ways of thinking distinctive to a particular region. In local-color literature, one can sense nostalgia and sentimentality. It was influenced by romanticism and realism.

Bret Harte's *The Luck of Roaring Camp* published in 1868 marked a significant development in the history of local colorism. Besides, Mark Twain[1]'s *The Celebrated Jumping Frog of Calaveras County* (1865), Hamlin Garland[2]'s *Main-travelled Roads* (1891), Edward Eggleston[3]'s *The Hoosier Schoolmaster* (1871), Harriet Beecher Stowe[4]'s *Old Town Folks* (1869) are representative works with local colorism.

地方色彩是一种文学潮流，在 19 世纪 60 年代末兴盛起来，在 20 世纪初开始衰落。该术语经常用来形容那些展现某个特定地区独特的生活、方言、习俗、服饰和思维方式的作品。在这样的作品中，读者

---

① Mark Twain (1835—1910) was an American writer noted for *The Adventures of Tom Sawyer* (1876) and *Adventures of Huckleberry Finn* (1885) which was called "the Great American Novel".

② Hamlin Garland (1860—1940) was an American writer best noted for his short stories *A Son of the Middle Border* (1917) and *A Daughter of the Middle Border* (1921).

③ Edward Eggleston (1837—1902) was an American novelist and historian.

④ Harriet Beecher Stowe (1811—1896) was an American author best famous for her anti-slavery novel *Uncle Tom's Cabin* (1852).

可以感觉到乡愁和伤感。它受到了浪漫主义和现实主义的影响。

布雷特·哈特在 1868 年出版的《咆哮营中的幸运儿》标志着地方色彩作品的极大发展。除此之外，马克·吐温的《卡拉维拉县著名的跳蛙》（1865）、哈姆林·加兰的《大路条条》（1891）、爱德华·艾格尔斯顿的《山区校长》（1871）、哈里特·比彻·斯托夫人的《老城的人们》（1896）都是非常重要的地方色彩的代表作品。

Locus Amoenus（安乐之所）

The literary term "locus amoenus", derived from Latin, means "pleasant place". It depicts a beautiful place, traditionally an idealized garden with tall trees, a green meadow, a clear river and cheerful birds... where people live in safety and comfort.

The Garden of Eden in the *Bible* is one of the earliest locus amoenus. The garden of Alcinous in Homer's *Odyssey* is also a typical locus amoenus.

该词来源于拉丁语，意思是"安乐之所"。它描写一个美丽的地方，传统上的理想乐园，有参天大树、碧绿草地、清澈河流、欢乐小鸟……人们安全舒适地生活。

《圣经》中的伊甸园可以说是最早的安乐之所。荷马《奥德赛》中的阿尔喀诺俄斯乐园也是一个典型的安乐之所。

Logocentrism（逻各斯中心主义）

The term "logos" is a Greek word meaning "word", "discourse", or "reason", but in philosophy it means a universal reason or eternal truth. "Logocentrism" was popularized by Jacques Derrida[1]in the late 1960s. According to Derrida, Western philosophy has had an authorizing centre or

---

① Jacques Derrida (1930—2004) was a French philosopher and founder of deconstruction.

Logos of thought since Plato. He used the term to "characterize any system structured by a valorization of speech over writing, immediacy over distance, identity over difference, and (self-) presence over all forms of absence"① . And applied deconstructive methods to collapsing logocentrism.

"logos" 是希腊词汇意思是"措辞""言语"或者"理性"，但是在哲学上意思是普遍理性或者永久真理。"逻各斯中心主义"一词是在 20 世纪 60 年代末经由雅克·德里达而被人熟知的。根据德里达所说，自从柏拉图开始，西方哲学就有思想的权威中心或者逻各斯。他用该词来"描述将言语与写作、直接与距离、认同与差异、（自我）在场与不在场……等相对立的所有体系"，并用解构方法来瓦解逻各斯中心主义。

Lost Generation（迷惘的一代）

"The Lost Generation" was an American literary trend that came into being after the First World War. In a narrow sense, it refers to a group of American notable writers, such as F. Scott Fitzgerald, T. S. Eliot, John Dos Passos, Waldo Peirce, Sherwood Anderson, Hart Crane, Erich Maria Remarque and so on. In a broad sense, it refers to the entire post-WWI American young generation.

Ernest Hemingway②, as a great spokesman of "the Lost Generation", quoted Gertrude Stein's remark: "you are a lost generation" as an epigraph for his first novel, *The Sun Also Rises*. The Lost Generation abominated imperialist wars, but couldn't find their way out, so they were "lost".

"迷惘的一代"是在第一次世界大战后形成的美国文学流派。从狭义上说，它是指美国一些著名的作家，例如司各特·菲茨杰拉德、

---

① Jasper P. Neel, *Plato*, *Derrida*, *and Writing*, Southern Illinois Univ Press, 1988 p. 175.

② Ernest Hemingway (1899—1961) was an American novelist and journalist, considered as one of the greatest writers in the 20th century.

T. S. 艾略特、约翰·多斯·帕索斯、沃尔多·皮尔斯、舍伍德·安德森、哈特·克莱恩、埃里希·玛丽亚·雷马克等。从广义上说，它是指整个第一次世界大战后美国的年轻一代。

厄内斯特·海明威是"迷惘的一代"的代言人，他在自己的第一部长篇小说《太阳照常升起》中引用格特鲁德·斯坦因的评论："你们就是迷惘的一代"作为题词。迷惘的一代憎恨帝国主义战争，却找不到出路，最终"迷惘"了。

Low Comedy（滑稽剧）

Low comedy, as opposed to high comedy, is a type of comedy aiming to make people laugh through horseplay, boasting, slapstick and other riotous activities rather than by witty language.

滑稽剧与高雅喜剧不同，是一种通过恶作剧、吹嘘、闹剧以及其他喧闹的行为而不是通过机智的语言来使人们大笑的喜剧。

Lyric Poetry（抒情诗）

The word "lyric" is the adjective form of "lyre" which means a musical instrument. In ancient Greece, a lyric was a poem sung to the accompaniment of the lyre. [1]Now lyric poetry is a type of poetry expressing the poet's emotion, thoughts and feelings in musical rhythm. Elegies, hymns, odes and sonnets belong to lyric poetry.

"lyric"一词是"lyre"（里拉琴是一种乐器）的形容词形式。在古希腊，抒情诗就是指由里拉琴伴奏而唱的诗。现在抒情诗是一种以音乐的旋律来表达诗人的情感、思想和感觉的诗歌。挽歌、赞歌、颂歌、十四行诗都属于抒情诗。

---

① David Mikics, *A New Handbook of Literary Terms*, New Haven: Yale University Press, 2007, p. 173.

M

Mannerism（矫饰主义）

The term "mannerism" is derived from Italian word "maniera" meaning style. Mannerism refers to an exaggerated style in paining, sculpture and architecture incorporating artificial color and unrealistic settings. It emerged in Florence and Rome at the end of the High Renaissance in about 1520 as a reaction to the harmonious ideals advocated by Leonardo da Vinci, Michelangelo, and Raphae. It lasted until the beginning of the 17th century. Parmigianino[①]and Pontormo[②]are typical Mannerist painters.

该词来源于意大利词汇"maniea"意思是风格。矫饰主义是指在绘画、雕刻和建筑中使用虚假的颜色和夸张的布景的风格。它是响应里奥纳多·达·芬奇、米开朗基罗以及拉斐尔所号召的和谐理想而在文艺复兴盛期末也就是1520年左右在弗罗伦萨和罗马兴起的。它一直持续到17世纪初。帕玛强尼以及蓬托尔莫都是典型的矫饰主义画家。

---

① Parmigianino（1503—1540）formerly known as Girolamo Francesco Maria Mazzola, was an Italian Mannerist painter. *Vision of Saint Jerome*（1527）and *Madonna with the Long Neck*（1534）were his representative paintings.

② Pontormo（1494—1557）formerly known as Jacopo Carucci, was an Italian Mannerist painter renowned for his masterpiece such as *Joseph in Egypt*（1517—18）, *The Deposition of the Cross*（1528）, etc.

Magic Realism（魔幻现实主义）

Magic realism, also called magical realism, was a literary genre that was popular in Latin-America in 1950s as a reaction against the domination of Portugal and Spain. The term was first coined by Franz Roh (1890—1965) in his *After Expressionism*: *Magical Realism*: *Problems of the Newest European Painting* in 1925.

Professor Matthew Strecher defines magic realism as "what happens when a highly detailed, realistic setting is invaded by something too strange to believe". [①]That is, magic realism narrates magical elements which actually break the rules of our real world in a reliable tone.

魔幻现实主义，也称"魔幻写实主义"，是在 20 世纪 50 年代反抗葡萄牙和西班牙的统治而在拉丁美洲兴盛的一种文学形式。该术语是最先由弗朗茨·罗（1890—1965）在 1925 年在《后期表现主义：魔幻现实主义：当前欧洲绘画的若干问题》中提出的。

马修·史崔彻是这样定义魔幻现实主义的："在非常详细、真实的背景中发生了奇怪的令人难以置信的事情"。也就是说，魔幻现实主义用非常可信的口气来描述事实上违背现实世界规律的魔幻因素。

Malapropism（荒唐的用词错误）

The term "malapropism" is named after Mrs Malaprop who was a character in Richard Brinsley Sheridan's play *The Rivals* (1775) and often misused words ridiculously (such as "contagious countries" for "contiguous countries"). Malapropism is also known as Dogberryism which comes from Officer Dogberry (a character in Shakespeare's *Much Ado About Nothing*) who also made such

---

① Mattew C. Strecher, "Magical Realism and the Search for Identity in the Fiction of Murakami Haruki", *Journal of Japanese Studies*, Volume 25, 1999, p. 267.

mistakes. Malapropism in literature means the incorrect use of words due to similar pronunciations, resulting in confusion and misunderstanding.

该词是以理查德·布林斯利·谢里丹的喜剧《情敌》（1775）中的马勒普太太命名，她经常荒谬地误用单词（例如"传染的国家"来代替"邻近的国家"）。莎士比亚的《无事生非》中的道格伯利警官也犯类似的错误，以他命名的词也有此意。在文学中，荒唐的用词错误是指因为发音相似而错误地使用单词最终造成混淆和误解。

Marxist Literary Criticism（马克思主义文学批评）

Marxist literary criticism is a sociological criticism which views literary works as reflections of political ideas and stances, analyzes the class, race, and attitudes in the works based on the principles of Marxism, and focuses on social and political elements rather than aesthetic and artistic elements of a text. Karl Marx（1818—1883）and Friedrich Engels（1820—1895）are its founders. Leon Trotsky（1879—1940）, Frederic Jameson（1934—）, Theodor Adorno（1903—1969）, Geoge Lukács（1885—1971）, Terry Eagleton（1943—）are Marxist literary critics of the 20th century.

马克思主义文学批评是一种社会批评，它将文学作品看成是政治观点和立场的反映，根据马克思主义原则来分析作品中的阶级、种族和态度，并且关注作品中的社会与政治因素而不是美学与艺术因素。卡尔·马克思（1818—1883）与弗里德里希·恩格斯（1820—1895）是其奠基人。列夫·托洛茨基（1879—1940）、弗雷德里克·詹明信（1934—）、迪奥多·阿多诺（1903—1969）、乔治·卢卡奇（1885—1971）、特里·伊格尔顿（1943—）都是 20 世纪的马克思主义文学批评家。

Masque（假面舞会）

The masque, as a form of courtly entertainment or artistic performance, emerged in Italy and became popular in Europe in the 16th and early 17th centuries. There were often dances, music, acting, gorgeous costumes and masked participants.

假面舞会作为一种宫廷娱乐或者艺术表演形式，始于意大利，在 16 世纪和 17 世纪初开始在欧洲流行。经常会有舞蹈、音乐、表演、华丽的服饰以及戴面具的参与者。

Melodrama（音乐剧）

The term "melodrama" originated from the French word mélodrame (Greek melos with the meaning of music, and French drame with the meaning of drama) in the late 18th century and early 19th century. Melodrama is a genre of drama in which orchestral music or song was played underneath or between delivered lines to emphasize the emotional aspects of the plot or the characters. The characters are often stock or stereotyped characters and the the plots, even though complex, always have happy endings with good triumphing over evil.

Melodrama appeared on the stage in the 18th century, and then became popular in various ways, but began to decline in the 21st century. However, melodramatic plots are still popular in comics and cartoons.

"音乐剧"这个词在 18 世纪末 19 世纪初起源于法语单词 mélodrame（希腊语 melos，意思是音乐，还有法语 drame 意思是戏剧）。音乐剧是戏剧的一种，管弦音乐和歌曲作为说台词或者台词间歇时的背景音乐来强调情节或者人物的情感方面。人物通常是小丑或者老套的人物，情节虽然很复杂但总是成功打败邪恶的悦人结局。

音乐剧在 18 世纪出现在舞台上，然后在各种形式上大受欢迎，但是在 21 世纪开始衰落。然而，音乐剧的情节仍然在喜剧和动画片中盛行。

Metafiction（元小说）

Metafiction, fiction about fiction, is a term used to describe fictional writing, in which the author usually describes the fictional status openly by using irony and self-reflection to make readers conscious of reading a fictional work and to pose questions about the relationship between fiction and reality.

Although metafiction, primarily associated with Modernism and Post-modernism, became prevalent in the 1960s, it can be found at least as early as Homer's *Odyssey*, Chaucer's *Canterbury Tales* in the 14th century and Cervantes's 17th-century *Don Quixote.*

John Fowles[①]'s *The French Lieutenant's Woman* (1969) is a typical example of the genre.

元小说是关于小说的小说，用来形容虚构的写作。在元小说中作者通常使用讽刺和自我反省来公开地描写小说的虚构身份使读者意识到自己正在读虚构的小说，并提出了小说与现实之间的关系问题。

虽然元小说通常与现代主义和后现代主义相联系，在 20 世纪 60 年代盛行，但是最早可以追溯到荷马的《奥德赛》、乔叟 14 世纪的《坎特伯雷故事集》还有塞万提斯 17 世纪的《堂吉诃德》。

约翰·福尔斯的《法国中尉的女人》（1969）是该类型小说的典型代表作。

Metaphysical Poetry（玄学派诗歌）

Metaphysical poetry is a term coined by John Dryden (1631—1700) to describe John Donne (1572—1631) but was later used by Samuel Johnson (1709—1784) to refer to a group of 17th-century English poets like Donne,

---

① John Fowles (1926—2005) was an English novelist and essayist, notable for *The French Lieutenant's Woman* (1969), *The Ebony Tower* (1974), *A Maggot* (1985) and so on.

whose poems were characterized by utilizing conceits, imagery, pun, paradox and harsh expression. The topics of this kind of poetry are usually death, love and religion.

John Donne was the leading figure of the school. In addition, George Herbert (1593—1633), Andrew Marvell (1621—1678), Henry Vaughn (1622—1695) and Abraham Cowley (1618—1667) were also notable. Some modern poets, such as T. S. Eliot and Allen Tate were affected much by Metaphysical poetry.

玄学派诗歌首先由约翰·德莱顿（1631—1700）形容约翰·邓恩（1572—1631）的时候提出来的，但是后来塞缪尔·约翰逊（1709—1784）用其来指 17 世纪像邓恩的英国诗人，他们的诗使用幻想、想象、双关、矛盾和粗糙的表达。该类型诗歌的话题通常是死亡、爱情和宗教。

约翰·邓恩是该派的代表人物。除此之外还有乔治·赫伯特（1593—1633）、安德鲁·马威尔（1621—1678）、亨利·沃恩（1622—1695）以及亚伯拉罕·考利（1618—1667）都比较出名。像 T. S. 艾略特和爱伦·泰特这样的现代诗人都受到了玄学派诗歌的很大影响。

Miracle Play（奇迹剧）

The miracle play, as a type of medieval European drama, evolved from liturgical plays in the 10th century. The plays became vernacularized and began to be performed at public festivals in the 13th century, reaching the height in the 15th century. They mainly depict the lives of saints and martyrs.

奇迹剧是中世纪欧洲戏剧的一种，在 10 世纪左右起源于礼拜剧。奇迹剧在 13 世纪的时候开始用方言表演并在公共节日演出，在 15 世纪达到巅峰。奇迹剧主要描述的就是圣人和布道者的生活。

Mock Epic（模拟史诗）

Mock epic is a form of poetry which employs epic's lofty manner and styles to deal with trivial subjects. It applies satire for mockery and laughter. Alexander Pope's *The Rape of the Lock*（1712—1714）is a typical example of mock epic.

模拟史诗是一种使用史诗高尚的形式和风格来描写一些琐碎事情的诗歌类型。它使用讽刺以达到愚弄和嘲笑的效果。亚历山大·蒲柏的《夺发记》（1712—1714）是模拟史诗的范例。

Modernism（现代主义）

According to Dr Samuel Johnson（1709—1784）in *The Dictionary of English Language*, the term "modernism" was first coined by Johnathan Swift（1667—1745）in a letter to Alexander Pope（1688—1744）. Charles Bordelaire（1821—1867）, a French poet, gave it a new meaning, and his famous work, *Les Fleurs du mal*（*The Flowers of Evil*）published in 1857, marked the beginning of modernism in literature.

Influenced much by Darwinism, Marxism, Freud's psychology, and Sir J. Frazer（1854—1941）'s anthropology expressed in *The Golden Bough*（1890—1915）, modernism was applied to a wide-scale range of movements or schools, such as aestheticism, expressionism, imagism, stream of consciousness, existentialism and theatre of the absurd. Though the shoots sprang up in the 19th century, it is generally considered to embrace the period from 1910 to the early years after WWII. Virginia Woolf once said: "On or about December 1910 the human character changed. All human relations shifted-those between masters and servants, husbands and wives, parents and children. And when human relations shift there is at the same time a change in religion, conduct, politics, and literature. "

Self-consciousness, breaking with all tradition, loss of civilization and connection with nature, alienation, decline of the significance of religion, spontaneity and discovery in creation, new narrative modes (discontinuous narrative) are characteristics of modernism.

Modernism is a cultural and philosophical movement widely spread in arts, architecture, literature and music in the late 19th and early 20th centuries. It takes Sir J. Frazer's anthropology (expressed in *The Golden Bough*), Darwin's theory of evolution, Freud's psychoanalysis and so on as the theoretical cases. It rejects established rules, conventions, Enlightenment thinking and even religious belief, meanwhile it stresses the importance of showing inner life and affirms that human beings are able to create, improve, and reshape their environment with knowledge and technology.

Ezra Pound (1885—1972) T. S. Eliot (1888—1965), Sinclair Lewis (1885—1951), Ernest Hemingway (1899—1961), James Joyce (1882—1941), Virginia Woolf (1882—1941), W. B. Yeats (1865—1939), Joseph Conrad (1857—1924), William Faulkner (1897—1962), Scott Fitzgerald (1896—1940), Arthur Miller (1915—2005) and Eugene O'Neil (1888—1953) are considered notable representatives of modernism.

根据塞缪尔·约翰逊（1709—1784）在《英语词典》中所说，"现代主义"这个词最先是由乔纳森·斯威夫特（1667—1745）在对亚历山大·蒲柏（1688—1744）的信中提到。法国诗人查尔斯·波德莱尔（1821—1867）给予了该词新意，其1857年出版的著作《恶之花》标志着文学现代主义的开始。

受到达尔文主义、马克思主义、弗洛依德的精神分析、J. 弗雷泽（1854—1941）在《金枝》（1890—1915）中的人类学的影响，现代主义用来指多种运动或者流派，例如美学、表现主义、意象主义、意识流、存在主义以及荒诞剧等。虽然在19世纪开始萌芽，但是通常认为它是指从1910年到第二次世界大战早期。弗吉尼亚·沃尔夫曾经说过："在 1910 年十二月左右，人们的性格变了。所有人际关系改变了——主人与仆人、丈夫与妻子、父母与孩子。当人际关系改变时，同时在宗教、行为、政治和文学中也出现了变化。"

现代主义的特点包括：自我意识、与传统割裂、文明缺失、与自然的联系减少、疏离感、对宗教重要性的否认、创作的自发性与发现、全新的叙事模式（间断叙事）等。现代主义是在 19 世纪末 20 世纪初广泛见于艺术、建筑、文学和音乐中的一个文化、哲学活动。它以 J. 弗雷泽的人类学（在《金枝》中的观点）、达尔文的进化论还有弗洛伊德的精神分析等作为理论基础。它摒弃已确立的规则、传统、启蒙思想甚至宗教信仰，同时强调真实展现内心世界的重要性，并声称人类是可以用知识和技术来创造、改善和改造他们的环境的。

埃兹拉·庞德（1885—1972）、T. S. 艾略特（1888—1965）、辛克莱·刘易斯（1885—1951）、厄内斯特·海明威（1899—1961）、詹姆斯·乔伊斯（1882—1941）、弗吉尼亚·沃尔夫（1882—1941）、威廉·巴特勒·叶芝（1865—1939）、约瑟夫·康拉德（1857—1924）、威廉·福克纳（1897—1962）、司各特·菲茨杰拉德（1896—1940）、亚瑟·米勒（1915—2005）以及尤金·奥尼尔（1888—1953）被认为是现代主义杰出的代表。

Monologue（独白）

The term "monologue" is derived from the Greek "monologos" meaning "speaking alone". In literature and drama, a monologue is a speech delivered by a character to express his thoughts and emotions directly to the audience or any other character on the stage.

该词来源于希腊词"monologos"意思是"自己说话"。在文学或者戏剧中，独白是由演员直接向观众或者其他台上的演员表达自己的思想和情感的话语。

Morality Play（道德剧）

The morality play, as a type of allegorical drama, first appeared in the beginning of 15th century and became popular in the 16th century in Europe. In a morality play, the protagonist personifies moral virtues to teach the masses moral lessons. *Pride of Life* (1350) and *Everyman* (1509) are famous morality plays.

道德剧是一种寓言剧，15 世纪初刚开始出现，16 世纪时在欧洲颇受欢迎。在道德剧中，主人公就是道德美德的化身，以此来给大众进行道德教育。《排场》（1350）以及《每个人》（1509）就是有名的道德剧。

Mummers' Plays（哑剧）

Mummers' plays, as seasonal folk plays acted by some mummers or guisers, began in Britain and then spread to other parts of the world in the Middle Ages and Renaissance. The plays are often based on the legend of St. George and the dragon and are often performed outdoors or in private houses.

哑剧是由很多哑巴演员或者假扮哑巴的演员来表演的季节性的民间戏剧，起始于英国，后来在中世纪和文艺复兴时期传到世界各地。哑剧通常是基于圣乔治和龙的传说而成，经常在户外或者私人家里表演。

Muses（缪斯）

Muses refer to the nine daughters of Zeus and Mnemosyne in Greek mythology. They were the goddesses of music, science, drama, song and dance. Meanwhile, they were also the writers', artists' and poets' creative inspiration.

缪斯是指希腊神话中宙斯和漠涅摩叙涅的九个女儿。她们是音乐、科学、戏剧、歌曲和舞蹈女神。同时，她们也是作家、艺术家和诗人的创作灵感。

Myth and Mythology（神话与神话学）

The term "myth" comes from the Greek word "muthos" meaning "story". Myths are traditional or legendary stories employing supernatural elements to explain the early history of people, phenomena or events. They are often associated with religious belief.

Mythology is the study of myths or the collection of myths.

神话一词来源于希腊词汇"muthos"，意思是"故事"。神话就是使用超自然的因素来解释人类的早期历史、现象或者事件的传统故事或者传说故事。它们经常与宗教信仰相联系。神话学是指对神话的研究或者神话的收集。

N

Narrative Poem（叙事诗歌）

Narrative poem is one of the oldest types of poem that often uses rhythm, thyme and repetition to tell a story. It has its own narrator, characters and plot. Epic poems like *Iliad* and *Odyssey* are narrative poems.

叙事诗歌是经常使用韵律、韵脚和重复来讲述故事的一种最古老的诗歌类型之一。它有自己的叙述者、人物和情节。史诗例如《伊利亚特》和《奥德赛》都属于叙事诗。

Naturalism and American Naturalism（自然主义与美国自然主义）

Naturalism is a literary movement which began in the late 19th century. It is a branch of realism, trying to depict reality as closely as possible.

In the last decade of the nineteenth century, influenced much by Darwinism and Herbert Spencer's Social Darwinism, American Naturalism began to prevail. It held that men were helpless in the cold, Godless, amoral, indifferent and hostile world. So in most representative works, gloomy and ugly sides of the society were often shown to readers objectively. Its representatives are Stephen Crane①, Frank Norris②and Theodore Dreiser③.

自然主义是起始于 19 世纪末的一场文学运动。它是现实主义的一个分支，努力尽可能地描绘事实。

在 19 世纪最后的 10 年，由于受到了达尔文主义和赫尔伯特·斯宾塞的社会达尔文主义的影响，美国自然主义开始盛行。它认为在这个残酷、没有上帝、不道德、冷漠、敌对的世界里，人类是无助的。所以在大部分代表作品中，社会的阴暗丑陋的一面比较客观地展露在读者面前。其代表作家有斯蒂芬·克莱恩、弗兰克·诺里斯和西奥多·德莱塞。

Neoclassicism（新古典主义）

Neoclassicism was developed in Rome in the eighteenth century and then spread widely to Europe and America in the fields of decoration, architecture, arts, theater, music and literature. It was a protest against Baroque and Rococo, that is, it was against the luxurious decoration and for the plain style. It proposed a revival of interest in the classical art and culture of Ancient Greece or Ancient Rome.

The Neoclassic period ranged from the Restoration in 1660 to the end of the eighteenth century when Wordsworth and Coleridge's *Lyrical Ballads* was published. This marked the beginning of Romanticism. Members of neoclassicism held that the classical works of famous ancient Greek and Roman writers such as Homer and Virgil should be studied carefully as models.

---

① Stephen Crane (1871—1900) was an American prolific writer whose works marked the beginning of American Naturalism. His *Maggie: A Girl of the Streets* (1893) is considered the first American Naturalism work.

② Frank Norris (1870—1902) was an American journalist and novelist, famous for his *McTeague* which is called the manifesto of American Naturalism.

③ Theodore Dreiser (1871—1945) was an American novelist and practitioner of Naturalism. His best known works include *Sister Carrie* (1900) and *An American Tragedy* (1925).

Milton, Bunyan, Dryden, Defoe, Richardson, Fielding, Smollett and Elizabethan Ben Jonson were representatives.

18 世纪新古典主义在罗马兴起，然后快速扩展到欧洲和美洲，遍布装饰、建筑、艺术、歌剧、音乐和文学领域。它反对巴洛克和洛可可，也就是说，它反对奢华的装饰，支持朴素的风格，倡导对古希腊、古罗马经典艺术和文化的复古。

新古典主义时期从 1660 年的复辟开始，结束于 18 世纪末华兹华斯和科勒律治的《抒情歌谣集》的出版，它标志着浪漫主义的开始。新古典主义者认为著名的古希腊和古罗马的作家例如荷马和维吉尔他们的经典作品应该像模版一样仔细研究。

弥尔顿、班扬、德莱顿、笛福、理查森、菲尔丁、斯摩莱特和伊丽莎白·本·琼森是其代表人物。

Neoplatonism（新柏拉图主义）

Neoplatonism is a modern term referring to a philosophical school that took shape in the 3rd century A. D. and ended with the closing of the Platonic Academy in 529 A. D. by Justinian I. Ammonius Saccas was the founder of Neoplatonism, but his student Plotinus（204—270）was considered the most important proponent in the school. In *Enneads*[1], Plotinus put forward the theory of three "hypostases" which had great influences on Christianity: the one, the intelligence and the sou. Neoplatonism was rooted in Plato's philosophy but transformed it in many aspects. It had more religious and mythical elements.

新柏拉图主义是一个现代词汇，用来指在公元 3 世纪形成，在 529 年查士丁尼一世关闭了柏拉图学院而随之结束的哲学流派。摩尼阿斯·萨卡斯是该流派的创始人，但是其学生普罗提诺（204—270）

---

① *Enneads* is Plotinus's collection of writings, compiled by his student, Porphyry.

被认为是该流派最重要的提倡者。在《九章集》中，普罗提诺提出了对基督教有这深远影响的三大"本体"论：太一、理智、灵魂。新柏拉图主义根源于柏拉图的哲学却在很多方面进行了全新的解释。它有着更多的宗教和神秘元素。

New Comedy（新喜剧）

New comedy was the most popular comedy in the late 4th century B. C. and declined in the mid 3th century B. C.

It often employs stock characters to tell some romantic love stories with fewer personal attacks and focuses on the plot drawn from bourgeois personal life. The chorus is just used to provide musical interlude. Menander[①], Diphilus[②] are notable writers of the genre.

新喜剧在公元前 4 世纪最为流行，在公元前 3 世纪渐渐衰落。

新喜剧经常使用小丑角色来讲述浪漫的爱情故事，不再有讽刺批评，关注于中产阶级私人生活的情节。歌曲仅仅用来作为音乐分段。米南德与狄菲卢斯都是该类喜剧的著名作家。

New Criticism（新批评）

New Criticism is a type of literary criticism that originated in the 1920s and began to decline in the 1950s. It ignores biographical and historical interpretations of literary works, and emphasizes "close reading" and the relationships between a text's ideas and its form. So it belongs to a formalist movement. New Criticism had developed before it was named after John Crowe Ranson's *The New Criticism* (1941). T. S. Eliot was the pioneer,

---

① Menander (342 B. C. —291 B. C.) was a Hellenistic Greek dramatist and the most famous representative of Athenian New Comedy. *The Arbitration* and *The Girl from Samos* are his notable works.

② Diphilus (350? B. C. —290? B. C.) was a Greek poet of New Comedy, most of whose poems were lost. Roman playwrights Plautus and Terence were influenced much by him.

whose *Tradition and The Individual Talent* published in1919 was actually a building block. In addition, T. A. Richards' *Practical Criticism*: *A Study of Literary Judgment* (1929) and *The Meaning of Meaning* (1923), William Empson's *Seven Types of Ambiguity* (1930) were of great importance for the development of New Criticism.

新批评是一种文学批评理论，起始于 20 世纪 20 年代，在 20 世纪 50 年代开始衰落。它忽视对文学作品进行传记和历史阐释，强调"细读"以及文本的观点与形式之间的关系。所以它是一种形式主义运动。新批评是以约翰·克罗·兰瑟姆的《新批评》（1941）命名，但是之前就已经有所发展。T. S. 艾略特是其先锋人物，他 1919 年出版的《传统与个人才能》实际上就是奠基石。除此之外 T. A. 瑞恰慈的《实用文艺批评》（1929）及《意义之意义》（1923）、威廉·燕卜荪的《复义七型》（1930）对于新批评的发展极其重要。

New Historicism（新历史主义）

New Historicism, first coined by Stephen Greenbratt[①]in 1982 in his introduction to *The Power of Forms in the English Renaissance*, is a literary theory which developed in the 1980s and became popular in the 1990s. New Historicism, also called Cultural Poetics, reintroduces the concept of history into literary studies, holding that "all history is subjective, written by people whose personal biases affect their interpretation of the past. History can never provide us with the truth or give us a totally accurate picture of past events or the worldview of a group of people. History is one of many discourses, or ways of seeing and thinking about the world"[②]. New Histori-

---

① Stephen Greenblatt (1943—) is an American critic, scholar and writer, considered as one of the founders of New Criticism.

② Charles E. Bressler. *Literary Criticism*: *An Introduction to Theory and Practice.* 3rd Edition, Pearson Education Inc., 2002, p. 181.

cists try to study a literary work within the author's and critic's historical context as well as the cultural history in a literary work.

Jonathan Dollimore①, Louis Montrose②and Hayden White③are notable New Historicists.

新历史主义由斯蒂芬·格林布莱特在 1982 年的《英国文艺复兴时期形式的权力》中首次使用，它是 20 世纪 80 年代发展而来，并在 90 年代开始颇受欢迎的文学理论。新历史主义，也叫"文化诗学"，将历史的概念重新引入到文学研究当中，认为"历史是主观的，是人写出来的，他们的个人偏见会影响着对过去历史的阐释。历史决不会提供给我们无论是真相还是过去事情完全准确的图景，也不会提供一大群人的准确的世界观。历史就是一个话语，或者看待思考世界的方法"。新历史主义者们努力在作者和批评者的历史背景下研究一部文学作品，也研究文学作品中的文化历史。

乔纳森·多利莫尔、路易斯·蒙特罗丝以及海登·怀特都是著名的新历史主义者。

New York School（纽约派）

New York School refers to a group of creative American poets in the 1950s and 1960s in New York City, including John Ashbery（1927—），James Schuyler（1923—1991），O'Hara（1926—1966），Kenneth Koch（1925—2002），Barbara Guest（1920—2006）and other poets. Influenced much by modernism and surrealism, New York School's poems were ironic. The School had great effects on later poets.

纽约派诗人是指 20 世纪 50 年代和 60 年代在纽约活跃的一群富有

---

① Jonathan Dollimore（1948—）is an English socialist, theorist and academic scholar in many fields.

② Louis Montrose is an American scholar and theorist. Now he is a professor of English literature in University of California.

③ Hayden White（1928—）is an American historian in literary criticism.

创作力的美国诗人，包括约翰·阿什贝利（1927—）、詹姆斯·斯凯勒（1923—1991）、奥哈拉（1926—1966）、肯尼斯·科赫（1925—2002）、巴巴拉·盖斯特（1920—2006）以及其他诗人。受现代主义和超现实主义的影响，纽约派诗人的诗都是讽刺诗。该派对于后来的诗人影响深远。

Nonfiction Novel（纪实小说）

Nonfiction novel is a literary genre which depicts real people and actual events using story-telling techniques. Truman Capote claimed to have been the inventor of the genre with his book *In Cold Blood* published in 1966. Autobiographies, biographies, memoirs belong to this genre.

纪实小说是一种用讲故事的技巧来描述真人真事的文学形式。楚曼·卡波第声称自己1966年出版的《冷血》开创了该类小说的历史。自传体小说、传记、回忆录都属于该类小说。

Novel and Novella（小说和中篇小说）

The term "novel" comes from the Italian "novello" which means "the small new thing". A novel is a long fictional narrative dealing with human experiences and events in the form of a sequential story.

A novella is a form of prose, shorter than a novel but longer than a short story.

该词来源于意大利词"novello"，意思是"小的新事物"。小说是指以连续故事的形式讲述人的经历和事件的长篇虚构故事。

中篇小说是一种比长篇小说短，比短篇小说长的小说形式。

Novel of Manners（社会风俗小说）

A novel of manners is a form of realistic novel that focuses on the values, cultures, customs, morals and ways of thinking of a particular group of people situated in a particular time and place. It often presents the conflict between a person's desires and the social reality in details. Jane Austen is considered as the master of the genre. Her *Sense and Sensibility* (1811), *Pride and Prejudice* (1813) and *Emma* (1815) are quintessential models. Besides, Henry James, Edith Wharton[①], and Evelyn Waugh[②] are also writers of the novel of manners.

　　社会风俗小说是一种现实主义小说，它关注于在特定的时间和地点中的特定人群的价值观、文化、风俗、道德观和思维方式。它经常详细地描绘个人的欲望与社会现实之间的矛盾冲突。简·奥斯汀被认为是该类小说的大师。她的《理智与情感》（1811），《傲慢与偏见》（1813）与《爱玛》（1815）都是典型的范例。除此之外，亨利·詹姆斯、伊迪丝·沃顿以及伊芙琳·沃都是社会风俗小说家。

---

① Edith Wharton (1862—1937) was a prolific American short-story writer and designer, best known for her *The Age off Innocence* (1920), *Hose of Mirth* (1905), and *Ethan Frome* (1911).

② Evelyn Waugh (1903—1966) was an English writer. *Decline and Fall* (1928), *A Handful of Dust* (1934), *Brideshead Revisited* (1945) are his notable works.

O

Objective Correlative（客观对应物）

Objective correlative is a literary term popularized by T. S. Eliot in his essay *Hamlet and his Problems* (1919). He wrote: "The only way of expressing emotion in the form of art is by finding an 'objective correlative'; in other words, a set of objects, a situation, a chain of events which shall be the formula of that particular emotion; such that when the external facts, which must terminate in sensory experience, are given, the emotion is immediately evoked."[1] That is, objective correlative refers to a set of objects, a situation or a sequence of events which evokes a reader's particular emotion.

客观对应物是 T. S. 艾略特在《哈姆雷特与他的问题》(1919) 中使其流行的一个文学术语。他写道："以艺术形式表达情感的唯一方式就是找到'客观对应物';换句话说,是用一些物体、情境、一连串事件来表现某种特定的情感;当只能用情感来慢慢体会的外部事实出现,情感就立刻被唤醒。"也就是说,客观对应物是指能够激起读者特殊情感的一些事物、情境或者一系列事件。

---

① T. S. Eliot, *The Sacred Wood*. London: Methuen, 1964, p. 100.

Objectivism（客观主义）

Objectivism is a philosophy for living on the earth that was formulated by Ayn Rand（1905—1982）, who was a Russian-American writer. Objectivism has many principles.

First, existence exists and one shouldn't escape from reality but face it courageously. Second, happiness or rational self-interest is a moral virtue. Third, supernatural notions should be abandoned, including God. Fourth, it supports pure, laissez-faire Capitalism.

In literature, the term "objectivism" was first used by William Carlos Williams[1]in 1930 and then expanded by Louis Zukofsky[2]in 1931 to refer to an influential movement in America in the early 1930s which advocated not to use metaphorical devices, focused on viewing poems as objects, emphasized the analysis of mechanical features of a poem rather than its ostensible content. George Oppen（1908—1984）, Charles Reznikoff（1894—1976）, Carl Rakosi（1903—2004）and Lorine Niedecker（1903—1970）were notable objectivist poets.

客观主义是由俄裔美国作家艾因·兰德（1905—1982）提出来的在世上生活的哲学。客观主义有很多原则：

第一，存在状况的存在，人不应该逃避现实只能勇敢地面对现实。第二，幸福或者合理的自利是道德目的。第三，超自然的概念，包括上帝都应该摒弃。第四，它支持纯洁、自由的资本主义。

在文学中，该词是由威廉·卡洛斯·威廉姆斯在 1930 年首先使用，在 1931 年由路易斯·朱科夫斯基对进行扩展，用来指 20 世纪 30

---

① William Carlos Williams（1883—1963）was a revolutionary poet in America, as well as a doctor, best know for imagery in his poems.

② Louis Zukofsky（1904—1978）was an American poet, best noted for being one of the founders of the Objectivist group of poetry.

年代早期美国非常具有影响力的运动。该运动倡导不使用比喻，将诗歌看成是客体，强调对诗歌的机构特点而不是其表面的内容进行分析。乔治·奥本（1908—1984）、查尔斯·列兹尼科夫（1894—1976）、卡尔·拉考西（1903—2004）以及洛琳·尼德克（1903—1970）是著名的客观主义诗人。

Octameter（八步格）

Ocameter refers to a poem consisting of eight metrical feet in each line. It is seldom used in English verse.

八步格是指每行有八个韵脚组成的诗歌。在英语诗歌中很少使用八步格。

Ode（颂歌）

Ode, originating in Ancient Greece, is a lyric poem expressing strong emotions or respect for someone or something. John Keats (1795—1821) was into odes and he wrote series of odes: *Ode to a Nightingale*, *Ode on Melancholy*, *Ode on a Grecian Urn*, *Ode to Psyche and Ode to Autumn.*

颂歌，起源于古希腊，是一种表达强烈的情感或者对某人或者某事的尊重。约翰·济慈（1795—1821）非常喜欢颂歌并创作了一系列的颂歌：《夜莺颂》《忧郁颂》《希腊古瓮颂》《赛姬颂》以及《秋颂》。

Oedipus Complex（俄狄蒲斯情结或恋母情结）

The term "Oedipus Complex" was coined by Sigmund Freud (1856—1939) in his psychoanalytic theory based on Sophocles's *Oedipus Tyrannus* (427 B. C.). It refers to a boy's desire for his mother and his feeling of anger towards his father because of jealousy brought about by sharing his mother's affections.

该词是由西格蒙德·弗洛伊德（1856—1939）根据索福克勒斯的

《俄狄浦斯王》（公元前 427 B. C.）在自己的精神分析理论中首次使用。它是指男孩对母亲的渴望，以及由于与父亲共享母亲的爱而心生妒忌对父亲产生仇恨的情感。

Old Comedy（旧喜剧）

Old comedy was a form of Ancient Greek comedy known through Aristophane[①]'s works. Performed usually in honor of Dionysus[②], old comedy had a lot of satire of public people and affairs. Aristophane's *Acharnians* (425 B. C.) and *The Birds* (414 B. C.) are notable works of the genre.

旧喜剧是一种古希腊喜剧，通过阿里斯托芬的作品被人熟知。旧喜剧通常是为了纪念狄奥尼索斯而演出，对公众人物和事件进行大量讽刺。阿里斯托芬的《阿卡奈人》（公元前 425）以及《鸟》（公元前 414）都是该类喜剧的代表作。

Omniscient Narrator（全知叙述者）

Omniscient narrator, also known as third person narrative, means that the narrator knows all the characters' thoughts and feelings, and the events in the story, giving readers a sense of reliability. Charles Dickens used omniscient narrator in his *Bleak House* (1853). In addition, Henry Feilding[③], Nathaniel Hawthorne[④], Thomas Hardy[⑤]and other writers also used the form

---

① Aristophanes (446 B. C. —385 B. C.) was the greatest writer of Old Comedy in ancient Greece, considered as the "Father of Comedy".

② Dionysus, as the son of Zeus and Semele, was the god of wine and fertility in Greek mythology.

③ Henry Fielding (1707—1754) was an English novelist and playwright, best known for *Joseph Andrews* (1742) and *Tom Jones* (1749).

④ Nathaniel Hawthorne (1804—1864) was an American novelist noted for *The Scarlet Letter* (1850) and *The House of the Seven Gables* (1851).

⑤ Thomas Hardy (1840—1928) was a Victorian writer whose *Far From the Madding Crowd* (1874), *The Mayor of Casterbridge* (1886), *Tess of the D'Urbervilles* (1891) and *Jude the Obscure* (1895) made him a famous writer in British literature.

of narration in their works.

全知叙述者也叫第三人称全能叙述，是指叙述者知道所有角色的思想和情感，以及故事中的所有事件，这样能够给读者一种可信感。查尔斯·狄更斯在《荒凉山庄》（1853）中便使用全知叙述者。除此之外，亨利·菲尔丁、纳撒尼尔·霍桑、托马斯·哈代，还有其他的作家也在他们的作品中使用了该种叙事法。

Ossianism（奥西恩风格）

The term is named after Ossian who was a third-century warrior and poet of the Scottish Highlands. In the 1760s, with James Macpherrson[①]'s publication of *Fragments of Ancient Poetry Collected in the Highlands of Scotland*, Ossian's two epic poems—*Fingal*（1762）and *Temora*（1763）—came on the literary scene, which had great influences on the writers in Europe. Many poets were interested in Ossian style, such as Johann Gottfried von Herder（1744—1803）, Johann Wolfgang von Goethe（1749—1832）, and Johann Christoph Friedrich von Schiller（1759—1805）.

该词以 3 世纪苏格兰高地的武士及诗人奥西恩命名。在 18 世纪 60 年代，随着詹姆斯·麦克弗森《收集于苏格兰高地的古诗片断》的出版，奥西恩的两部史诗——《芬格尔》（1762）以及《特摩拉》（1763）——步入到文学舞台，这对欧洲作家产生极大的影响。很多诗人对奥西恩风格感兴趣，例如约翰·哥特弗雷德·冯·赫尔德（1744—1803）、约翰·沃尔夫冈·冯·歌德（1749—1832）以及约翰·克里斯托弗·弗里德里希·冯·席勒（1759—1805）。

Ottava Rima（八行体）

Ottava rima, originating in Italy, is an eight-line stanza, rhyming ab-

---

① James Macpherrson（1736—1796）was a Scottish writer, best known as the translator of Ossian's poems.

ababcc. Giovanni Boccaccio (1313—1375) is believed to be the earliest user of ottava rima in his Teseida (1340—1841) and Filostrato (1340), making ottava rima the standard form for epics in Italy. In English verse, Lord Byron (1788—1824) used ottava rima often in his *Don Juan* (1818—1823).

八行体，起源于意大利，是以 ababbcc 押韵的八行诗。乔万尼·薄伽丘被认为是在其作品《泰萨依德》（1340—1841）和《爱的摧残》（1340）中最早使用八行体的作家，最终使八行体成为意大利史诗的标准模式。在英语诗中，拜伦（1788—1824）在《唐璜》（1818—1823）中大量使用八行体。

Oxymoron（矛盾修辞法）

Oxymoron is a figure of speech which puts two contradictory words together to reveal a paradox. Oxymorons are often pairs of words but sometimes can also be found in sentences. In Oscar Wilde's *The Picture of Dorian Grey* (1890): "As for believing things, I can believe anything, provided that it is quite incredible." In the sentence "believe" and "incredible" just create an oxymoron. Shakespeare often employed oxymoron in his works, for example, *Romeo and Juliet* (1597).

矛盾修辞法是一种将两个矛盾的词放在一起来揭示悖论的修辞方法。矛盾修辞法经常是以对词形式出现，但有时也可以在句子中使用。奥斯卡·王尔德的《道林格雷的画像》（1890）中写道："至于相信与否，除非实在是无稽之谈，否则我都一概相信。"在该句子中，"相信"与"无稽之谈"便是矛盾修辞法。莎士比亚也经常在作品中使用该法，例如《罗密欧与朱丽叶》（1597）。

P

Palindrome（回文）

The term "palindrome", derived from the Greek "palindromos" meaning "running back again", refers to a word or a sentence which reads the same from either direction, backwards or forwards. For example, level, eye, civic and so on.

该词来源于希腊词汇"palindromos"，意思是"又回来了"，它是指一个单词或者一个句子无论是从前往后读还是从后往前读，读法都一样。例如，level（水平）、eye（眼睛）、civic（城市的）等。

Panegyric（颂词）

Panegyric is a speech or written text delivered to praise someone or something. Andrew Marvell[1]'s Horatian Ode on Cromwell's return from Ireland is one of the best known panegyrics in English. [2]

颂词是为了赞扬某人或者某事而做的演讲或者文章。安德鲁·马维尔为了欢迎克伦威尔从爱尔兰返回而作的贺拉斯式颂词就是英语中

---

[1] Andrew Marwell（1621—1678）was one of the best English metaphysical poets.

[2] David Mikic. *A New Handbook of Literary Terms*, New Haven: Yale University Press, 2007, p. 220.

最著名的颂词。

Parable（寓言）

Parable is a literary term used to refer to a didactic story in which two different objects or ideas are compared to help readers better understand a concept, a value, or a moral. Parables are different from fables: fables are based on imaginary stories with talking animals and plants as heroes, while parables are often associated with spiritual or religious beliefs. In the Bible, there are many parables.

寓言是一个文学术语，用来指两种不同的物体或者观点进行比较以帮助读者更好地理解一个概念、价值观或者道德观的说教故事。Parable 与 Fable 都是"寓言"之意，区别在于：Fable 是想象的故事，会说话的动物和植物是主角，而 Parable 经常与精神或者宗教信仰相关。在《圣经》中，就有很多寓言。

Parody（戏仿）

Parody is a special kind of comedy, imitating the style of a well-known literary work and ridiculing the original by humorous and exaggerated mimicry. Simon Dentith has defined parody as "any cultural practice which provides a relatively polemical allusive imitation of another cultural production or practice"[1].

Parody is related to burlesque, satire and criticism. But it is different from burlesque in that a parody is a fine amusement while a burlesque is a miserable buffoonery. In English, Henry Fielding (1707—1754) and James Joyce (1882—1941) are representative parodists.

戏仿是一种特殊的喜剧，仿照著名文学作品的风格，通过幽默、

---

[1] Simon Dentith, *Parody (The New Critical Idiom)*, Routledge, 2000, p. 9.

夸张的模仿来嘲弄原著。西蒙·邓提斯是这样定义戏仿的："它是指对一部文化作品进行的任何具有挑衅、影射性模仿的文化尝试"。

戏仿与滑稽模仿、讽刺、批评有关。但是它有别于滑稽模仿，它是非常好的娱乐而滑稽模仿就是可怜的搞笑。在英语中，亨利·菲尔丁（1707—1754）和詹姆斯·乔伊斯（1882—1941）是非常有代表性的戏仿者。

Pastoral （田园诗）

Pastoral was originated by Theocritus, who established the conventions of European ancient pastoral poetry. It idealized a rural world or a shepherd's life which is close to nature in an artificial manner. It usually describes beautiful scenery and carefree shepherds to compare the peace and innocence of the simple life with the chaos and corruption of city life.

Christopher Marlowe's "The Passionate Shepherd to His Love", Virgil's "Eclogues and Georgics" and Edmund Spenser's "The Shepheardes Calender" in the Renaissance are influential examples of the genre.

田园诗是由忒俄克里托斯首创的，他为欧洲古代田园诗建立了规则。它用人为的方式使农村生活或者与自然接近的牧民生活理想化。它通常描述美丽的景色和无忧无虑的牧民，将简单生活的宁静与无邪同城市生活的混乱与腐败进行对比。

文艺复兴时期克里斯托弗·马洛的《热恋中的牧羊人致情人》、弗吉尔的《牧歌与农事诗》以及埃德蒙·斯宾塞的《牧人月历》都是具有影响力的田园诗代表作。

Pathetic Fallacy （情感的误置）

The term "pathetic fallacy" was coined by John Ruskin[1] in the third

---

[1] John Ruskin (1819—1900) was a great critic of art and architecture in Victorian Age. He was also a member of Pre-Raphaelites.

volume of *Modern Painters* published in 1856. It refers to attributing human emotions and actions to nonhuman objects of nature. Poets often use pathetic fallacy in their poems, for example, Lord Tennyson[①]'s *Maud* (1855) and Edgar Ellen Poe[②]'s *Raven* (1845).

该词是由约翰·罗斯金在 1856 年出版的《现代画家》第三卷中首次使用。它是指将人类的情感和行为用到自然界的非人类物体上。诗人经常在诗歌中使用情感的误置，例如丁尼生的《莫德》以及埃德加·爱伦·坡的《乌鸦》（1845）。

Pathos（同情）

Pathos means using language, situations or images to evoke readers' emotions of sympathy.

同情是指使用语言、情境或者意象来激发读者的同情心。

Phenomenology（现象学）

Phenomenological inquiry in philosophy dates back to G. W. F. Hegel's *Phenomenology of Mind* (1807)[③]. Then Husserl[④]initiated modern phenomenology in his *Logical Investigations* (1900—1901). He thinks that phenomenology is a form of methodological idealism, seeking to explore an abstraction called "human consciousness" and "a world of pure possibilities"[⑤], and we should use our consciousness to understand phenomena, combing "the

---

① Lord Tennyson (1809—1892) was one of the most famous Victorian poets, best known for *Ulysses* (1842) and *Tithonus* (1860).

② Edgar Ellen Poe (1809—1849) was an American writer and literary critic, notable for his tales of mystery. *The Fall of the House of Usher* (1839) is his representative work.

③ David Mikics, *A New Handbook of Literary Terms*, New Haven: Yale University Press, 2007, p. 230.

④ Edmund Husserl (1859—1938) was a German philosopher, regarded as the "father of phenomenology."

⑤ Terry Eagleton. *Literary Theory: An Introduction*, U of Minnesota Press, 1996, p. 49.

outside thing with the inward thinking"①.

哲学中的现象学理论可以追溯到黑格尔的《精神现象学》（1807）。后来胡塞尔在《逻辑研究》（1900—1901）中提出现代现象学。他认为现象学就是一种唯心主义方法论，探索"人类意识"与"完全可能性世界"之间的抽象关系，我们应该用意识来理解现象，将"外部事物与内心思想"结合在一起。

Picaresque Novel（流浪汉小说）

A picaresque novel refers to fiction which relates a flawed but endearing picaro's adventures from one place to another in pursuit of his survival. The form of the novel is often first-person narration, combing travel, adventure, comedy and satire together.

The anonymously authored *Lazarillo de Tormes* was published in 1554 in Spain, which marked the beginning of the picaresque novel. Then in the 17th and 18th century, picaresque novels flourished throughout Europe. Thomas Nash's *The Unfortunate Traveler or the Life of Jack Wilton* (1594) was considered as the first picaresque novel in English. Henry Fielding's *Tom Jones* (1749), Lord Byron's *Don Juan* and Charles Dickens's *The Pickwick Papers* (1836) also belong to this type of novel.

流浪汉小说是指讲述一个有缺点但是招人喜欢的流浪汉为了生存从一个地方到另一个地方的冒险故事的小说。该类小说经常以第一人称叙述，将旅行、冒险、喜剧和讽刺结合在一起。

1554 年在西班牙匿名出版的《小癞子》标志着流浪汉小说的开始。在 17 世纪和 18 世纪，该类小说在整个欧洲蓬勃发展。托马斯·纳什的《不幸的旅行者或者杰克·威尔顿的生活》（1594）被认为是第一部英语

---

① Qin Bailan, *Defending Husserlian Phenomenology From Terry Eagleton's Critique*, Advances in Literary Study, Vol. 1, 2013, p. 11.

流浪汉小说。亨利·菲尔丁的《汤姆·琼斯》、拜伦的《唐璜》以及查尔斯·狄更斯的《匹克威克外传》（1836）也属于该类小说。

Poetic License（诗的破格）

Poetic License means that a poet can depart from conventional form or reality to create an effect.

诗的破格是指诗人为了营造效果可以偏离传统的形式或者现实。

Poetic Justice（理想的赏罚）

Poetic Justice, as a literary term coined by Thomas Rhymer in *The Tragedies of the Last Age*（1678）, means that good characters are rewarded and bad characters are punished to convey moral principles to readers and audience.

该词是由托马斯·雷默在《上个时代的悲剧》（1678）首次提出，意指好人有好报，恶人有恶报，以此为读者和观众传达道德准则。

Postcolonial Studies（后殖民研究）

Postcolonial studies began with Edward Said[①]'s *Orientalism*（1978）, which is regarded as the foundation text in the field. Since then, the field has been gaining prominence. It focuses on the literal, political, economic, cultural and historical effects Western European and American colonialism have had on the rest of the world, especially on the former British Empire colonized areas.

后殖民研究开始于爱德华·萨义德的《东方主义》（1978），该书被认为是后殖民研究的奠基之作。自此，该领域一直都颇具声望。它

---

① Edward Said（1935—2003）was a Palestinian-American literary critic, scholar and professor, known as the founder of post-colonialism.

主要研究西方欧洲与美国的殖民主义对世界其他各地，尤其是对前英国殖民地的政治、经济、文化和历史的影响。

Postmodernism（后现代主义）

The word "postmodern" was first used by John Watkins Chapman in 1870s to suggest "a Postmodern style of painting" as a way to depart from French Impressionism. ①But not until 1972 was it officially inaugurated in literature, when the first issue of *Boundary* 2, subtitled "Journal of Postmodern Literature and Culture" was published.

Postmodernism means to "come after modernism". It embraces the period from about 1980 to the present, and covers many areas, including architecture, art, music, literature, film, sociology and technology. It developed from modernism but is a departure from it. Criticizing modernity is its quintessence. Postmodernism holds that the world is a very complicated and uncertain place; truth is relative to one's viewpoint and stance; facts are useless. It emphasizes the differences and uncertainties, opposes traditional authority and centrism, and advocates diversification and skeptical interpretation of literature, culture, art, history, and architecture... It favors self-consciousness, narrative fragmentation, and ambiguity, and underlines pastiche, parody, bricolage, playfulness and irony.

Some famous writers, such as Thomas Pynchon (1937—), Donald Barthelme (1931—1989), Joseph Heller (1923—1999) are associated with postmodernism.

"后现代主义"在 19 世纪 70 年代首次由约翰·沃特金斯·查普曼

---

① Ihab Hassan. *The Postmodern Turn*, *Essays in Postmodern Theory and Culture*, Ohio University Press, 1987, p. 12.

用"后现代绘画"来与法国印象主义区分。但是直到 1972 年，带有副标题为《后现代文学和文化的期刊》的《边界 2》的第一期出版，它才正式应用于文学之中。

后现代主义意思是"现代主义之后"，它是指从 1980 年到现在的时期，涵盖了很多领域，包括建筑、艺术、音乐、文学、影视、社会学和技术。它由现代主义发展而来，同时又背离现代主义。批判现代性是其精髓。后现代主义认为世界是一个复杂且不确定的地方；真理是与个人的观点和立场有关；事实是不足信的。它强调差异和不确定性，反对传统的权威和中心主义，倡导多元化和对文学、文化、艺术、历史、建筑等的质疑……它提倡自我意识、叙事上的破碎以及模糊性，并强调模仿、戏仿、拼贴、戏谑和反语。

一些著名的作家，例如托马斯·品钦（1937—）、唐纳德·巴塞尔姆（1931—1989）、约瑟夫·海勒（1923—1999）等都是后现代主义的代表。

Post-structuralism（后结构主义）

Post-structuralism, a philosophical movement or theory growing as a response to structuralism, emerged in France in the late 1960s and early 1970s. Absorbing Jacques Derrida's deconstructionism, Jacques Lacan's psychoanalytic theories and Michel Foucault's historical critiques, post-structuralism denies the binary oppositions of structuralism and emphasizes plurality of meaning and instability of concepts.

Derrida (1930—2004), Lacan (1901—1981), Foucault (1926—1984), Jean-François Lyotard (1924—1998), and Gilles Deleuze (1925—1995) are notable representatives of post-structuralism.

后结构主义是对结构主义进行回应的一个哲学运动或者理论，在 20 世纪 60 年代末 70 年代早期起源于法国。后结构主义吸收了雅克·德里达的解构主义、雅克·拉康的精神分析理论和米歇尔·福柯的历史批评，否定结构主义的二元对立，强调意义的多重性以及概念的不稳定性。

德里达（1930—2004）、拉康（1901—1981）、福柯（1926—1984）、让－弗朗索瓦·利奥塔（1924—1998）以及吉尔·德勒兹（1925—1995）是著名的后结构主义的代表。

Pre-Raphaelites（拉斐尔前派）

Pre-Raphaelites, also known as the Pre-Rapharlite Brotherhood, was founded by John Everett Millais（1829—1896）, Dante Gabriel Rossetti（1828—1882）, and William Holman Hunt（1827—1910）in 1848. It was an influential group of English painters, poets and critics opposing the Royal Academy's promotion of the Renaissance master Raphael（1483—1520）.

The second phase of the movement began in about 1860 and emphasized the symbolic meaning in poetry, which had great influence upon the Decadence.

拉斐尔前派，也称作拉斐尔前派兄弟会，是由约翰·埃弗利特·米莱斯（1829—1896）、但丁·加百利·罗塞蒂（1828—1882）以及威廉·霍尔曼·亨特（1827—1910）在 1848 年建立。它是由一群极具影响力的英国画家、诗人以及评论家组成，他们反对皇家学院对文艺复兴时期的大师拉斐尔（1483—1520）的推崇。

该运动的第二个阶段从 1860 年左右开始，强调诗歌的象征意义，这对颓废派诗人影响巨大。

Prologue（前言）

Prologue, as a literary device, is an opening or introduction in the beginning of a novel, play or poem. It can be as short as a poem or as long as a chapter, mainly setting the tone, previewing the characters, providing some background details and other information. In a drama, prologues are often given to the audience by one or more actors. In Greek and Elizabethan drama, it often took the form of a character's monologue or dialogue. After the Restoration, prologues began to fade in English Theaters. Compared with the modern prologues, the ancient Greek prologues were more important.

前言是一种文学手段，它是指在小说、戏剧或者诗歌开头的开篇或者简介。它可以像一首诗一样短，也可以像一个章节一样长，主要是设置基调、介绍人物、提供背景以及其他信息。在戏剧中，前言经常是由一个或者更多的演员说给观众。在希腊戏剧和伊丽莎白戏剧中，前言以人物独白或者对话形式出现。在复辟时期过后，前言在英国剧场开始衰落。与现代的前言相比，古希腊时期的前言要更为重要。

Psychoanalytic Criticism （精神分析批评）

Psychoanalytic criticism is a literary criticism employing psychoanalytic theories to analyze literary characters and their authors. Sigmund Freud (1856—1939) is one of the most important psychoanalysts associated with the criticism. According to him, the human mind can be divided into conscious mind (ego) and unconscious mind (id and superego). The ego balances the demands of the id and the superego. A Literary work is the reflection of the author's mind, expressing the author's unconscious desires and anxieties. The theory is significant in psychoanalytic criticism. Besides, Freud's Oedipus complex is also an enduring theory used in literary criticism. His theory of "penis envy" created a public sensation.

Jacques Lacan is another important psychoanalysts that inspired literary criticism. He emphasized the idea of narcissism and the unconscious behind the language of the text.

精神分析批评是用精神分析理论来分析文学人物及作家的文学批评理论。西格蒙德·弗洛伊德（1856—1939）是与该批评相关的最重要的精神分析学者。根据他所说，人类的心理可以分为有意识的心理（本我）以及无意识的心理（自我和超我）。本我能够平衡自我与超我的需求。一部文学作品就是作者的心理反映，表达了作者无意识的欲望和渴望。该理论对于精神分析批评非常重要。另外，弗洛伊德的俄狄浦斯情结也是一个在文学批评中经常使用的理论。

雅克·拉康是另一个重要的激发文学批评灵感的精神分析学者。他强调自恋的观点以及文本语言背后的无意识。他的理论"阳物崇拜"曾轰动一时。

Psychological Realism（心理现实主义）

Psychological realism, as a modern movement, emerged in the late 19th century founded by Henry James (1843—1916). It focused on the exploration of characters' interior world—their thoughts and motivations. Thus, first-person narrator is often used to make readers believe what characters perceive is real. Henry James' *The Ambassadors* is reckoned as a masterpiece of psychological realism.

According to Sali Zaliha Mustapha: "psychological realism allows for the theoretical possibility of infinite meanings and it recognizes the impossibility of the reader's 'mastering' a text, but gives the reader the freedom to establish a single, though partial, interpretation. Psychological realism also allows readers to interpret texts in a different manner depending on what aspects of the text they want to study and from which angle they want to study texts from."[1] In the 1960s and 1970s, psychological realism was put to its new height by Wright Moris[2], John Updike[3]and Joyce Carol Oates[4].

---

[1] Sali Zaliha Mustapha. "Psychological Realism in The Study of Literary Texts", *The English Teacher*, Vol xxiii, October, 1994. http://www.melta.org.my/ET/1994/main5.html.

[2] Wright Moris (1910—1998) was an American writer and photographer, best known for his "photo-texts".

[3] John Updike (1932—2009) was an American writer, notable for his "Rabbit" series.

[4] Joyce Carol Oates (1938—) is a prolific American writer and distinguished professor in Princeton University. *Them* (1969), *Black Water* (1992), *Blonde* (2000) are her representative works.

心理现实主义是 19 世纪末兴起的现代运动，由亨利·詹姆斯
（1843—1916）发起。它强调探索人物内心世界，也就是他们的思想
和动机。因此，经常使用第一人称叙述来让读者相信人物所想便是现
实。亨利·詹姆斯的《奉使记》被认为是心理现实主义的经典之作。

根据萨利·匜丽哈·穆斯塔法所说："心理现实主义使无限意义
成为理论可能，它认识到读者'掌握'文本是不可能的，但是却给读
者进行单独解释（虽然有些片面）的自由。心理现实主义也使读者可
以根据自己想要研究的方面和角度用不同的方式来解释文本。"在20
世纪 60 年代和 70 年代心理现实主义被赖特·莫里斯、约翰·厄普代
克以及乔伊斯·卡罗尔·奥茨推向了新的高峰。

Pulp Fiction（低俗小说）

Pulp fiction descended from the magazines of the 19th century which
were printed on the cheaply made wood-pulp paper and published thrilling,
exciting and fantastic fiction for the American public.

低俗小说起源于 19 世纪，印刷在劣质的木浆纸上，为美国大众发
表惊悚、刺激、怪诞小说的杂志。

Pure Poetry（纯诗）

Pure poetry refers to the poetry which focuses on the musical and color-
ful nature of language rather than educational or didactic purpose. Edgar Allan Poe, Stéphane Mallarmé[1]and Paul Verlaine[2]were practitioners of pure
poetry.

纯诗是指注重语言的音乐与色彩本性，而不是为了教育或者说教
的目的。埃德加·爱伦·坡、斯特凡·马拉梅以及保罗·魏尔伦都是

---

① Stéphane Mallarmé（1842—1898）was a French poet and one of the leaders of the Symbolist
movement in poetry.

② Paul Verlaine（1844—1896）was a French symbolist poet and the founder of Decadence.

纯诗的实践者。

Puritanism（清教主义）

Puritans were originally members of a division of the Protestant Church in England, who tried to purify their religious beliefs and practices through worship and doctrine. In 1620, about one hundred puritans sailed to America aboard Mayflower to escape from political persecution and became the first settlers in America. They accept the doctrine of predestination, original sin and total depravity, and limited atonement. Puritanism is Puritans' practices and beliefs, most of which were piety, dressing simply, and living a modest life. It had a very profound influence on American Literature and is famous for its fresh and direct style of writing.

清教徒原是英国新教分支的成员，他们努力通过信仰与教义来净化自己的宗教信仰与实践。在 1620 年，一百多个清教徒为了逃避政治迫害乘坐"五月花"号到达美国，成为美国的第一批居民。他们接受预定论、原罪、性恶说以及限定的救赎的教义。清教徒的行为与信仰就是清教主义，他们提倡虔诚、着装朴素、生活简朴。清教主义对美国文学影响深远，也因为它清新、直接的写作方式而闻名遐迩。

Q

Quatrain（四行诗）

Quatrain is a four-line stanza or poem with alternate rhymes. abab is the most common pattern，as in Thomas Gray[①]'s *An Elegy Written in a Country Churchyard* (1751).

四行诗就是一个有交替押韵的四行诗节或者诗歌。abab 是最常见的模式，例如托马斯·格雷的《墓畔挽歌》（1751）。

Queer Theory（酷儿理论）

Queer theory，coined by Teresa de Lauretis[②]in 1991，is a post-structuralist critical theory about sexuality and gender which was originally associated with gay and lesbian studies. It reverses the binary sexual regime of sexuality and gender. According to Teresa de Lauretis，lesbian and gay sexualities are "forms of resistance to cultural homogenization，counteracting dominant discourses with other constructions of the subject in culture"[③] . Queer

---

① Thomas Gray (1716—1771) was an English poet，best known as the author of the lyric poem *An Elegy Written in a Country Churchyard*.

② Teresa de Lauretis (1938—) is an Italian-born writer and professor at the University of Californian.

③ Theodora A. Jankowsk. *Pure Resistance*：*Queer Virginity in Early Modern English Drama*，University of Pennsylvanian Press，2000，p. 7.

theory aims at the disruption of the dominant social text not via separatism, but through "demanding political representation while insisting on... material and historical specificity"① . Michel Foucault, Judith Butler, and Eve Kosofsky Sedgwick are important theorists and forerunners of queer theory.

酷儿理论，是由特瑞莎·德·劳利提斯于 1991 年首次使用，最初是与同性恋研究相关的关于性与性别的后结构主义批评理论。它颠覆了二元对立的性别政治。根据特瑞莎·德·劳利提斯所说，同性恋就是"反对文化的同质化，用文化中的其他主体结构来抵制主权话语"。酷儿理论旨在"通过要求政治表现同时坚持物质与历史的特异性而不是通过分裂主义来瓦解具有统治地位的社会文本"。米歇尔·福柯、朱迪斯·巴特勒、伊芙·科索夫斯基·赛奇维克是酷儿理论重要的理论家和先驱。

① Teresa de Lauretis, "Queer Theory: Lesbian and Gay Sexualities: An Introduction", *Differences: A Journal of Feminist Cultural Studies.* 1991. 3 (2): iii, extracted from Shane Phelan, Sexual Strangers: Gays, Lesbians, and Dilemmas of Citizenship, Temple University Press, 2001, p. 111.

R

Reader-response Criticism（读者反映论）

Reader-response criticism is a literary criticism starting with "affective fallacy" called by New Critics. It lays emphasis on the reader's interpretation of a literary work while ignoring the author and the text's contents. I. A. Richards's *Practical Criticism* (1929) and Hans-Robert Jauss①'s lecture in 1967②are the sources of reader-response criticism. It was popularized by Norman Holland (1927—), Stanley Fish (1938—), Roland Barthes (1915—1980) and others in the1970s.

读者反映论起源于新批评学者称为"情感谬误"的文学批评理论。它强调读者对文学作品的解释，忽视作者和文本的内容。I. A. 瑞恰慈的《实用文艺批评》（1929）以及汉斯·罗伯特·姚斯在 1967 年的评论是读者反映论的源泉。在 20 世纪 70 年代，诺曼·霍兰德、斯坦雷·费什、罗兰·巴特等人将读者反映论推广。

Realism（现实主义）

Realism is a literary movement that began in the middle of the 19th cen-

---

① Hans-Rober Jauss (1921—1997) was a German academic and theorist, notable for establishing Reception Aesthetics.

② Jauss's lecture in 1967 was entitled "Literary History as a Challenge to Literary Theory", calling for a new approach to literary studies.

tury in France as a reaction to and a rejection of Romanticism. It then spread to other European countries and America, extending until the beginning of the 20th century. Realism, in literature, refers to an approach of describing everyday activities in a matter-of-fact manner to show life as it is, instead of romanticized or stylized presentation.

Mark Twain, William Howells, William Burroughs[①], George Eliot, Charles Dickens, Thomas Hardy, and Norman Mailer[②]belong to realists.

现实主义是对浪漫主义进行回应与摒弃，在 19 世纪中期起始于法国，然后传到欧洲国家和美国，一直持续到 20 世纪早期。在文学中，现实主义是指用现实的方法来描写日常的行为动作以真切地展示生活的本来面貌，而不是用浪漫手法或者非写实手法呈现。

马克·吐温、威廉·豪威尔斯、威廉·巴勒斯、乔治·艾略特、查尔斯·狄更斯、托马斯·哈代、诺曼·梅勒都属于现实主义者。

Refrain （叠句）

Refrain refers to a set or a group of lines that appears at intervals throughout a song or poem, usually at the end of a stanza. A refrain can be an exact repetition, or it may have slight variations. Sebastian Barker[③]'s *The Uncut Stone* is a poem with a typical refrain.

叠句是指出现在歌曲或者诗歌停顿部分，经常出现在诗节的末尾的一组诗句。叠句可以是精确的重复，也可以有些许的改变。

赛巴斯蒂安·巴克的《未切割的石头》便是有典型叠句的诗。

---

① William Burroughs (1914—1997) was an American writer, best known as a primary figure of the Beat Generation.

② Norman Mailer (1923—2007) was an American writer, famous for his *The Naked and The Dead* (1948).

③ Sebastian Barker (1945—2014) was a British writer of many books of poetry and editor of London Magazine, famous as a master of meter and rhyme.

Regency Period（摄政时期）

The Regency period refers to the nine years of the reign of the Prince of Wales (later George IV) from 1811 to 1820, when George III was so seriously ill that his son, the Prince of Wales, assumed the role of Prince Regent. It lasted until 1820 when George III died and the Regent became king George IV.

Jane Austen, Walter Scott, Susan Ferrier[1] were famous writers in the period.

摄政时期是指威尔士王子（后来的乔治四世）从 1811 年到 1820 年的统治时期，当时乔治三世病重，他的儿子威尔士王子开始王子摄政。直到 1820 年乔治三世去世，摄政王才成为乔治四世。

简·奥斯汀、沃尔特·司各特、苏珊·费里尔是该时期的著名作家。

Renaissance（文艺复兴）

Renaissance, derived from the French word, "renaissance" and the Italian word "rinascità", meaning "rebirth", was an artistic and cultural movement that began in Northern Italy in the 14th century, spread to the rest of Europe in the 15th century, and finally ended in the 17th century. It witnesses the demise of the Middle Ages and the beginning of Early Modern Age.

As one of the three greatest ideological emancipation movements in Europe, renaissance was known for the renewed interest in classical art, architecture and literature. It caused revolutions in many fields, such as educa-

---

[1] Suan Ferrier (1782—1854) was a Scottish novelist. She wrote three novels: *Marriage*, *The Inheritance* and *Destiny*.

tion, society and politics, but the most distinguished achievement was fulfilled in art, with Leonordo da Vinci, Michelangelo, Raphael and Titian as its representatives.

In literature, renaissance also saw the emergence of many great writers like Francesco Petrarca①, Shakespeare, Christopher Marlowe②, John Donne, Ben Johnson and so on.

文艺复兴一词来源于法语词汇"renaissance"和意大利语词汇"rinascità"意思是"复兴",是在 14 世纪起始于北部意大利,在 15 世纪传到欧洲其他国家,最终在 17 世纪结束的艺术与文化运动。它见证了中世纪的衰败和早期现代时期的兴起。

作为欧洲三次最大思想解放运动之一,文艺复兴因重新燃起对经典艺术、建筑和文学的兴趣而闻名遐迩。它引发了在教育、社会和政治领域的革命,但是最为卓越的成就是在艺术方面的体现,其代表人物有里奥纳多·达芬奇、米开朗基罗、拉斐尔和提香。

在文学中,文艺复兴时期出现了很多著名的作家,例如弗朗西斯科·彼特拉克、莎士比亚、克里斯托弗·马洛、约翰·邓恩、本·琼森等。

Restoration Comedy(复辟时期喜剧)

Restoration comedy, also the comedy of manners, is a form of English comedy, which developed from the Restoration of the Stuart monarchy in 1660 to about 1700. Witty dialogue, obscene words, cynical sarcasm, intricate plots and amoral behaviors are its common features. According to American literary theorist M. H. Abrams, "It deals with the relations and in-

---

① Francesco Petrarca (1304—1374), also known as Petrarch, was an Italian writer in Renaissance Italy. He is called "the father of Humanism".

② Christopher Marlowe (1564—1593) was a poet, best known for his establishment of dramatic blank verse.

trigues of men and women living in a sophisticated upper-class society, and relies in large part on the wit and sparkle of the dialogue for comic effect— often in the form of repartee, a witty conversational give and take which constitutes a verbal fencing match—and to a lesser degree, on the violations of social standards and decorum"① .

George Etherege (1636—1692)'s *The Man of Mode* (1676), William Wycherley (1640—1715)'s *The Country Wife* (1675), and William Congreve (1670—1729)'s *The Way of the World* (1700) are notable examples of Restoration comedy.

复辟时期喜剧，也叫做社会风俗喜剧，是英国喜剧的一种，从 1660 年斯图亚特王朝复辟发展到 1700 年左右。诙谐的对话、淫秽的话语、愤世嫉俗的讽刺、错综复杂的情节和非道德的行为都是其共同特征。根据美国文艺理论家艾布拉姆斯所说："它是关于生活在上层社会的男女关系和阴谋诡计，在很大程度上通过诙谐和智慧对话来渲染喜剧效果——经常是妙语连珠的对话，也就是能够形成唇枪舌剑的机智对话——在很小程度上通过违反社会道德和礼仪来取得喜剧效果。"

乔治·埃思里奇（1636—1692）的《时髦男子》（1676）、威廉·威彻利（1640—1715）的《村妇》（1675）以及威廉·康格里夫（1670—1729）的《如此世道》（1700）都是复辟时期喜剧的代表之作。

Revenge Tragedy（复仇悲剧）

The revenge tragedy, as a genre of drama popular during the Elizabethan and Jacobean eras in England, describes a protagonist's seeking revenge for his relative's or friend's injury or death. Seneca (4 B. C. —65 A. D.), a Roman playwright, popularized the genre with his works. Thomas

---

① 罗选民：《英美文学赏析教程（小说与戏剧）》，清华大学出版社 2006 年版，第 588 页。

Kyd①'s *The Spanish Tragedy*（1587）established the revenge tragedy on the English stage and Shakespeare's *Hamlet* perfected the genre.

复仇悲剧，是在英国伊丽莎白和雅各布时期颇受欢迎的戏剧形式，讲述主人公为了给亲人或者朋友的伤害或者死亡进行复仇。罗马剧作家塞内加（公元前4年—公元65年）使该类型得以普及。托马斯·基德的《西班牙悲剧》（1587）将复仇悲剧搬上了英国的舞台，莎士比亚的《哈姆雷特》将该类戏剧达到极致。

Rhyme Royal（帝王韵）

Rhyme royal is a form of English verse which consists of seven-line iambic pentameter stanzas rhyming ababbcc. Geoffrey Chaucer first employed the form in *The Parlement of Foules*（1382）and *Troilus and Criseyde*（1385）. King James I of Scotland（1394—1437）used the form in his Charcerian poem *The Kingis Quair*, which is the origin of the Royal title.

帝王韵是一种英语诗歌形式，它是由五音步抑扬格的七行诗诗节组成，按 ababbcc 押韵。杰弗雷·乔叟最开始在《火鸟议会》（1382）和《特洛伊罗斯和克丽西达》（1385）中使用该形式。苏格兰国王詹姆士一世（1394—1437）在其乔叟式诗歌《国王书》中使用该形式，这也是该词冠以帝王的原因。

Romanticism（浪漫主义）

Romanticism, as an artistic, literary and intellectual movement, originated in Europe in the late 18th century and came into being under the impetus of the Industrial Revolution and French Revolution. It went against Classicism, laying emphasis on the individual's feelings and emotions as well as

---

① Thomas Kyd（1558—1594）was an English playwright in Elizabethan era, best known for *The Spanish Tragedy*.

criticizing the conventions and social rules. The publication of the *Lyrical Ballads in* 1798 by William Wordsworth and Samuel Taylor Colevidge marked the beginning of the Romantic Age, and Walter Scott's death in 1832 was the end of it. American romanticism rose after the Civil War. It is the first creative period for American literature, during which many famous writers such as Melville, Whitman, Dickinson, Emerson published many distinguished works.

浪漫主义，作为一种艺术、文学及知识运动，于 18 世纪后期起始于欧洲并受到工业革命和法国革命的推动最终形成。它与古典主义对立，主要强调个人情感同时对传统和社会统治进行鞭挞。由威廉·华兹华斯和塞缪尔·泰勒·柯勒律治于 1798 年出版的《抒情歌谣集》标志着浪漫主义时代的开始，并随着沃尔特·司各特在 1832 年去世而结束。美国浪漫主义在内战后出现。这是美国文学史上第一次真正有创造性的时期，很多著名作家，例如麦尔维尔、惠特曼、狄金森、爱默生都出版了杰作。

Round Character（圆形人物）

A round character, as opposed to flat character, is also known as "a multidimensional character". In his *Aspects of the Novel* published in 1927, E. M. Forster (1879—1970) first coined the phrase to refer to a full delineated person who has complicated and contradictory personality traits. He or she can change with the development of a story. Harry in *Harry Porter* is a typical round character.

圆形人物，与扁平人物相反，也被称为"多维人物"。在爱德华·摩根·福斯特（1879—1970）1927 年出版的《小说面面观》中第一次使用该词来指一个被全面刻画、有着复杂矛盾个性特点的人物。他（她）会随着故事的发展而改变。《哈利波特》中的哈利就是一个典型的圆形人物。

S

Saga （萨迦）

In the original sense, a saga referred to a historical tale written between 1120 and 1400, dealing with the battles, adventures and customs of the first families that settled in Iceland or Norway. Today, a saga means a long and complicated story with many details.

从原始意义上来看，萨迦是指在 1120 年到 1400 年间写的关于最先到冰岛或者挪威定居的家庭的战争、冒险和习俗的历史传说。现在，萨迦是指情节复杂、突出细节的长篇故事。

Science Fiction （科幻小说）

Science fiction is a new literary genre in western modern literature which deals with the influences that imaginative science and technology will have on individuals and society in the future. The story in science fiction often happens in space or in a different universe with imagined and attractive plots. Science, imagination and fiction are the three elements of the genre.

Jules Verne (1828—1905), a French writer, wrote many adventure novels, such as *Journey to the Center of the Earth* (1864), *Twenty Thousand Leagues Under the Sea* (1870), and *Around the World in Eighty Days*

(1873), which had great effects on science fiction, so he was called the "father of science fiction".

科幻小说是西方现代文学的一种新的文学体裁,描写想象中的科学和技术对于未来的个人和社会将要产生的影响。科幻小说的故事经常发生在太空或者一个不同的星球,情节都是想象的并引人入胜。科学、想象和小说是该类体裁的三大要素。

法国作家儒勒·凡尔纳 (1828—1905) 创作了很多冒险小说,例如《地心历险记》(1864)、《海底两万里》(1870)、《八十天环游世界》(1873),这些对科幻小说影响深远,所以他被称为"科幻小说之父"。

Semiotics (符号学)

Semiotics is the study of the signs and symbols to explore how meaning is created. Ferdinand de Saussure[1] propelled the use of semiotics in modern linguistics in the 19th century. Saussure divided the sign into two components: signifier (the sound of the word) and signified (the concept indicated by the sound). The signifier means something that can be seen, heard, felt, smelled, or tasted, while the signified does not need to be a real object. Charles Sanders Peirce (1839—1941), as the founder of pragmatics, is another important person in the field of semiotics. Syntactics, semantics and pragmatics are three branches of semiotics.

符号学是研究符号和象征的学说,旨在探索意义的产生。费尔迪南·德·索绪尔在 19 世纪推动了符号学在现代语言学中的使用。索绪尔将符号分为两个组成部分:能指(音响形象)和所指(音响形象所暗含的概念)。能指是指能够看到、听到、摸到、闻到或者尝到的东西,而所指不一定是真的事物。查尔斯·桑德斯·皮尔士 (1839—1941)

---

[1] Ferdinand de Saussure (1857—1913) was a Swiss linguist and semiotician, best known as one of the two founders of semiotics.

是语用学的创始人，也是符号学领域中另一个重要人物。句法、语义学及语用学是符号学的三个分支。

Sensation fiction（奇情小说）

Sensation fiction was a literary genre popular in the 1860s in Britain. Similar to Gothic fiction, sensation fiction is filled with crime, suspense, sex, adultery, insanity, thriller and so on for exciting, shocking or moving effects.

Wilkie Collins[①]'s *The Woman in White* (1860), Charles Dickens's *Great Expectation* (1860—1861), Ellen Wood[②]'s *East Lynne* (1861) belong to the genre.

奇情小说是在 19 世纪 60 年代在英国流行的文学体裁。与哥特式小说相似，奇情小说为了刺激、震惊或者感人的效果，充满了犯罪、悬疑、性、出轨、疯狂、恐怖等情节。

威尔基·柯林斯的《白衣女人》（1860）、查尔斯·狄更斯的《伟大前程》（1860—1861）、爱伦·伍德的《东林怨》（1861）都属于该类型。

Sentimentalism（感伤主义）

Sentimentalism was an important literary genre in England that emerged in the process of Enlightenment in the middle of the 18th century. It struggled against the feudalism, attacked the injustices brought about by the industrial revolution, showed sympathy for the poverty-stricken peasants, blamed reason and appealed to sentiment.

---

① Wilkie Collins (1824—1889) was an English writer, whose *The Moonstone* (1868) is considered the first modern English detective novel.

② Ellen Wood (1814—1887), also known as Mrs. Henry Wood, was an English novelist, famous for *East Lynne*.

It brought the elements of individualism and objective fantasy into artistic writing, which had a great influence on romanticism, and thus it was also called "pre-romanticism".

The representative writers include Samuel Richardson[1], Laurence Stern[2] and Oliver Goldsmith[3].

感伤主义是英国一种重要的文学形式，是 18 世纪中叶在启蒙运动中产生的。它反对封建主义，抨击工业革命带来的不公平，同情贫困的农民，谴责理性，倡导感性。

它把个人主义和主观幻想的因素带入到文艺创作中，对浪漫主义产生了巨大的影响，因此它也被称为"前浪漫主义"。

其代表作家有塞缪尔·理查森、劳伦斯·斯特恩和奥利弗·哥德史密斯。

Sestina（六节诗）

Sestina is a complicated verse form which consists of six stanzas of six lines each, followed by a three-line envoy. The end words of the first stanza are repeated in a different order as end words in each of the subsequent five stanzas; the closing envoy contains all six words, two per line, placed in the middle and at the end of the three lines. The patterns of word repetition are as follows, with each number representing the final word of a line, and each row of numbers representing a stanza:[4]

Stanza 1: 1 2 3 4 5 6

---

① Samuel Richardson (1689—1761) was an English writer and printer, notable for his three novels: *Pamela* (1740), *Clarissa* (1748) and *The History of Sir Charles Grandison* (1753).

② Laurence Stern (1713—1768) was an Irish-Anglo writer, best known for *Tristram Shandy* (1759—67) and *A Sentimental Journey* (1768).

③ Oliver Goldsmith (1730—1774) was an Anglo-Irish dramatist, poet and novelist, famous for *The Deserted Village* (1770) and *The Vicar of Wakefield* (1766).

④ http: //www. poetryfoundation. org/learning/glossary-term/sestina.

Stanza 2：6 1 5 2 4 3

Stanza 3：3 6 4 1 2 5

Stanza 4：5 3 2 6 1 4

Stanza 5：4 5 1 3 6 2

Stanza 6：2 4 6 5 3 1

Envoy：Variable.

Arnaut Daniel, a Provencal troubadour of the 12th century, invented the form.

六节诗是一种复杂的诗歌形式，由六节六行诗句和一节三行诗句组成，第一诗节六行诗句中的末尾单词以不同的顺序在紧接下来的五个诗节的末尾重复出现；结尾诗句包含所有这六个词，两个为一行，放在末尾三行的中部和尾部。单词的重复模式如下，每个数字代表一行的最后一个单词，每行数字代表一个诗节：

第一诗节：1 2 3 4 5 6

第二诗节：6 1 5 2 4 3

第三诗节：3 6 4 1 2 5

第四诗节：5 3 2 6 1 4

第五诗节：4 5 1 3 6 2

第六诗节：2 4 6 5 3 1

结尾诗节：变化的

12 世纪的普罗旺斯行吟诗人阿尔诺·丹尼尔创造了该诗体。

Setting（情境）

Setting refers to the time, place and the social environment in which a novel, play or poem happens. The setting can be an actual city or an imagined world. It has a great influence on the plot, theme and characters.

情境是指小说、戏剧或者诗歌所发生的时间、地点以及社会环境。情境可以是真实的城市也可以是一个想象中的世界。它对情节、主题和人物有着很重要的影响。

Silver Fork Novel（银叉小说）

Silver fork novel was a form of novel that flourished in Britain from the 1820s to the 1840s and depicted the elegance, fashionable etiquette and manners of the upper class's lives in detail, exposing the downsides and mocking aristocratic characters. It was named by William Hazlitt in 1827 in an article on "The Dandy School" after the upper-class's use of two silver forks to eat fish. [①]William Makepeace Thackeray's *Vanity Fair* (1848) was influenced much by the form.

Benjamin Disraeli (1804—1881), Theodore Hook (1788—1841), Susan Ferrier (1782—1854), Catherine Gore (1798—1861), Lady Charlotte Bury (1775—1861), Lady Caroline Lamb (1785—1828) and other writers were silver fork novel writers.

银叉小说是 19 世纪 20 年代到 40 年代在英国兴盛的小说类型，它详细地描写上层阶级生活的优雅、时髦的礼节和礼仪，揭露其消极的一面并嘲讽贵族阶级。该词是根据威廉·黑兹利特在 1827 年关于"上流社会"的文章中写的上层阶级用两个银叉子吃鱼得名而来。威廉·梅克比斯·萨克雷的《名利场》（1848）就受到了该形式小说的影响。

本杰明·迪斯雷利（1804—1881）、西奥多·胡克（1788—1841）、苏珊·费里尔（1782—1854）、凯瑟琳·高尔（1798—1861）、夏洛特·百利（1775—1861）、卡洛琳·兰姆夫人（1785—1828）等等都是银叉小说的作家。

Social Realism（社会现实主义）

Social realism, as an international art movement, originated from the

---

① William Hazlitt. *The Complete Works of William Hazlitt.* London: Dent, 1934, p. 146.

Ashcan School movement①in the beginning of the 20th century and peaked in America during the Great Depression. Social realists focused on racial conflict and the working class's bad working conditions and poor life to express their social and political protest edged with satire.

社会现实主义是一个国际性的艺术运动，在 20 世纪初起始于垃圾箱派运动，并在大萧条时期在美国达到巅峰。社会现实主义者关注种族冲突及工人阶级恶劣的工作条件和贫苦的生活，表达他们对社会和政治的具有讽刺意味的反抗。

Socialist Realism（社会主义现实主义）

Socialist realism is the officially sanctioned style of art which was developed in the Soviet Union under the guidance of Stalin in 1932. It was the only criterion for measuring literary works and theoretically dominated art production until the disintegration of the Soviet Union in 1991. Socialist realist fiction often depicts positive and glorified characters to advocate communist values.

社会主义现实主义是在 1932 年斯大林的指导下在苏联发展起来的官方批准的艺术形式。它是衡量文学作品的唯一标准并且在理论上掌控艺术出版直到 1991 年苏联解体。社会主义现实主义小说经常描写的是正面、美化的人物以倡导共产主义价值观。

Soliloquy（独白）

Soliloquy is a device often used in drama when a character discloses his or her own inner thoughts, audible only to the audience.

独白是经常在戏剧中使用的手段，是指人物出声地仅向读者暴露自己的内心想法。

---

① Ashcan School, sponsored by Robert Henri (1865—1929), was an artistic movement in America in the early 20th century, best known for the realistic portraying of daily life in New York. It had great effects on modern art.

Sonnet（十四行诗）

As a lyric poem consisting of 14 lines written in iambic pentameter, sonnet, originating in Italy, was created by Giacomo Da Lentini[①]in the 13th century and then spread to other European countries. Generally speaking, there are two categories of sonnet: Italian sonnet and English sonnet.

Italian sonnet, also known as Petrarchan sonnet, is comprised of two quatrains followed by two tercets, following the rhyme scheme: abba abba cde cde or cdc dcd.

English sonnet, also known as Shakespearean sonnet, is comprised of three quatrains and a final couplet, following the rhyme scheme: abab cdcd efef gg.

十四行诗是用五音步抑扬格所写的十四行抒情诗，起源于意大利，是贾科莫·达·伦蒂尼在 13 世纪创始的，然后传到欧洲其他国家。总的说来，有两种十四行诗：意大利十四行诗和英国十四行诗。

意大利十四行诗，也叫做彼特拉克式十四行诗，由两个四行诗再跟两个三行诗组成，韵律模式为：abba abba ced cde 或者 cdc dcd。

英国十四行诗，也叫做莎士比亚式十四行诗，由三个四行诗跟着一个两行诗组成，韵律模式为：abab cece efef gg。

Spenserian Sanza（斯宾塞体诗节）

Spenserian stanza is a verse form invented by Edmund Spenser (1552—1599) in his poem *The Faerie Queene*. It is comprised of 8 lines of iambic pentameter and a final line of iambic hexameter, with the rhyming scheme ababbcbcc.

---

① Giacomo Da Lentini (1210—1260) was an Italian senior poet of the Sicilian school, known as the inventor of the sonnet.

斯宾塞体诗节，是由埃德蒙·斯宾塞在《仙后》中创造的诗歌形式。它是由八行五音步抑扬格以及结尾的一行六音步抑扬格组成，押韵模式为 ababbcbcc。

Stream of Consciousness（意识流）

In literary criticism, stream of consciousness is a literary narrative technique, which is characterized by a flow of thoughts（a character's thoughts, feelings and images are depicted as they occur without cohesion or a coherent structure）. Thus, it is often regarded as a form of interior monologue.

It is William James that first coined "stream of consciousness" in his *The Principles of Psychology*（1890）and May Sinclair in 1918 first used it in a literary context.

It is employed by many well-known writers in their masterpieces, for example, James Joyce（1882—1941）'s *Ulysses*（1922）, Virginia Woolf（1882—1941）'s *The Waves*（1931）, William Faulkner（1897—1962）'s *The Sound and The Fury*（1929）and Marcel Proust（1871—1922）'s *à La Recherche Du Temps Perdu*.

在文学评论中，意识流是一种文学叙述方式，以思想流为特征（即人物的思想、情感和意向一发生就描述出来，没有凝聚力或者连贯的结构）。因此，通常也被认为是一种内心独白的形式。

威廉·詹姆斯首先在其 1890 年出版的《心理学原理》提出"意识流"，然后在 1918 年梅·辛克莱尔首先将其运用在文学作品中。

有很多著名的作家在自己著作中使用该手法，例如：詹姆斯·乔伊斯（1882—1941）的《尤利西斯》（1922）、弗吉尼亚·伍尔夫（1882—1941）的《海浪》（1931）、威廉·福克纳（1897—1962）的《喧嚣与骚动》（1929）以及马塞尔·普鲁斯特（1871—1922）的《追忆似水年华》。

Structuralism（结构主义）

Structuralism was an intellectual movement beginning in the 1950s. It is an approach of analyzing the relationships between fundamental elements in linguistics, sociology, anthropology, philosophy, psychology or literature to explore a complex system combined with the elements.

Ferdinand de Saussure is considered as the forerunner of structuralism and the anthropologist Claude Levi-Strauss①was one of the most important practitioners.

In the late 20th century, structuralism became one of the commonly-used methods to analyze linguistics, culture and society.

结构主义是在 20 世纪 50 年代兴起的知识运动。它是分析语言学、社会学、人类学、哲学、心理学或者文学中基础因素之间的关系，目的在于探索由这些因素组成的复杂体系。

费尔迪南·德·索绪尔被认为是结构主义的先驱，人类学家克劳德·列维－斯特劳斯是最重要的实践者之一。

在 20 世纪后半叶，结构主义成为了分析语言学、文化和社会领域的最常用方法之一。

Style（风格）

Style in literature refers to the way in which the author writes and conveys his thoughts. Along with theme, plot, setting and characters, it is considered to be one of the essential components of literary works. Every author has his/her own writing style, which makes him or her different from others.

According to Richard Nordquist, style is "narrowly interpreted as those

---

① Claude Levi-Strauss（1908—2009）was a French anthropologist and structuralist. Along with James George Frazer and Franz Boas, he has been called "the father of modern anthropology".

figures that ornament discourse; broadly, as representing a manifestation of the person speaking or writing. All figures of speech fall within the domain of style"① .

文学中的风格是指作者写作、传达自己思想的方式，连同主题、情节、情境和人物一起，被认为是文学作品中至关重要的组成部分。每位作家都有使自己与他人相区分的写作风格。

根据理查德·诺奎斯特所说，风格"狭义地来说，就是美化语言的修辞方法；广义地来说，就是一个人说话或者写作方式的标志。所有语言形式都属于风格的范畴"。

Subplot（陪衬情节）

A subplot is a secondary plot that is related and auxiliary to the main plot to increase tension and make a story more complicated. A subplot also has a beginning, a climax and an ending, often appearing in novels, plays, movies and TV shows.

陪衬情节就是一个次要情节，与主要情节相关并对其进行补充以增添紧张气氛，使故事更加复杂。陪衬情节也有开头、高潮和结局，经常出现在小说、戏剧、电影和电视剧中。

Surrealism（超现实主义）

Surrealism is a revolutionary movement in sculpture, painting, music, arts and literature that was launched in France by André Breton's *Manifesto on Surrealism* published in 1924. It developed out of Dadaism during World War I, aiming at "resolving the previously contradictory conditions of dream and reality" by engendering a negative art and literature that would destroy the false values of modern bourgeois society. Affected by Freud's psychoanal-

---

① http：//hubpages. com/literature/Writing-Styles-of-English-Literature.

ysis, surrealism tried to represent the subconscious mind, and considered that only in the surreal and unconscious world can we get rid of all the bounds and truly show the fact.

Notable surrealists include H. T. Rousseau, Joan Miro, Salvador Dali, M. Emst, R. Magritte, and so on. Many writers were influenced much by surrealism, such as Dylan Thomas[1], Henry Miller[2], William Burroughs, and Thomas Pynchon[3]. Flights of fantasy, hallucinative writing, startling consequences and black humor are the results of the influence.

超现实主义是在法国由安德烈·布勒东在 1924 年出版的《超现实主义宣言》中发起的一场在建筑、绘画、音乐、艺术和文学中的革命运动。它从第一次世界大战期间的达达主义发展而来，目的是通过创作出负面的能摧毁现在资本主义社会错误价值观的艺术与文学来"解决以前的梦想与现实的矛盾状况"。受到了弗洛伊德的精神分析的影响，超现实主义努力展现潜意识，并认为只有在超现实、无意识的世界里我们才能摆脱所有的束缚，真实地展现事实。

超现实主义艺术家主要有卢梭、米罗、达利、恩斯特以及雷尼·马格里特等。很多作家受到了超现实主义的影响，例如迪兰·托马斯、亨利·米勒、威廉·巴勒斯、以及托马斯·品钦。幻想飞跃、幻想写作、惊人结局和黑色幽默都是其影响下的产物。

Suspense（悬念）

Suspense is a literary device used by an author to attract audience. It is deliberately instilled in readers by the author to make them hold their breath

---

① Dylan Thomas (1914—1953) was a Welsh poet and writer best known for his poem "Do Not Go Gentle Into Good Night.

② Henry Miller (1891—1980) was an American writer whose *Tropic of Cancer* (1934) is considered as a masterpiece of American post-modernism.

③ Thomas Pynchon (1937—) is an American postmodernist writer famous for his obscure and complicated novels.

and expect more information. With suspense, the audience has an intense desire to go on reading through the book to dig out the outcome of certain events. M. H. Abrams (1912—2015), quoted in *A Teacher Writes*, defined suspense as "a lack of certainty, on the part of a concerned reader, about what is going to happen". Cliffhanger, dramatic irony, verbal cues and so on are the ways often used to create suspense. Shakespeare's *Othello* is a typical play with dramatic irony to create suspense.

悬念是作者用来吸引读者的一种文学手段，它是作者特意使用的，以让读者能够屏气凝神，期望更多的信息。有了悬念，读者便有一种强烈的想要继续读下去找到结果的欲望。M. H. 艾布拉姆斯（1912—2015）在《教师笔记》中这样定义悬念："从读者角度来说，悬念就是要发生事物的不确定性。"惊险、戏剧性的反讽、口头暗示等都是制造悬念的手段。莎士比亚的《奥赛罗》就是一部典型使用戏剧性的反讽来制造悬念的戏剧。

Symbol（象征）

A symbol is a mark, sign or word that stands for or indicates an idea, belief, or relationship. The explanation of symbol as "something which stands for something else" was first recorded in 1590, in Edmund Spenser's *Faerie Queene*. A symbol combines a literal quality with an abstract aspect, allowing people to associate what they see with very different concepts.

According to Campbell[①], "a symbol, like everything else, shows a double aspect. We must distinguish, therefore between the 'sense' and the 'meaning' of the symbol. It seems to me perfectly clear that all the great and little symbolical systems of the past functioned simultaneously on three lev-

---

① Joseph Campbell (1904—1987) was an American writer, best known for his works in comparative mythology and comparative religion.

els: the corporeal of waking consciousness, the spiritual of dream, and the ineffable of the absolutely unknowable. The term 'meaning' can refer only to the first two but these, today, are in the charge of science —which is the province as we have said, not of symbols but of signs. The ineffable, the absolutely unknowable, can be only sensed. It is the province of art which is not 'expression' merely, or even primarily, but a quest for, and formulation of, experience evoking, energy-waking images: yielding what Sir Herbert Read has aptly termed a 'sensuous apprehension of being'"[1].

象征是一个标记、符号或者言语，能代表或者暗示一种观点、信念或者关系。"能代替其他事物的某种事物"这种解释最开始出现在 1590 年埃德蒙·斯宾塞的《仙后》中。象征把字面意义与抽象意义结合在一起，使人们可以将其所见到的事物与截然不同的概念联系在一起。

根据坎贝尔所说："象征，就像所有的事物一样都有双面性。因此我们要区分象征的'感知'和'意义'。所有过去的无论是伟大还是微小的象征体系都是同时在三个层面发挥作用：清醒的意识层面、梦想的精神层面，还有完全不可知事物的无法言表的层面。'意义'一词只是指前两个层面，如今，科学上主要使用这两个层面——这就是我们已经说到的符号领域，而不是象征。难以言表的完全不可知的事物只能通过感知。这就是艺术的领域，它不仅仅是'表达'，更主要地，它是一种唤醒经历、激发能量的探索和构想：最终产生赫伯特·里德所说的'对事物感官上的理解'。"

Symbolism（象征主义）

Symbolism was an artistic and literary movement developing in France in the 1880s. Jean Moréas's *The Symbolist Manifesto* in *La Figaro* published

---

[1] Joseph Campbell. *Flight of the Wild Gander: The Symbol without Meaning*. California: New World Library, 2002, p. 153.

in 1886 popularized it. The symbolists tried to use metaphorical or symbolized language to express personal emotion or consciousness. Stéphane Mallarmé (1842—1898), Paul Verlaine (1844—1896), Jean Nicolas Arthur Rimbaud①and Charles Pierre Baudelaire②were the leading figures in the movement. Symbolism had great influences on 20th century literature

象征主义是在 20 世纪 80 年代在法国兴起的艺术与文化运动。让·莫雷亚斯在 1886 年的《费加洛》报上发表的《象征主义宣言》使象征主义开始流行。象征主义者使用比喻或者象征的语言来表达个人的情感或者意识。斯特凡·马拉梅、保尔·魏尔伦、让·尼古拉·阿蒂尔·兰波以及夏尔·皮埃尔·波德莱尔是该运动的领导人。象征主义对 20 世纪的文学有很大的影响。

---

① Jean Nicolas Arthur Rimbaud (1854—1891) was a marvelous French poet, gaining reputation as a symbolist.

② Charles Pierre Baudelaire (1821—1867) was a French poet, best known for his *The Flowers of Evil*.

T

Terza Rima （三行体）

Terza rima, invented by Dante Alighieri (1265—1321) in *The Divine Comedy* in the 13th century, is an Italian verse form consisting of an interlocking three-line rhyme scheme, usually in iambic pentameter. That is, the end-word of second line of each stanza sets the rhyme for the following stanza. A final line is used at the end of a poem which rhymes with the end-word of the second line of the last stanza. Thus, the rhyme scheme is "aba bcb cdc ded... yzy z". Many poets favored terza rima, including Boccaccio, Petrach and Chaucer.

三行体诗是由但丁·阿利吉耶里（1265—1321）在 13 世纪创作的《神曲》中首先使用的，它是由三行连锁押韵，经常用五音步抑扬格的形式组成的意大利诗歌形式。也就是说，每个诗节的第二行的最后一个单词是紧随其后诗节的韵脚。诗歌最后的结尾行只有一行，其韵脚是最后一个诗节中的第二行的末尾单词。因此，韵脚为"aba bcb cdc ded... yzy z"。很多诗人喜欢用三行体诗，包括薄伽丘、彼特拉克以及乔叟。

Textual Criticism （文本批评）

Textual criticism, as a branch of literary criticism, refers to the identification and elimination of transcription errors in texts (including manuscripts and printed books).

Editors of classical Greek and Latin texts have practiced textual criticism by means of recension (selection after the examination of all available materials) and emendation (elimination of errors) in order to produce or reconstruct as closely as possible a "critical edition" of the original writing.

Three German scholars, Friedrich Wolf (1759—1824), Immanuel Bekker (1785—1871), and Karl Lachmann (1793—1851), contributed much to the application of critical methods in textual criticism.

文本批评，作为文学批评的一个分支，是指鉴别和删除在文本中（包括手稿和出版书籍）的抄写错误。

经典希腊和拉丁文本的编辑们通过修改（在验查所有可得资料后做出选择）和修订（删除错误）的方式将文本批评付诸实践，为了尽可能创作出或者重建与原版极其接近的"批评版本"。

三位德国学者弗里德里希·伍尔夫（1759—1824）、伊曼努尔·贝克尔（1785—1871）以及卡尔·拉赫曼（1793—1851）发展了文本批评中的批评方法。

Tragedy（悲剧）

Tragedy, as a literary genre established by ancient Greek playwrights, refers to a serious play which depicts a series of obstacles and unfortunate events undergone by the protagonist in a dignified manner. The end of a tragedy is often the protagonist's failure or destruction.

Sophocles[①], Euripides[②], and Aeschylus[③] were ancient Greek masters

---

① Sophocles (496 B. C—405 B. C.) was one of the greatest tragedians in Ancient Greece, best known for *Oedipus the King*, *Electra*, and *Antigone*.

② Euripides (480 B. C—406 B. C.) was a productive tragedian in Ancient Greece, best known for *Medea* and *The Trojan Women*.

③ Aeschylus (525 B. C—456 B. C.) was one of the greatest tragedians in Ancient Greece, notable of *Prometheus Bound*, *Agamemnon* and *Eumenides*.

of tragedy. Shakespeare was the greatest writer of tragedy in English litera-ture. *Hamlet*（1603）, *Othello*（1603）, *King Lear*（1605）and *Macbeth*（1606）were Shakespeare's "four great tragedies".

悲剧是由古希腊剧作家创作的一种文学体裁，是指严肃地讲述主人公所遭遇的一系列困难和不幸的正剧。悲剧的结尾经常是主人公的失败或死亡。

索福克勒斯、欧里庇得斯、埃斯库罗斯是古希腊的悲剧大师。莎士比亚是英国文学史上最伟大的悲剧作家。《哈姆雷特》（1603）、《奥赛罗》（1603）、《李尔王》（1605）以及《麦克白》（1606）是莎翁的"四大悲剧"。

Tragicomedy（悲喜剧）

Tragicomedy, as a literary genre, contains both tragic and comic forms. Dramatic literature often employs tragicomedy. A tragedy containing many comic elements or a serious play with a happy ending are both tragi-comedies.

As John Fletcher（1579—1625）wrote in his preface to *The Faithful Shepherdess*（c. 1610）, tragicomedy "wants（i. e., lacks）deaths, which is enough to make it no tragedy, yet brings some near it, which is enough to make it no comedy, which must be a representation of familiar people... A god is as lawful in（tragicomedy）as in a tragedy, and mean people as in a comedy".

Shakespeare's *Merchant of Venice*, *Cymbeline* and *The Winter's Tale* were written in this mode.

Tragicomedy, using both tragic and comic elements, can reflect society from many aspects, widening the extension and depth of a drama reflecting life.

悲喜剧，作为一种文学形式，包含悲剧和喜剧形式。戏剧文学经常使用该体裁。包含很多笑点的悲剧和带有大团圆结局的正剧都属于悲喜剧。

正如约翰·弗雷彻（1579—1625）在《忠实的牧羊女》（约，1610）的前序中写道：悲喜剧"需要（即缺少）死亡，这就足以使之不能成为悲剧，但又让剧中的人物濒临死亡，这也足以使之不能成为喜剧，而这必定表现了我们所熟悉的人……（悲喜剧里）神的存在和悲剧里神的存在一样合情合理；悲喜剧里普通人的存在也和喜剧中普通人的存在一样合情合理"。

莎士比亚的《威尼斯商人》《辛白林》以及《冬天的故事》都是用该形式写成。

悲喜剧，使用悲剧和喜剧因素，能多方面地反映社会，加大戏剧反映生活的广泛性和深刻性。

Transcendentalism（超验主义）

Transcendentalism, also known as American Transcendentalism or American Renaissance, originated in New England in the 1830s as a protest against the general state of culture and society, as well as the doctrine of established religions. It is a religious, philosophical and literary movement, whose members are well-educated people and believe in the inherent goodness of nature and people. Transcendentalists emphasize spirit, thinking that an ideal spiritual reality exists and transcends the empirical and scientific and is knowable through intuition. Meanwhile, they stress the importance of the individual. Ralph Waldo Emerson and Margaret Fuller are representatives.

Transcendentalism is a great ideological emancipation movement in America, and inspires many distinguished writers such as Thoreau, Hawthore and so on.

超验主义，也被称为"美国超验主义"或者"美国文艺复兴"，于 19 世纪 30 年代兴起于新英格兰，是当时反对文化、社会以及宗教教义的产物。这是一次宗教、哲学和文学运动，其成员都是受过良好教育的人，他们相信自然与人类"性本善"。超验主义者强调精神，认为一种理想的精神实体存在并超越经验和科学，只能通过直觉感知。同时，他们强调个人主义。拉尔夫·沃尔多·爱默生和玛格丽特·福勒是其代表人物。

超验主义是美国一次伟大的思想解放运动，激发了很多像梭罗、霍桑这样杰出的作家。

Trochee（扬抑格）

Trochee, derived from the Latin word "trochaeus" meaning "to run", is a metrical foot consisting of a stressed syllable followed by an unstressed syllable, or a long syllable followed by a short one.

抑扬格，来自拉丁语中的"trochaeus"意思是"跑"，它是一种韵脚，由一个重读音节后面再跟一个非重读音节，或者一个长音节后面跟着一个短音节组成。

Triplet（三行联句）

Triplet, as a type of tercet that follows specific rules, is a three-lined stanza or poem that follows the same rhyme, aaa. It is a rare stanza form in poetry but it is more customarily used in verse of heroic couplets or other couplet verse to emphasize meaning. Alfred Tennyson's "The Eagle" is a typical example.

The Eagle

By Alfred Tennyson

He claps the crag with crooked hands; [a]

Close to the sun in lonely lands, [a]

Ring'd with the azure world, he stands. [a]

The wrinkled sea beneath him crawls；［b］

He watches from his mountain walls，［b］

And like a thunderbolt he falls.［b］

三行联句，是一种有着具体规则的三行押韵诗句，它是有着相同韵律（通常是 aaa）的三行诗节或者诗歌。三行联句在诗歌中很少见，通常情况下，它在英雄双行体或者其他对句中使用以强调某种意思。阿尔弗雷德·丁尼生的《鹰》就是一个典型的例子。

《鹰》

阿尔弗雷德·丁尼生

他用蜷曲的爪子抓着巉岩，

背顶着寂寂大地上的太阳，

那周围是一片淡淡的蓝天。

他下面是蠕动着的皱海面，

他栖在墙似的山岩上凝望，

刹时间向下扑去迅如雷电。

——黄杲炘译

Troubadour（行吟诗人）

Troubadours were a group of poets and musicians appearing in southern France，northern Italy，and northern Spain during the High Middle Ages (1100—1350). Troubadours wrote and sang songs and poems chiefly on courtly love，creating new metrical forms. They elevated the art of the song to new heights and had great social influence.

行吟诗人是在中世纪盛期（1100—1350）时在法国南部、意大利北部和西班牙北部地区出现的一群诗人和音乐家。行吟诗人创作并吟唱主要关于宫廷爱恋的歌曲和诗歌，创作新的韵律。他们将歌曲艺术提升到了新的高度并产生了巨大的社会影响。

U

Understatement （低调陈述）

Understatement is a literary device used by writers to minimize the magnitude of something. That is, understatement makes the situation less significant than it is in reality. It is opposite to hyperbole.

低调陈述是作者用来降低事情的重要性的一种文学方法。也就是说，低调陈述把事说的没有事实上的那么重要。它与"夸张"恰恰相反。

University Wits （大学才子）

University Wits were an Elizabethan group of playwrights and pamphleteers, including Christopher Marlowe[1], Robert Greene[2], John Lyly[3], George Peele[4], Thomas Lodge[5], Thomas Nashe, all of whom were well-

---

① Christopher Marlowe (1564—1593) was a playwright and poet of Elizabethan era, known for the use of blank verse.

② Rober Greene (1558—1592) was a popular writer in the late 16th century, notable for his comedy *The Honorable History of Frier Bacon and Frier Bongay* (1594).

③ John Lyly (1553—1606) was a famous writer for his books *Euphues: The Anatomy of Wit* (1578) and *Euphues and His England* (1580).

④ George Peele (1556—1596) was an Elizabethan writer, known for *The Old Wives' Tale* (1591—1594).

⑤ Thomas Lodge (1557—1625) was an English writer, known for his prose romance *Rosalynde*, the source of Shakespeare's *As You Like It*.

educated in either Oxford or Cambridge and wrote in the late 16th century. Thomas Kyd[①]didn't have a university education but he also belonged to the group. They set up the theatrical tradition and paved the way for William Shakespeare.

大学才子是一群伊丽莎白时期的剧作家和小册子作者，包括克里斯托弗·马洛、罗伯特·格林、约翰·利利、乔治·皮尔、托马斯·洛奇、托马斯·纳什，他们在牛津或者剑桥接受良好的教育，在 16 世纪末期从事创作。托马斯·基德虽然没有受到大学教育，但是他也属于该群体。他们建立了戏剧传统并为威廉·莎士比亚铺平了道路。

Utopia（乌托邦）

The term "utopia" was first coined by Sir Thomas More（1478—1535）in his book *Utopia* published in 1516. In the book, utopia refers to an imagined island society in the Atlantic Ocean. Now a utopia is a non-existent society or world that is considered better than contemporary society or world.

Chronologically, the first recorded utopian proposal is Plato's *Republic*. There are many notable works describing utopia, including Tommaso Campanella's *City of the Sun*（1623）, Francis Bacon's *New Atlantis*（1627）, Edward Bellamy's *Looking Backward*（1888）, William Morris' *News from Nowhere*（1891）, Charlotte Perkins Gilman's *Herland*（1915）, and James Hilton's *Lost Horizon*（1934）.

"乌托邦"一词是由托马斯·莫尔（1478—1535）在 1516 年出版的书《乌托邦》中首次使用。在该书中，乌托邦是指在大西洋的一个想象的小岛。现在乌托邦是指一个被认为比当代社会或者世界更好的根本不存在的社会或者世界。

从时间上看，最早有乌托邦式建议的记载出现在柏拉图的《理想

---

① Thomas Kyd（1558—1594）was an Elizabethan writer, best known for *The Spanish Tragedy*.

国》。有很多描述乌托邦的著作，包括托马索·康帕内拉《太阳城》
（1623）、弗朗西斯·培根的《新大西洋》（1627）、爱德华·贝拉米的
《回顾》（1888）、威廉·莫里斯《乌有乡消息》（1891）、夏洛特·伯
金斯·吉尔曼的《他乡》（1915）以及詹姆斯·希尔顿的《消失的地
平线》（1934）。

V

Variorum （集注本）

Variorum is Latin word which refers to a collection of a writer's complete works or an edition of various notes and commentaries by scholars or critics on a particular piece of work.

该词是拉丁语词汇，是指一个作家的所有著作的合集或者是指学者、评论者们对于一部作品各种各样的注解和评论的合集。

Verbal irony （反讽）

Verbal irony is a kind of irony in which a person makes a comment with underlying meaning different from its literary meanings.

反讽是一种讽刺，是指一个人所说的话中暗含的意思与字面意思不一样的。

Victorian Age （维多利亚时代）

Victorian Age refers to Queen Victoria's reign from 1837 till 1901, when the Queen died. The Age saw great progress in economy, politics, literature, and art. It was a time of peace, prosperity, industrial development and imperial expansion.

During this Age, literature flourished, especially novels. Charles Dickens was considered as the most important novelist in the Victorian Age. There were many other notable novelists of the Age, including George Eliot, three Bronte sisters (Charlotte Bronte, Emily Bronte, Anne Bronte), William Thackeray, Thomas Hardy, Oscar Wilde etc.

维多利亚时代是指维多利亚女王从 1837 年继位到 1901 年去世的统治期间。该时代见证了经济、政治、文学与艺术的巨大进步。这是一个和平、繁荣、工业发展、帝国扩张的时代。

在该时代期间，文学繁荣发展，尤其是小说。查尔斯·狄更斯被认为是维多利亚时代最重要的作家。还有很多其他著名的小说家，包括乔治·艾略特、勃朗特三姐妹（夏洛蒂·勃朗特、艾米丽·勃朗特、安妮·勃朗特）、威廉·萨克雷、托马斯·哈代、奥斯卡·王尔德等。

Villanelle （维拉内拉诗或十九行二韵体诗）

"Villanelle", deriving from the Italian word "villa", is a traditional verse form in poetry. It consists of nineteen-line stanzas with usually five of the tercets rhyming aba, and a concluding quatrain rhyming abaa. Dylan Thomas[①]'s "Do Not Go Gentle into that Good Night" (1951—1952) is reckoned as the most famous villanelle.

"维拉内拉诗"，起源于意大利单词"villa"（别墅），是一种传统的诗歌形式。它由十九行诗组成，其中五个三行体，韵式为 aba，还有最后一个四行体，韵式为 abaa。狄兰·托马斯的《不要温柔地走进那个良夜》（1951—1952）被认为是最出名的维拉内拉诗。

Vorticism （漩涡派）

Vorticism is a short-lived 20th-century movement in art and litera-

① Dylan Thomas (1914—1953) was a Welsh writer and poet, best known for *Do Not Go Gentle Into That Good Night* and the play *Under Milk Wood*.

ture. In 1914, Wyndham Lewis advocated the movement in the first issue of *BLAST* published by vorticists, trying to combine arts with machines. It was influenced much by Cubism and Futurism, and complimented the vitality of machines and advocated the way of expression full of violence.

Other than Lewis, there were many people associated with the movement, such as Ezra Pound (1885—1972), Edward Wadsworth (1889—1949), David Bomberg (1890—1957), Cuthbert Hamilton (1860—1930) and Lawrence Atkinson (1906—1979).

漩涡派是一个存在时间较短的 20 世纪的艺术和文学运动。1914 年，温德姆·刘易斯在由漩涡派人士出版的《疾风》第一期就倡导该运动，试图将艺术与机器结合在一起。它受到立体主义和未来主义的影响很大，赞扬机器的活力并倡导充满暴力的表达方式。

除了刘易斯之外，还有很多人与该运动有关，例如埃兹拉·庞德（1885—1972）、爱德华·华兹华斯（1889—1949）、大卫·邦伯格（1890—1957）、库斯波特·汉密尔顿（1860—1930）以及劳伦斯·阿特金森（1906—1979）。

W

Well-made Play（佳构剧）

Well-made play, first introduced by the French dramatist Eugène Scribe (1791—1861) in the early 19th century, is a type of drama which employs strict technical rules, such as a predetermined pattern, suspense and a happy ending to construct a well-crafted plot. Then in the middle of the 19th century, it became a pejorative word because of its artificial action and plot.

佳构剧由法国戏剧家尤金·斯克莱伯（1791—1861）在 19 世纪早期首先提出，它使用严格的技术规则，例如预定的模式、悬疑和圆满的结局来建构一个结构精良的情节。在 19 世纪中期，因为做作的动作和情节，该词成为贬义词。

Women's Studies（妇女研究）

Women's studies is a multidisciplinary study centering on the relationship between power and gender, women's social status, and their contributions. It emerged in the late 1960s, closely associated with the second wave of the Feminist Movement. Now it has become more and more important.

妇女研究是一个多学科研究，关注于权力与性别的关系、妇女的社会地位以及贡献。妇女研究出现于 20 世纪 60 年代，与第二次女性主义运动密切相关。现在它变得越来越重要。

Z

Zeugma（轭式修饰法）

The word "Zeugma" is a Greek word meaning "yoking" or "bonding". Zeugma is a figure of speech where a word is used to modify or govern two or more other words grammatically, though it is correct logically with only one. For example, "He lost his coat and his temper".

该词是一个希腊词汇，意思是"轭"或者"联结"。轭式修饰法是一种修辞方法，是指一个单词在语法上同时用来修饰或者支配两个或者两个以上的词，但是只有其中一个符合逻辑的搭配句式。例如"他丢了衣服，大发雷霆"。

参考文献

艾略特：《传统与个人才能》，卞之琳、李赋宁译，上海译文出版社
　　2012 年版。

艾布拉姆斯：《文学术语词典》，吴松江译，北京大学出版社 2009 年版。

斑澜：《英美"新批评派"的方法论特征》，《内蒙古社会科学》1988
　　年第一期。

保罗·德曼：《美国新批评的形式与意向》，周颖译，《外国文学》
　　2001 年。

胡家峦：《历史的星空：文艺复兴时期英国诗歌与西方传统宇宙论》，
　　北京大学出版社 2001 年版。

胡经之：《西方文艺理论名著教程》，北京大学出版社 2003 年版。

胡燕春：《"英、美新批评派"研究》，中国社会科学出版社 2010 年版。

黄杲炘：《英国抒情诗歌 100 首》，上海译文出版社 1988 年版。

黄琼：英美新批评的批评，《宿州学院学报》2007 年 8 月。

勒内·韦勒克、奥斯汀·沃伦：《文学理论》，刘向愚、邢培明译，文
　　化艺术出版社 2010 年版。

李菡：《英国玄学派诗人约翰多恩爱情诗中的表象群赏析》，《解放军
　　外国语学院学报》2003 年第三期。

罗选民：《英美文学赏析教程（小说与戏剧)》，清华大学出版社 2006
　　年版。

秦旭:《J. 希利斯·米勒解构批评研究》，社会科学文献出版社 2011 年版。

特里·伊格尔顿:《当代西方文学理论》，中国社会科学出版社 1988 年版。

杨周翰:《十七世纪英国文学》，北京大学出版社 1985 年版。

尹建民:《艾略特的诗歌理论与新批评》，《青海师范大学学报》1996 年第七期。

约翰·克劳·兰瑟姆:《新批评》，王腊宝、张哲译，文化艺术出版社 2010 年版。

王佐良、何其莘:《英国文艺复兴时期文学史》，外语教学与研究出版社 1996 年版。

王佐良、李赋宁等:《英国文学各篇选著》，商务印书馆 1983 年版。

王佐良译:《彭斯诗选》，外国文学出版社 1985 年版。

张隆溪:《二十世纪西方文论述评》，生活·读书·新知三联书店 1986 年版。

张首映:《西方二十世纪文论史》，北京大学出版社 1999 年版。

赵毅衡:《新批评文集》，百花文艺出版社 2001 年版。

赵毅衡:《新批评与当代批判理论》，《英美文学研究论丛》2009 年第二期。

郭宏安等:《二十世纪文论研究》，中国社会科学出版社 1997 年版。

朱立元:《当代西方文艺理论》，华东师范大学出版社 1997 年版。

左金梅、申富英等:《西方女性主义文学批评》，中国海洋大学出版社 2007 年版。

Aristotle. *Poetics*. Perseus Digital Library, 2006.

Abrams, M. H. *A Glossary of Literary Terms*. Sixth Edition, Fort Worth: Harcourt Brace Jovanovich College Publishers, 1993.

Abrams, M. H. *A Glossary of Literary Terms*. Seventh Edition. Boston: Heinle & Heinle: 1999.

Abrams, M. H. *A Glossary of Literary Terms*. Peking University Press, 2009.

Apter, Emily & William Pietz. eds. *Fetishism as Cultural Discourse*. Ithaca: Cornell University Press, 1993.

Arnold, Mattew. *Culture and Anarchy*. Chapter 4, http://faculty.gvc. edu/ssnyder/Hum101/hebraism_ and_ hellenism. htm.

Bailan, Qin. "Defending Husserlian Phenomenology From Terry Eagleton's Critique", *Advances in Literary Study*. Vol. 1. 2013.

Baldick, Chris. *The Concise Oxford Dictionary of Literary Terms*. Oxford: Oxford University Press, 1990.

Baldick, Chris. *Concise Dictionary of Literary Terms*. Shanghai, Shanghai Foreign Language Education Press, 2000.

Baumgardner, Jennifer & Richards, Amy. *Manifesta: Young Women, Feminism, and the Future*. Macmillan, 2000.

Benson, Larry Dean. *The Riverside Chaucer*. Oxford University Press, 2008.

Beja, Morris. *Epiphany in the Modern Novel*. Seattle: University of Washington Press, 1971.

Beckson, Karl. *Literary Terms: A Dictionary*. New York: Farrar, Straus and Giroux, 1975.

Beja, Morris. *Epiphany in the Modern Novel*. Seattle: University of Washington Press, 1971.

Booth, Wayne. *The Rhetoric of Fiction*. University of Chicago Press, 1961.

Bressler, Charles E. *Literary Criticism: An Introduction to Theory and Practice*. 3rd Edition, Pearson Education Inc. 2002.

Bressler, Charles E. *Literary Criticism-An Introduction to Theory and Practice*. Higher Education Press, 2004.

Canter, H. V. "Digressio in the Orations of Cicero", *The American Journal of Philology*, Johns Hopkins University Press, Vol. 52, No. 4,

1931.

Cuddon, J. A. *A Dictionary of Literary Terms and Literary Theory*, Oxford: Oxford University Press, 1998.

Culler, Johnathan. *Literary Theory*, Oxford: Oxford University Press, 1997.

D'Ammassa, Don. "Encyclopedia of Adventure Fiction", *Facts on File Library of World Literature*. Infobase Publishing, 2009.

Dentith, Simon. *Parody (The New Critical Idiom)*. Routledge, 2000.

Derrida, Jacques. *Dissemination*, Jhonson, Barbara translated, London: Continuum, 2005.

Eagleton, Terry. *Literary Theory: An Introduction*. U of Minnesota Press, 1996.

Eliot, T. S. *The Sacred Wood*. London: Methuen, 1964.

Eliot, T. S. "Tradition and the Individual Talent", *II The Sacred Wood*. 1922. http://www.english.illinois.edu/maps/poets/a_ f/eliot/tradition.htm.

Gang, Zhu. *Twentieth Century Western Critical Theories*. Shanghai Foreign Language Education Press, 2001.

Glaisyer, Natasha & Pennell, Sara. *Didactic Literature in England*, 1500—1800. Ashgate, 2003.

Glotfelty, Cheryll. *The Ecocriticism Reader: Landmarks in Literary Ecology*. Athens: The University of Georgia Press, 1996.

Guerin, Wilfred L. *A Handbook of Critical Approaches to Literature*. Foreign Language Teaching And Research Press, 2004.

Hirsch, Edward. *A Poet's Glossary*. Houghton Mifflin Harcourt, 2014.

Honderich, Ted. *The Oxford Companion to Philosophy*. Oxford: Oxford University Press, 1995.

Jankowski, Theodora. *A Pure Resistance: Queer Virginity in Early Modern English Drama*. University of Pennsylvanian Press, 2000.

Knellwolf, Christa. *The Cambridge History of Literary Criticism: Volume 9*,

Twentieth-Century Historical, Philosophical and Psychological Perspectives. Cambridge University Press, 2008.

Lagasse, Paul. *Columbia Encyclopedia Sixth Edition*. Columbia University Press, 2000.

Lewis, C. S. *English Literature in the Sixteenth Century (Excluding Drama)*. New York: Oxford University Press. 1954.

Makayrk, Irena. *Encyclopedia of Contemporary Literary Theory*. Toronto: University of Toronto Press, 1993.

Mellor, Mary. *Feminism & Ecology*. New York: New York University Press, 1997.

Mikics, David. *A New Handbook of Literary Terms*. New Haven: Yale University Press, 2007.

Moi, Tori. *Feminist Literary Criticism*. reprinted in Modern Literary Theory by Ann Jefferson and David Robey, 1991.

Moore, Dafydd. *Ossian and Ossianism: The pomes of Ossian*。London and New York: Routledge Taylor & Francis Group, 2004.

Morris, Wesley. *Toward a New Historicism*. Princeton University Press, 1972.

Paulk, Sarah F. *The Aesthetics of Impressionism: Studies in Art and Literature*. Ann Arbor: University Microfilms International, 1979.

Phelps, William Lyon. *The Beginnings of the English Romantic Movement*. Boston: Ginn & company, 1893.

Preziosi, Donald. *The Art of Art History: A Critical Anthology*. Oxford University Press, 2009.

Selden, Raman. *A Reader's Guide to Contemporary Literary Theory*. Foreign Language Teaching And Research Press, 2004.

Simone de Beauvoir. *The Second Sex*. translated by H. M. Parhsley, New York: Vintage Books, 1989.

Scott, A. F. *Current Literary Terms: A Concise Dictionary of Their Origin*

And Use. New York: St. Martin's Press, 1971.

Veeser, Harold. *The New Historicism.* Routledge, 2013.

Willett, John. ed. and trans, *Brecht on Theatre.* New, York: Hill and Wang, 1964.

Yelland, H. L. Jones, S. C. & Easton. *K. S. W. A Handbook of Literary Terms.* New York: Philosophical Library, 1950.

Yuval-Davis, *Nira. Gender and Nation.* Sage Publications, 1997.